ABOUT THE AUTHOR

CW01467456

Jeff Dowson began his caree actor and a director specialising in productions of modern British and European playwrights.

From there he moved into television as an independent writer/producer/director. Substantial screen credits include arts series, entertainment features, drama documentaries, drama series and TV films.

Turning crime novelist, he introduced Bristol private eye Jack Shepherd in *Closing the Distance*. The second thriller, *Changing the Odds*, was published the following year. *Cloning the Hate* is the latest in the series.

Born in northeast England he now lives in Bristol. He is a member of BAFTA and the Crime Writers Association.

Visit: www.jeffdowson.co.uk

Book Cover Design by Andy Bone

ISBN 9781911266648

Williams & Whiting (Publishers)
15 Chestnut Grove, Hurstpierpoint,
West Sussex, BN6 9SS

Thanks to...

The Bristol people of all colours and creeds whose words helped to inform this book

Mariette and Andy of Jackson Bone for their design skills and advice

Phil Rowlands and Jim Knight for reading the manuscript

My old friend Peter Nash, south Bristol born and bred, for lending me his name

Mike Linane of Williams and Whiting, publisher of the Jack Shepherd series for his enthusiasm and support

Also by Jeff Dowson
from Williams & Whiting

Jack Shepherd Thrillers:

Closing The Distance
Changing The Odds

For information about these and other books published
by Williams & Whiting go to:
www.williamsandwhiting.com

For Mary... Priceless

CLONING THE HATE

A Jack Shepherd thriller

Jeff Dowson

WILLIAMS AND WHITING

PRELUDE

Alfie Barnes was found a few minutes before 8 o'clock, by a Red Setter who galloped up to investigate the shape lying on the grass. The dog licked Alfie's bruised and battered face, got no response, and sat down beside the body. His owner called the police.

Alfie didn't have an enemy in the world, so why the hell would anyone want to beat him to death? Most of the time he was in his own loop, apparently unaware of the world outside its orbit and listening to music the rest of us couldn't hear. And that made him the kind of person you had to look out for, not stumble over before breakfast in a copse of trees on the Downs.

Alfie was extra-ordinary. 26 years old, fifteen years younger than his sister Linda. A late addition to the Barnes family, arriving when his mother Joanna was 39. A mistake, but loved to bits nonetheless, even though living his life was a complicated process. He lost vital moments of oxygen during his birth, which left him with sensory disorders and some speech problems. Five days before his death he had stopped using sentences and instead précised them into phrases. He had taken to repeating actions over and over again. But he listened intently when someone spoke to him and took time to process what was being said. He smiled readily at those he knew, eyes that glowed with recognition and lips that revealed sparkling white teeth which he cleaned and polished and flossed for twenty-five minutes each morning.

Joanna and Patrick were devastated by the loss. Both in their mid-60s, they had embraced retirement and the long anticipated joy of being at home and close to their beautiful, vulnerable son, around the clock. Their world was blown apart in a handful of brutal moments on a warm September morning. Alfie was taking the walk he did every day at 7.30, winter or summer, rain or shine.

Nobody saw what happened. The dog and his owner knew who Alfie was – the trio met regularly during their early morning exercise. A uniformed constable wrote down all the man could tell him. Then in the company of a detective from Redland Police Station, he knocked on the Barnes' front door at 10 minutes to 9. Half an hour later, Linda was visited by two uniforms in a patrol car.

When the police left, Linda took the few steps from her office door to mine and paused on the threshold. The lady is 43 years old, beautiful, smart and funny. She was my wife's closest friend and her empathy with Emily's cancer was instinctive. Emily battled hour by hour to stay alive and spent eight months dying. Linda supported the Shepherd family day after day, right down to the wire.

Today it was my turn to be friend and counsellor.

I looked up from behind my desk. She stared at me as if we had forever. I got to my feet.

"Jack …" she said.

* * *

The human mind has an eject button. Of sorts. And if you possess a super kind of resolve you can use it. Until you discover it's not really what you want after all. Because you still pick up the photograph and choose to remember the moment it was taken, or listen to the song and reap the memories it evokes.

A slow revving murder investigation doesn't help with the grieving. No progress had been made in the eight days since the discovery of Alfie's body, and the list of possibilities was endless. The Murder Investigation Team was headed by my old friend Superintendent Harvey Butler, almost thirty years a detective and a man with more insight into the nature of the human condition than anyone I know. MIT had rounded up a catalogue of characters – known violators of law and order, heavies on the rise, losers with convictions for aggravated assault and grievous bodily harm, back lane hard cases, street enders, nonces, plain and simple felons – with absolutely no result. Close to one hundred interviews had been conducted and no one was talking. Which meant they all embraced a mighty code of silence, or the murder was a random affair committed by someone who had never appeared on the MIT radar. Or it had been carefully planned and executed to look that way.

CHAPTER ONE

When you open a can and there are prunes in it, it's a can of prunes. Confirms all your expectations. But open a can of worms and your expectations go viral. Especially if the can is offered to you by Danny Malone.

"I don't like you, Shepherd, but I trust you," he said.

Malone had walked into my office without knocking. Served me right for leaving the door open. But then, I shouldn't have been sitting in my office on a Saturday morning. The intention was to spend time with my accounts. My financial year runs September to August and Linda had been threatening to send me a bill this time – unlike last year and the year before – if I didn't get my arse in gear. The current hiatus was useful. Or so I had imagined.

"How did you get in?" I asked.

"I told the Security Man I was an old friend and I wanted to surprise you."

The Saturday man was a locum. I made a mental note to take this up with *Harbour Security*.

There is nothing in the private investigator's manual which says you have to like your client. But the Shepherd detective manual says you do. And Danny Malone was as far away from likeable as it was possible to be. Fifteen years ago, I had helped take him down. Hard as nails and seriously disturbed, he left the Special Crimes Unit squad room with his belongings in a cardboard box, swearing to get even with me. He had done some deal with the ACC. Not prosecuted for the odious bastard he was – charged

4

with having sex with a fifteen year old girl he had frightened into not testifying – he was simply kicked out onto the street. The last time I'd heard of him was eighteen months ago. He was in the bodyguard business, working for a local captain of industry with an inglorious disregard for straight dealing, protocol, and compliance. But then due diligence was never Danny's forte either. He had not delivered the pounding he had promised me, and right now he looked as if he had stumbled into a rigid steel joist. He was standing on the other side of my desk, with a face like a yard of bad road and his neck in a whiplash collar. Six feet four tall and at least two thirds of that wide. He was a genuine monster.

I stared at him.

"Car accident," he offered.

"I'm not wondering about your welfare," I said.

"No hard feelings though?"

"I've got the nightmares down to one or two a month."

"I don't do violence anymore."

"Not since you took Eddie Winston's top set out with a pair of rusty pliers."

"That was then."

He seemed to think that was explanation enough. It wasn't.

"And this is now," I said. "Take your proposition and leave."

He responded by sitting down in one of my client chairs, clearly in no mind to consider my request.

"You look to be in good shape," he said.

A little under six feet tall, still with my own hair, my own teeth and thirty-two inch waist. I eat sensibly and battle daily to keep away from biscuits and chocolate between meals.

"Do you go to the gym?"

"I run a couple of miles round the Ashton Court Estate three times a week. There's a rowing machine in my summerhouse."

New additions to the garden, both. The summerhouse arrived on the back of a lorry six weeks ago. Adam – my daughter's long-time partner – and I put it together one Saturday morning with the help of the women in our lives and an ongoing chorus of satire. The rowing machine is inside it because there's no space inside the house, a three bedroom semi-detached in Redland. The house Emily and I bought not long before we got married, the house Chrissie grew up in, the house I've lived in for twenty-five years.

I looked at Malone again, endeavouring to convey my distaste at this unscheduled reunion. If he hadn't been swathed in bandages I'd have heaved him out of the chair and back into the corridor. Although, on reflection, maybe not. Even if he had slowed down a bit over the past decade, he could still out-reach and out-thump me.

He shifted his position in the chair and got to the point.

"I want to hire you, and I can pay," he said.

"I don't want your money."

"It's clean."

"Maybe now. But it probably didn't start out that way."

There was a beat. Malone took a moment to measure his reaction to the insult, decided to ignore it and changed tack.

"I hear you're not exactly snowed under with clients."

"Nothing you hear has any base in reality."

The right-hand corner of his mouth drooped, the eye above it narrowed – in historical terms, the prelude to an act of extreme brutality. I slid my chair back three feet. Malone locked his eyes onto mine, satisfied he could still frighten the shit out of me.

"Give me ten minutes of your time," he said.

I decided I could extend him that much courtesy, especially if the alternative was a month in traction. And if I could drive the conversation, at least to begin with...

I asked him what he did for a living these days.

"Whatever my employer asks," he said.

"And he is?..."

"Gerald Gaghan. At least he's the boss of the firm. They specialise in -"

I interrupted Malone. "I know what they do."

Gaghan Nash hired muscle. Legal muscle. Acted as an agency for High Court Enforcement Officers – lawfully sanctioned bailiffs on speed. If A has a county court judgement against B for anything from £600 upwards, and is unhappy with the way the County Court Bailiffs are working, he can instruct an HCEO to take it on. They are enforcers authorised by the Lord Chancellor's Office and work as freelancers or for private companies. Unlike bailiffs, who are salaried civil servants and employed directly by the courts, HCEOs earn their fees from the debtor – providing they can collect – and receive no income from an unsuccessful enforcement.

A financially precarious living you may think, but not so. They have a much tougher approach than bailiffs, who have no financial incentive to collect and tend to be more sympathetic to the debtors. As a result High Court enforcers have a significantly higher collection rate. Anyone called upon to assist them, even the police, must do so. Chasing down debtors, reclaiming property, evicting squatters... it's all in a day's work. They have the right to break into a property with whatever force they deem necessary and stay there until they have reparation. Inevitably they get thumped now and then, as the face in front of me bore witness, but in this age of privatised menace, what's the odd knock here and there.

"People tend to think I'm just a thug," Malone said.

No argument from me there.

"But if you were owed thousands of pounds and the court ordered you were entitled to get it back, wouldn't you hire Gaghan Nash to do it?"

In the normal run of things, no. Unless the debt was owed by the most malodorous man in town, in which case yes, absolutely. It would be a match made in hell. Gerald Gaghan had actually attempted to hire me on a couple of occasions.

"How is your boss?" I asked.

Malone grimaced. "Devious bastard. No sense of right and wrong."

That was choice, coming from an experienced body-breaker like Malone. I wanted him out of my office. I stood up. He did too. Four inches taller than me and with his knuckles close to the floor he looked terrifying.

"Don't you want to listen to my proposition?" he asked.

"Not even if it's to be the last conversation of my life."

Undeterred, he simply ploughed on. "Word is, nobody's getting anywhere with the murder of this Alfie Barnes kid."

That sentence changed the whole conversation.

I sat down again.

So did Malone. And beamed across the desk at me. At least, with his version of a beam. It was only slightly less sinister than his 'ready to pound me into the carpet' look.

"I heard he had a problem tying his shoes and he talked to his socks."

I took Malone by surprise. Reached across the desk, grabbed his jacket collars with both hands, pulled him out of his chair, then pushed down and slammed his forehead onto the desk top. I hauled him upright and let go. He fell back into the chair, which tipped over and deposited him on the floor. I moved around the desk. Malone rolled over and looked up at me. He couldn't see straight and was having trouble focusing.

"Jesus..." he groaned.

"Tell me what you know about Alfie Barnes," I said.

Malone tried to lever himself up onto his elbows. I put my foot on his throat and let it take my weight. He gurgled, choked, and lay back on the carpet. There was no wound on his forehead, but the skin was beginning to discolour, and if we stayed as we were for a while we would be able to watch a lump growing.

"Tell me about Alfie."

Malone swallowed, tried to breathe, and shook his head. I took my shoe off his Adam's apple, moved back to my desk, reached for the phone and picked up the receiver.

"Maybe you'll talk to the police about him."

Malone found his voice. "Call them and I'll say nothing. Fuck all."

I looked at the malice in his eyes.

We had a stand-off. I ignored the phone and sat down behind my desk. From there I couldn't see Malone, but I could hear him gurgling. Which was accompanied by a long groan as he rose into view, got to his feet and began to sway. He shuffled backwards across the office, reached behind him, closed the door and leaned against it. He was temporarily out of commission and far enough away to give me time to react if he pulled himself together.

I waited. Things could go either way at this point. Malone raised his right hand and began massaging his forehead.

"Christ," he moaned. "I'm going to look like the fucking Elephant Man in a couple of hours."

Hardly. But then he was no oil painting on the best of days. So by the time he'd added a bulging forehead to the scars and the whiplash collar, he'd probably be able to frighten the horses. He managed to concentrate enough to return to business.

10

"Does this mean you're turning me down?" he grunted.

"Tell me what you know about the killing of Alfie Barnes."

"That's no fucking bargaining position," he said.

"So don't take it," I suggested. "And you will have no need to darken my doorstep again. The bump on your head will mend, and this meeting will become another painful memory we can both lock away somewhere and eventually forget."

He straightened his body, stood upright and took a step towards the desk. I stood up too, prepared for something of an onslaught. Malone flapped his right hand as if he was attempting to wave away a wasp.

"I haven't the strength," he said. "Can I sit down again?"

I nodded and pointed to the chair on the floor. He ignored that and sat down in the other client chair. I ignored it, too. It seemed that what Malone did next was the thing to focus on. He took a deep breath and began prodding at his forehead again.

"What do I look like?"

He looked like Lurch from the *Adams Family*. I couldn't resist telling him so and prepared for a reaction. Instead, he grinned. Almost a real grin this time.

"Listen, Shepherd," he said, "I know a couple of people Alfie Barnes was hanging out with."

"Hanging out at the edges, or mixing with?"

"A couple of people he was tight with."

"And who are they?"

11

Malone shook his head without thinking of the state he was in and yelled in pain. He slouched in the chair, his head lolled back and he closed his eyes. I took advantage of the hiatus, moved around the desk and righted the other client chair. He looked up at me as I stood above him. Slid upright, slowly and carefully. Lifted his head enough to look straight into my eyes. Neither of us blinked. I waited for him to speak.

"My daughter is missing," he said.

I'd forgotten he had a daughter. And that at one point he'd asked me to be her godfather. A suggestion so preposterous I had laughed at him. Which he didn't take all that well. I was (a) amazed that Malone had found a wife, and (b) dismayed that he had planted his seed. But then, I suppose, he was as entitled as anyone else to pollute the gene pool.

"From where?" I asked. "From home?"

"No. She was with Rachel at her mother's place."

Rachel. Malone's short suffering wife. The daughter of a vicar – surprised all of us that – she and Danny had been married for a year and a half and Amy was only a couple of months old when she left him. He chased after his wife and daughter. Kicked down her parents' front door. Upstairs, locked in the bathroom, Rachel dialled 999. Two uniforms in a patrol car arrived to find Malone on the landing, hammering on the bathroom door. They realised who he was, summoned another patrol car, and called the Special Crimes Unit. I got to the house five or six minutes later with another young DC, George Hood. By that time, one of the PCs was dabbing at the bridge of his broken nose with a wet tea towel, and Malone was sitting sulking on a chair in the kitchen, handcuffed to the steel towel rail on the front of the Aga. The moment he saw Hood and me, he tried to get to his feet, handcuffs notwithstanding, like Christopher Lee's Monster in *The Curse of Frankenstein*. He didn't make much progress but we kept our distance.

It was downhill all the way from there for Malone. His wife moved again, this time without offering him an address. Retained by the SCU because when he was focused and in his right mind he was a useful detective, he then sat on a succession of branches and proceeded to saw them off. He swiftly used up all the credit he had accrued. Sex with a fifteen year old was his last act of stupidity. He survived the investigation because the girl was too terrified to make a statement, and the ACC agreed he could leave the force without an official stain on his character. None but the ACC knew why.

And now the bastard was sitting in my office, the lump on his forehead expanding by the second. I walked back around my desk and sat down in my chair.

"Who are these people?" I asked.

"What people?"

"The people Alfie was tight with."

Malone returned to his mantra. "Find my daughter and I'll tell you."

I stared at him. Finding people is what I do, the job on offer was my kind of business. But working for Danny Malone... Any ordinary mortal would prefer to stay at home and stick pencils in his eyes.

13

"Listen, Shepherd," he went on, "you're one of the best detectives I ever worked with."

He was the last person in the world I would have approached for a testimonial. And digging around in whatever pile of manure he had stirred up was likely to leave me smelling bad for weeks. But, as I remembered, a deal was always a deal to Danny Malone. Irrevocable. So...

"Let's be clear about this," I said. "If I find your daughter and tell you where she is, you will give me the names of people linked to Alfie's death?"

"Cast iron leads," he said. "If I could do this myself I would, but I can't."

"Why not?"

"I'm not a private investigator. I don't have your contacts. I'd probably fall over a real detective at some point, and Harvey Butler would come down on me like a thirty storey lift. I can't go up against the law. You have a better connection."

"Not once it's revealed that I'm working for you."

"Easy to ensure no one finds out."

"No it's not," I insisted. "Not the way I do things."

He grinned again. "I wish I could afford to have principles."

No he didn't. And sitting across my desk like some copiously satisfied ogre, he looked as despicable as I remembered. But he was holding a high card. He paused for a moment to enhance the dramatic effect and then played it.

"Amy doesn't have my surname. Or Rachel's. She uses her grandmother's name. Turner. My daughter is Amy Turner. The actress."

He stared at me, waiting for that morsel to sink in.

You couldn't miss Amy Turner in a blackout. 22 years old and the current soap princess. Returning TV drama gold, with a 'Rising Star' award and a couple of BAFTA nominations on her CV. *The Causeway* was based north west of Bristol, on the sprawling back lot of what used to be a Royal Mail sorting depot. In its fifth year and constantly top of the ratings. Not my choice to accompany a night in with a pizza, but I had watched a couple of episodes. Amy was an astonishingly beautiful girl – difficult to believe therefore that she was the result of a union with Malone – and according to the tabloids she had it all. She was on television five nights a week and five times on Sundays. Had an agent who looked after her as if she was her own daughter. I had seen Amy on the *Graham Norton Show*, relaxed, at ease and funny. There were no ill winds blowing across the Amy Turner garden. Apparently.

I asked Malone how long she had been missing. He didn't know.

"She had a three day break from recording – Monday to Wednesday. She was supposed to be back on set two days ago. She didn't show. The production company and crew are shooting around her. Everyone in the know is working under threat of dismissal if word leaks out. Basically, she disappeared after her scenes wrapped last Saturday."

"Has she done this before?"

"No. At least not that I know of."

"And why are you in the know, now?"

"Because Rachel called me." His mouth changed shape and he fell into a momentary sulk. "The first time she's spoken to me since Christmas. She thought I might still have enough connections to twist an arm or two. Have you got any painkillers?"

"No."

He reached up and massaged his forehead yet again. "Christ, you didn't have to do this."

"Yes I did."

"Will you take the job?"

We were back to the can of worms again. Expectations were low here. At least on my side of the desk. Limited to previous experience of a man who had little nobility of purpose in anything he did. Danny Malone was unfettered by responsibility or righteousness. He took my few seconds of musing as a positive sign and decided to gild the lily.

"You charge two hundred and fifty a day. I'll give you three hundred."

I must have looked unimpressed.

"All right. Three hundred and fifty."

"Give me the names you offered."

"If I do, you'll go chasing them down before you start working for me."

The phone on my desk rang. I picked up the receiver. Linda asked how I was. I told her I had someone in my office.

"Give me two minutes and I'll call you back."

I disconnected the line, picked up my mobile, got to my feet and looked at Malone.

"Stay here while I make this call."

I left the office and walked along the corridor to the kitchen. Filled the kettle and switched it on. Spooned instant coffee into a mug. Called Linda.

"Was that an important client I disturbed?" she asked.

"He might be, unhappily. How are you?"

"Okay."

"How's the rest of the family?"

"Trying to keep busy. You know how it is. Can you pick me up on Monday morning before the funeral? Then join us in the limousine?"

"Of course."

The conversation whispered into silence. Which morphed into a long pause. I asked Linda where she was.

"At home."

"Do want me to drive out and see you?"

"I'd like that, yes."

I looked at my watch. 9.25.

"I'll be with you around 10 o'clock."

"Good. Thanks."

Linda closed the line. I listened to the hum of static. The kettle hissed and began to boil. I pressed the end call button and put the mobile down on a worktop. The kettle switched off. I picked it up, made the coffee, stirred it, ran the spoon under the hot tap, picked up the mug and the mobile and walked back to my office.

Malone looked a trifle indignant. He stared at the mug.

"You didn't ask if I'd like some."

"No I didn't. And when I've drunk this, I have something important to do. So I'd like you to leave."

"I didn't come here to be told that," he said.

"There had to be a risk."

He stood up. "Shepherd..."

His 'don't fuck with me' face materialised again. I held up my left hand. I put the mug on my desk, tore a sheet off the top of a pad block, picked a pencil out of the holder on my desk and offered both to Malone. He watched all this, eyes glued to the action, then stared down at the pencil and paper as if they were booby-trapped.

"Give me your phone numbers. I'll get back to you."

"Tomorrow, yeah?"

"Tomorrow belongs to me. And Alfie's funeral is on Monday. Meantime, I'm not going to let anything get in the way."

I sat down and sipped at my coffee. Malone wrote on the paper and slid it across the desk top towards me.

"Get on with this soonest," he said, giving every syllable weight.

"There you go," I said. "Threatening me again."

"I'll be back if I don't hear from you."

He looked at me, in a menacingly relaxed kind of a way and let the silence fill. Then he turned and walked out of the office. I watched him go. One of nature's steamrollers.

Five minutes later, I got into my car and drove to Linda's house in Portishead. It was a little over forty-eight hours until the funeral. She just wanted me to be with her.

CHAPTER TWO

I heard the explosion as I stepped out of the shower. It slammed across Redland from the Downs Shopping Centre on Whiteladies Road, two miles away.

A youngish man, around five feet nine, chin bearded and brow hooded, had detonated the home-made device belted to his tee shirt. There wasn't enough of him left to put back together. The undisputed description of him was available because he had made mistakes – the job requirements for suicide bombers don't allow them to dress rehearse. He had stationed himself on the terrace pavement which stretches fifteen or so feet from the roadside bus stops to the shopping mall entrance. The first report to the police was made at 8.23 by the owner of *All About Art* – the artists' materials shop facing the street – when he arrived to prepare for opening up. Avon and Somerset Constabulary put into action a plan they had been rehearsing twice a month for the past two years.

Within sixteen minutes, eight armed officers, supported by twenty uniformed constables, moved into the rear of the shopping mall from the car park and began to clear every member of the public out of the two shops that were open – a dispensing chemist and a supermarket. At the same time, detectives and constables in plain clothes joined the two bus queues and began to warn putative passengers of the situation, asking them to stand by and wait for a signal to move. Three elderly people along with a blind man and his guide dog were escorted away from the scene, one at a time. Other officers replaced customers approaching and walking past the mall entrance. A hundred yards north along Whiteladies Road and the same distance south, police patrol cars began controlling the flow of traffic, gradually slowing it down and introducing, one by one, a stream of their own unmarked vehicles. Buses were halted. And four marksmen stationed themselves in street facing rooms in flats above the pub, the estate agent and the burger takeaway on the opposite side of the road.

All through these manoeuvres the bomber loitered on the pavement. It became clear he was waiting for something or some moment to arrive. He kept glancing to his left towards the pedestrian crossing twenty yards away.

And that allowed the plan to work.

Until 8.47, when Assistant Chief Constable Langley and his Task Force Commander ordered 'Go', and a policeman on the roof of the car park fired his Heckler & Koch 9mm machine gun into the air. The people in the bus queues, sprinted across the road. Those on the pavement parted like the waters of the Red Sea and fled. The marksmen prepared to fire. The bomber hesitated for precious moments, confused about what to do, perhaps trying to locate the source of the machine-gun fire. He pulled his hood back, looked around, then grabbed at something attached to the belt around his chest. The four marksmen fired in unison. The bomber jerked, staggered, fell backwards and exploded before he hit the ground.

Every window behind him disintegrated. Sections of the pavement rose into the air and rained back down in pieces. The bus queue people did as they had been instructed, throwing themselves face down onto the comparative refuge of the opposite pavement. They were showered by small bits of concrete, copious amounts of dust, and glass from windows above them blown out by the blast scorching across the street. Ten seconds later, brick dust still thick in the air, it was all over. Paramedics poured out of the doors of the pub onto the pavement, suddenly an alfresco triage station.

The incident made the 9.10 *BBC Breakfast* insert from *Points West* and cut short the interview with the latest *Strictly Come Dancing* announcee. And within half an hour, network camera cars, vans and satellite uplink trucks began to arrive.

By 9.30, ACC Langley was praising the work of all members of his squad for saving the lives of everyone in peril and giving his assessment of the situation. The theory he posited, was that the bomber had intended to blow himself up as a crocodile of children and parents moved over the pedestrian crossing on their way to Warwick Park Primary School, one hundred yards beyond the pub. What foiled the bomber was his lack of research. The school was operating an 'in service' day, hastily arranged after the staff had been informed of a visit by Ofsted in five days' time. There were no parents and children available to be blown up.

By the time I left home at 10 o'clock, a score of people had been interviewed on all the news channels in action.

22

The recorded police footage had been played and replayed on endless loops as the art shop owner and blast survivors told their stories, while a host of terrorist consultants, ex-Home Office department heads and dirty bomb-making experts were rushed into studios all over the country. And followed, as the morning went on, by political pundits, concerned community activists and even the local leaders of the hard right *British Political Action Group*.

I didn't have time for reviews and re-runs. I had my own date with the proceeds of cold blooded murder.

* * *

I stood next to Linda and her parents in the crematorium chapel as Alfie slipped from sight through the velvet curtains, accompanied by *I Fought the Law* from Joe Strummer and the Pogues – a song he had listened to round the clock on his MP3 player.

Chrissie was standing at the back of the chapel. She nodded at us as we walked past her and out into the sunshine. Adam was standing on the other side of the grassed quadrangle. Sam the Bearded Collie was sitting next to him on the end of his lead, still and quiet. He made no attempt to leap into his default greeting mode. He had captured the solemnity of the occasion. Chrissie joined the pair of them and took over lead duties. Adam crossed the road to pay his respects to Linda and her parents. Sam looked up at Chrissie. She reached down and stroked the top of his head. The dog woofed quietly and sighed.

Back at Joanna and Patrick's house, it was 2 o'clock by the time the last guest departed. There had been some conversation about the morning's bombing. A range of reactions from shock through resentment to anger. All sotto voce, as the day was about something else for us. Chrissie, Adam and I took charge of the clearing up while Linda and her parents rested. Afterwards we sat in the garden. Sam lay down on the grass and went to sleep. He began snoring softly. Adam asked if I would be interested in some good news. I said I would be. He took a deep breath.

"Your daughter," he said, "has finally agreed to marry me."

I looked at Chrissie. She shrugged.

"He wore me down."

Adam and Chrissie had been living together for close on four years. She had recently left university after making PGCE qualification look easy – which it isn't – and was about to take up her first teaching post, at Bedminster Primary School. So she had finally decided that forever with Adam was a good idea. The only person not sharing in the family celebration was Emily. Her death had been a massive punch in the guts, but three years on, the rest of us were closer because of it. Adam stood by Chrissie like the rock of ages, she and I had begun our relationship anew, and Linda had provided the glue which now bound the four of us together. And thus the Shepherd family, Sam included, was among those celebrating Alfie's life.

Linda joined us in the garden.

"You look exhausted," Chrissie said.

Linda nodded. I asked her if she was staying overnight. She shook her head.

"I offered but..." She paused, distracted, then started over. "Will you take me home?"

"Of course."

I got to my feet. Sam woke up, saw Linda and barked a greeting. She smiled at him.

"Hello Sam."

The dog stood up wagging his tail, padded over to Linda and leaned against her legs. She looked down at him and said, "Thank you, Sam." He crooned a little grace note and settled down again at Linda's feet.

I said my goodbyes to Joanna and Patrick. He shook hands with me, Joanna told me to take care. Inside the Healey, I switched on the ignition, pressed the starter and the straight six rumbled into life. Linda looked at me.

"I thought you had an offer for this car."

I had owned the 3 litre Austin Healey for fifteen years. It was closer than a best friend and valued like a wardrobe of old clothes. Ace mechanic Mr Earl had the six cylinders running like a great piece of music, but the body needed some work I couldn't afford. A dealer who knew a dealer I knew, wanted to buy the car, and had made an offer which, given the state of my bank account, I would be mightily irresponsible to refuse. The idea had always been to enjoy the Healey as a second car. But I had never been able to afford to run two, and those halcyon days of bowling around country lanes with the top down are long gone. And British motorways are not places where a three litre engine can stretch its legs. I had decided to allow another forty-eight hours or so to talk myself into it, but I knew that the beautiful machine had to go.

We had been on the road two minutes when Linda's mobile rang.

"Don't - " was as much as I managed.

Linda pressed the respond button, offered her name, listened for a second or two and said "Yes". Then after a pause, "Do you know where my office is?" Another second or two, then "Can you get there now?" was followed by "Fine, thirty minutes," and then "Not at all."

She closed the call. Stared ahead through the windscreen.

"I'm supposed to be taking you home," I said.

"I need something to do."

"Not today surely?"

"Especially today."

She breathed in, let the breath out slowly and looked at me, dead centre. I turned my attention back to the traffic in front of us. We said no more for the rest of journey.

* * *

Our adjacent offices are on the fifth floor of a converted tobacco warehouse. It sits on the north bank of the Avon, between the river and the Cumberland Basin. The conversion retains the stone floor red bricked lobby, which is furnished with a quartet of repro chesterfield sofas, half a dozen armchairs, a couple of side tables, a large yucca in a stone pot, and a big reception desk manned by persons from *Harbour Security*.

Jason, the best greeter in the world, popular with tenants and guests alike, was gone for a while. Finally considered an elite athlete after being shamefully ignored for three years by UK Athletics, he was in full time training for the World Championships and leading the men's kayaking team. Eric, the man who had led the day security shift and who had been given to patrolling the corridors ramrod straight and resolutely user-unfriendly had gone, too. Walter, his successor, was in his early 40s, almost as wide as he was long, shaven-headed, red-faced and mostly monosyllabic, although the broadness came with a wide smile. Damon, long and slim and looked as if he worked out, was off shift. Walter waved a fistful of letters at Linda. He gave me a brown envelope with a window in it.

"And one for you, Mr Shepherd…"

At the lift, Linda pressed the call button. There was a rattle, a thud and a sigh, and the lift door opened. We moved into it and rode up to the fifth floor. We stepped out on to the landing and walked along the corridor.

I asked, "Are you sure you want to meet this man?"

"Yes."

We stopped outside her office door. Linda leaned into me. I held her close. I felt her breath on the side of my neck.

"Thank you, Jack."

She unlocked the office door and stepped inside. I did the same, a few paces along the corridor.

Shepherd Investigations had begun life in the spare bedroom; the intention being to eliminate overheads and for me to work more user friendly hours than I had done on the Special Crimes Unit. The reality proved to be flawed. There was tension throughout every case I worked on and disharmony when I wasn't working at all. I finally accepted that personal and business affairs needed to be separated, preferably by some distance. Truthfully, Emily ran out of patience. She decided that the separation, while unlikely to improve relationships or business opportunities, would at least provide definition. Linda announced that the office next door to her was empty, the landlord offered me the first two months' rent free, and so I moved in.

Shepherd Investigations had been told to stay away from the Alfie Barnes murder. Harvey Butler had looked me straight in the eyes and reminded me it was an open case, best left to Avon and Somerset Constabulary to pursue. The private sector, no matter how motivated, had no business anywhere near it. I mumbled some protest, which was stifled by the steeliest of unblinking, blue-eyed stares. But intentions on both sides were clear. Those of the best copper in town, driven by the mission he got out of bed for every day, to protect and serve; and a private investigator driven by frustration and anger – never the best way to solve a murder.

I sat at my desk. Stared gloomily at the laptop screen and the dozen in box emails. The salespersons were on my case again. A company with absolutely no idea of the size and state of my garden was offering a year's horticultural care for £35 a month. An online comparison site was assuring me I was paying way over the odds for my house and contents insurance and offering to cut my payments by thirty percent. And my bank had got in on the act; praising me for having an account in the black – just about – and insisting I could take advantage of this by signing up to *Account Plus* and all the savings that would accrue if I continued being so fiscally responsible. Other emails looked as if they might prove worthy of study, but in the end I was doomed to disappointment.

The phone on my desk rang. A lady asked me if I could find her estranged husband, a plumber, because she wanted him back. To fix a leak, presumably. I was as polite as I could possibly be. Told her I was, regretfully, too busy to take on more work.

I opened the letter Walter had handed me. A Dutch mail order company – where the hell did these people get my address from? – was insisting I was extremely lucky to be the only person in my postcode area to get into the last stage of their latest prize draw. All I had to do to earn the cheque, along with a swift reply bonus which might be a TV set, a DVD player, or a 5.1 home sound system, was to buy one item from the catalogue worth a minimum of £11.95p, and respond within eight days of receiving this outstanding offer.

There was nothing in any of this stuff which could lay claim, even remotely, to helping the world turn.

Meanwhile, a young man had blown himself apart in Clifton and Alfie Barnes had been murdered.

* * *

"A lot of people thought Alfie was just nerdy," Linda said.

29

I had managed to get her home by half past four. We were sitting in the tiny garden, balanced on the cliff-top overlooking the Severn Estuary. One of the best views in old Portishead. The tide was high and the water sparkled in the sunshine. We were drinking tea and there was a plate of chocolate digestives on the table between us.

"He was light years beyond nerdy," I suggested. "In a way, the problem wasn't his. That lay with the rest of us."

"In the family, we've done a lot of reading about Autism Spectrum Disorders," Linda said. "One percent of UK children are born with an ASD condition. We swiftly took on board that there was no cure for Alfie. But to begin with, the drug regimens the doctors tried caused grotesque personality swings. They got it as good as it was going to be eventually, but some of the versions of Alfie we coped with during the tests and the experiments were horrendous. He swung from amazingly gifted to severely challenged. There were days when nobody could have guessed he had anything wrong with him at all, and then there were days of extraordinary behaviour. Huge mood swings, no communication with any of us, angry outbursts... He'd lock himself in his room and stare at the walls. Then he would come out of it like he was on speed and become obsessively interested in something or someone. What he responded to mostly was music. But then he'd find a piece which connected with something in his brain and he'd listen to it over and over again."

She looked at the plate of biscuits.

"Are we finished with these?"

I nodded, she picked up the plate and the empty coffee mugs and went into the house.

CHAPTER THREE

The traffic on Whiteladies Road was moving again by 6 o'clock in the evening. The pub and the takeaway burger place had re-opened for business, albeit with a couple of windows boarded up. The twisted bus stop poles had been dug out of the ground, the holes filled and temporary poles on stands positioned on the pavement. The entrance to the shopping mall had been inspected and pronounced sound, but ingress was barred as contractors were re-laying the pavement outside. Television news channels were still speculating on who the bomber might have been. Avon and Somerset Constabulary were saying no more than ACC Langley had offered ten hours earlier.

I ate at home, watched some TV and went to bed early.

* * *

I didn't hear from Linda for a couple of days. I decided not to bombard her with 'are you all rights?'

The car dealer called at my house, handed me a cheque for £18,500, and drove the Healey away. I didn't watch him go. I banked the cheque, took a bus ride across the city to the Honda dealership in Brislington, turned my back resolutely on the Jaguar franchise on the opposite side of the road, and bought a two years old, dark blue, two litre Accord.

Two days after the funeral, I drove east to visit Auntie Joyce and Uncle Sid in Suffolk.

He had something to celebrate. An exhibition of his work at the Southwold Arts Festival. Since retiring, he had quadrupled the size of his garden shed, imported crates of arc welding stuff, and courtesy of 'Gently' Bentley Murdoch – a boat breaker and scrap dealer along the estuary – monster pieces of iron and steel, which he cut, hammered and brutalised into mighty works of art. It took three of Gently's trucks to transport the art to its installation site, a twenty yards square deck built out from the promenade onto the beach.

And it was a sensation. Southwold raised its collective hat to the new, 67 year old, arc welding genius. Press and TV descended on the town. As the festival closed, the town council hastily convened an extraordinary general meeting and voted unanimously for the installation to stay right where it was for the foreseeable future. What a coup. Auntie Joyce, who had suffered through the noise and the violence of Uncle Sid's extended metamorphosis from engineer into artist, was as proud as anyone could be.

As were all of us raising a glass to Uncle Sid. He had spent the entire week at the installation site. The preview was held on Thursday lunchtime. Feted and congratulated by press people, local artists, town councillors, tourists, and friends he had known for years. Uncle Sid took on all the questions asked of him and beamed in delight as he responded. By mid-afternoon he looked tired and a little short on concentration. He insisted it was caused by all the work and the excitement. I noticed Auntie Joyce catching his eye from time to time.

In high spirits, we sat down to tea and scones at 4 o'clock. Gently and his wife Eileen joined us. Now relaxed, Uncle Sid seemed himself again. Auntie Joyce had ceased being concerned. We ate and we talked and the day wound down. I managed to excuse myself from joining Gently for a couple of bottles of his home made cider.

At 5.30, I took my leave and set out to drive home.

* * *

My return to the fallout from Alfie's murder was less joyful.

I called Linda when I got home. She said she would be in the office the following morning and we could catch up then. I walked into the building at a just after 9. Her office door was open. I hovered at the threshold.

She looked up from behind her pc screen.

"Good morning," she said.

I stepped into the office.

"Every day I'm scared of tomorrow," she said. "Tomorrow when something else might be taken away."

She had no cause to feel like that, but Alfie's loss had cut deep. Brought about by numbness of the heart. He wasn't just a brother. He was a gifted, brilliant, marvellous boy, who had battled the peculiarities of the lifetime illness he had been handed and had accepted how his world was going to be. He had worked from his bedroom as an Imagineer for animation production companies and games devisers. The job description was all in the title. He thought up ideas and then made them work. Edited stories based on those ideas, devised and wrote code for new games.

34

Linda's eyes were not the eyes I had looked into a couple of weeks ago and toasted the future. They had lost their glow. Her face was thinner. The funny, dark haired, relaxed, sexy lady I knew was unfocused. Talking to me yes, but not really part of the conversation. Her hands roamed all over the place while she was speaking; not making gestures, simply not being still. She had understood why I'd stayed away from the police investigation, but both of us knew it was inevitable I was going to join the fray sooner or later.

She looked at me.

"Jack..."

"I'm going to call George Hood," I said.

"I was about to say that you - "

"Never mind."

I went into my office, sat down behind my desk, lifted the phone receiver and called the Murder Investigation Team. A woman answered the call.

"DS Hood please."

"He's no longer with MIT," she said. "I'm DS Mailer, can I help?"

"Where is he?" I asked.

"He's now a DI with the Special Crimes Unit."

So he had taken the promotion he passed on when those who settle things like this had offered him Vice. At that time he had opted to stay with MIT. Harvey had been pleased, but George Hood is a bright copper and the next offer was clearly better.

"Can I help?" DS Mailer repeated.

A bit of quick thinking was required here. Hood might have helped unofficially with what I was about to propose, but Harvey would hate it. However, I was on my way down the road with this...

"Can you put me through to Superintendent Butler?"

"Can I ask your name?"

"Jack Shepherd."

The voice at the other end of the line changed dramatically. "Well, well, well," DS Mailer said, "We finally get to talk. Jack Shepherd... You're something of a celebrity round here."

"Is Superintendent Butler in?"

"No. He's upstairs in a strategy meeting."

"I bet he's loving every minute."

"I can't comment on that," DS Mailer said.

Deep in the clarts now, there was only one way forward.

"Ask him to call me please. He knows my number."

"I'm sure he does. Personally, may I say I'm looking forward to meeting you, Mr Shepherd?"

"Oh Jack, please."

"Bye, Jack," DS Mailer said.

Well that was a job half done. Now Harvey had been given notice that I was up to something. I spent a moment or two musing on how long it would be before he called.

I sat in my chair, feet up on the desk, staring at the office door. A sort of pale blue colour. *Shepherd Investigations* had occupied this twelve by twelve space for nine years. I was getting older in the midst of one hundred and forty-four square feet of space, rented out at £10 per square foot. The landlord had recently jacked up the price because he had begun to believe that the age of austerity was now behind us and receding into the distance. *Brexit* had further cheered him, until he found that half a dozen of his tenants had lost European contracts and given notice that they couldn't afford the rent hike.

The office inventory... One double pedestal mahogany desk with inlaid red leather top and a matching swivel chair, two client chairs with arms but not very substantial cushions, a three drawer mahogany filing cabinet, four book shelves, and a tray on a corner table with a tin of tea bags, a tin of coffee, a cafetière and three mugs on it. By no means a desperate place when compared to Bob Cratchit's office, but there were occasions when I grimaced as I crossed the threshold. I'd lost count of the number of times I'd considered a move. On good days the cocoon of walls is comforting, and often I manage to do some constructive thinking and planning. But on days like this day in history, stuff like purpose and motivation get tossed into the grinder, and my office is the last place I want to be.

And the last person I wanted to have on my case, was Danny Malone. He was carrying around a fifty quid grudge in a five quid box. Still mad as hell at the world, still raging against circumstance and the odds. It was never going to be otherwise, and never going to be life-enhancing. Especially for those unlucky enough to be on his radar.

I transferred my attention to the clock on the wall. Nearing high noon.

On reflection, *High Noon* was apropos. I was sitting in my office watching the time tick by, waiting for the guy on the right side of the law to ring and order me to be sensible, or the guy on the wrong side to kick down the door and menace me all over again.

Harvey called first. "Let me buy you lunch," he said. "The *Nova Scotia*. 12.30."

It would have been churlish to refuse. Harvey Butler is a clever, tough, compassionate, straight-arrow copper. Five or six years older than me and with all the experience that grows alongside a passion for law and order, and an instinctive grasp of the difference between right and wrong. Nobody better to head up the Murder Investigation Team. He doesn't approve of private investigators and he regards what I do, at best, as borderline. But he has always accepted that we're usually allies – in a 'what the hell are you doing?' sort of a way – even though we work from opposite sides of the street. He operates with a copy of *Moriarty's Police Law* tucked under his arm, I sneak into places through the side entrance. Sometimes our interaction is right on the note, sometimes it resembles the relationship between a terrorist and his hostage.

Harvey arrived with DS Mailer. We sat down at a table on the quayside. He went into the pub to order food and drinks. DS Mailer smiled at me. She nodded towards the pub door.

"The Super said we ought to meet."

She held out her right hand. I shook it and said 'hello'.

"Elizabeth. Liz," she said. "I have your name, you should have mine."

She was a very striking lady. Around five feet six, black skin, short black hair, and dark eyes created for mesmerising. Wearing tight jeans and carrying the right amount of weight. She gave me time to make the survey without getting upset, then supplied everything else I needed to know.

"I was born in St Pauls, went to Bristol Grammar School, then on to Sheffield to study psychology. I met a couple of top coppers on graduation day, who told me I ought to consider a police career. So here I am."

Harvey arrived with a tray.

"All aspects of the political correctness debate wrapped up in one bundle," he said. "A woman, black, a first class degree and on a fast track."

"Not that the Superintendent is being cynical you understand."

"God forbid," I said.

"And he missed out lesbian."

Not the ghost of a reaction from Harvey. He put the tray on the table and dispensed the drinks. Then sat down and raised his glass.

"Cheers."

I reciprocated, swallowed a mouthful of beer and put the glass on the table. Harvey looked me straight in the eyes.

"So?..."

I'd rehearsed this bit, but suddenly it felt as if I hadn't worked on it enough. I decided to hold out for an update on the Alfie investigation.

"DS Mailer is in charge of co-ordinating everything," Harvey said, and he gestured for Liz to continue.

"What do you want to know, Jack?" she asked. "Specifically."

Specifically, I didn't want to be seduced by this double barrelled dose of helpfulness. It felt suspiciously like an act of indulgence that I would have to account for later. I offered a question I hoped might reveal something to work on.

"Is there no progress at all?" I looked from the fast tracker to her boss. Neither of them said anything. I ploughed on. "Linda is seriously distressed. And she's wondering why I'm not getting involved."

Mailer responded. "There are gaps in Alfie's days, on a regular basis. Which is out of character, considering the way he did things. His timetable was well established and written down. But there are omissions. We have yet to discover what he was doing during those unrecorded periods."

"Maybe he wasn't doing anything at those times," I suggested.

"Then he would have written that down too," Mailer said. "Everything in his life, especially time, was logged. But he was off the grid during those periods.   Engaged in something, I believe, that eventually got him killed."

"Over how long a period?" I asked.

"Ten months," Mailer said. "Three times a week on Monday, Wednesday and Thursday. And also on Friday evenings."

"How many hours altogether?"

"Twelve each week."

"What do Joanna and Patrick say about that?"

"Way back, when they asked him what he did, he said he went out and walked around. That's as plausible as everything else he did. They knew better than to dig for more. Just asked him to be careful."

"And that's all you have. Holes in Alfie's diary and a hunch about why?"

"Yes."

"He didn't drive a car," I said. "So someone must have seen him out and about somewhere. Have you trawled bus drivers and taxi firms?"

"We are doing that, Jack," Harvey said. "No result with taxis. It appears he didn't use them. He took buses everywhere. He kept a list of all the routes in the city."

I stared at him. Mailer picked up the story.

"Every single one. Bus numbers, roads and stops."

"A list?"

Mailer nodded.

"But not a log of which, when, and where to?"

"Not that we've found," she said. "And checking routes, chasing up drivers and passengers is taking up huge chunks of time. There are nine different bus services which call at stops within a half mile radius of his house."

She picked up her glass of cider and drank from it. The landlord stepped out of the pub door with three plates of scampi and chips.

* * *

The investigation into Alfie's death needed a helping hand. And, unhappily, the likelihood was Danny Malone was it. I rang his mobile from my office. His voice invited me to leave a message. I told him to call me soonest.

With nothing else to do, I decided to make a stab at the old telephone directory ploy. Sometimes it works. The last time I had heard, Rachel Malone was living in Henleaze. Five R Malones were listed in the post code area, one RB Malone and one RS. The first call was answered by a lady called Renee, who told me she was a pensioner and politely wished me well. The second number offered a message from Rhonda Malone. The third, a message from Richard Malone. The fourth, a live and at home response from Rowland, and the fifth from Robert – 'call me Bob'. RB Malone was Randolph Brian and RS was Rose Sylvia.

A fruitless half hour on balance. And the odds on success with Turner were even longer.

At which point I chided myself for not making this simpler. I called Adam, at the *Bristol Evening Post*. The call was transferred to his mobile. He was in Clevedon, out with Sam on Poets Walk – a footpath which climbs the hillside at Marine Lake, skirts the channel shore, and ends by looping around the tiny church of Saint Andrew and the graveyard with stunning views across the water. I asked how he was. He said he was fine. I told him I needed his help.

"Okay. But I'm a little busy tonight. I've got some copy to file and then there's a drinks do somewhere. Will it wait until tomorrow?"

I said it would.

"Come over mid-morning," he said.

"Let me just ask you one thing. You've heard of the actress Amy Turner?"

"Of course. Swiftly rising star."

"Will the *Post* have copy about her?" I asked.

"Lots of it," he said. "Why?"

"I'll tell you tomorrow."

CHAPTER FOUR

The local news at breakfast the following morning wasn't good. Overnight there had been a series of knife attacks in Easton.

Shortly after 11.30, Zuhair Ashraf was found by two constables in a police patrol car, stabbed and bleeding on the pavement outside the mosque he attended. At five minutes to midnight, Samir Malik was attacked two streets away from the house in which he was born and brought up. An hour later, another man, James Rashid, staggered into Stapleton Road Police Station, bleeding from wounds to his thigh and his groin.

Easton, an old fashioned, thickly populated area northeast of the city centre, has been an Asian neighbourhood for two generations, the sporadic troubles of the 60s and 70s now long consigned to memory. But these days are unsteady, tempers are short, and perceived foreigners – especially those with Muslim names and connections – are treated with all the suspicion the new 'little Englanders' can muster. The chemists and the grocers and the newsagents who set up their shops way back when, are afraid. White friends and neighbours have morphed into unpredictable malcontents.

* * *

Adam and Chrissie live on Dial Hill in Clevedon, in a short terrace of impressive Edwardian houses, with a view from the north end over the golf course and Margaret's Bay.

I walked up the garden path, arrived at the doorstep, planted my feet, distributed my weight evenly, and rang the doorbell. A mighty fusillade of barking erupted inside the hall. The door opened. Sam launched himself over the threshold, a rocket powered, whirling mass of excitement. He reared up onto his back legs planted his front paws firmly at trouser belt level and danced forwards. I did a corresponding dance backwards until I managed to twist away. He dropped onto all four legs and swung to face me once more. I yelled 'Sit' and the dog froze almost in pre-leap. I shot him the fiercest expression I could muster. He sorted the likely opportunities in order of possibility, decided on discretion at this point and sat down, tongue hanging out, his tail thrashing from side to side over the lawn, like the blade of a rotary grass cutter. From behind me I heard his master's voice, quiet but firm.

"Sam..."

The dog shook his head. His ears flapped and his choke chain rattled. Then he got to his feet, executed a neat swerve around me, padded to the front door and on into the hall.

"Welcome," Adam said. "Chrissie's at work of course. Her first week as a new teacher."

Sam was bribed with biscuits and a dog chew. Adam rustled up scones and jam. We ate, then took mugs of tea into the study.

The instant topic for discussion was the overnight stabbings. Both of us were angry that our city – which has been feted for so long for its inter-racial harmony – was once again gripped by despair and back in the headlines

45

courtesy of people whose zeal was unnatural, whose knee-jerk reaction was to hate rather than to welcome.

Eventually we got to the purpose of my visit. Adam logged into the *Post* archive and opened Amy Turner's folder.

"Okay... What is it you want to know?"

"Actually, I want to know something about her mother."

Adam turned back to the keyboard, tapped at it again. Paused. Grimaced. Then scrolled down the page he was on.

"Not much here. A couple of references. Erm... Divorced... proud of her daughter's success... happy she's a level-headed girl..."

"Okay. An address?

"No."

"Is there anything on her grandmother?"

Adam tapped keys again. Waited. Dragged the mouse over some copy and double clicked.

"Here we are. Thelma Turner. An interview with her last year about her granddaughter's BAFTA."

"Done where?"

"Where?"

"Yes. Indulge me."

Adam began reading the interview. "At home. With a lot of local born and bred stuff in the piece."

"And home is?"

He scrolled through the article. "In Harriet Street. Runs along the side of Brandon Hill. The piece doesn't give the full address, understandably. Sarah Kingland –

the reporter who filed the story – will have it. Take Sam into the garden and throw his latest toy around. I'll call her."

Sam, never a dog to do things by halves, threw himself around too, making a series of spectacular mid-air catches. He was dropping the toy at my feet for the umpteenth time when Adam called from the living room window.

"I have what you want."

I told Sam that was all for now. I handed him his toy. He grabbed it, waited for me to set in motion whatever excitement was coming next. I retreated into the house. He dropped his toy and barked at me, then overcome by gloom, he lay down, stretched for his toy and began to chew it.

I got into the Accord an hour later, fished my mobile out of the glove compartment and called Malone. Again, no response. I left another message. I looked at my watch. 12.45. A visit to Thelma Turner unannounced was looking more likely by the minute. I resolved to give Malone another couple of hours to call, then if he didn't, to carry on regardless.

Which was the afternoon matinee on Film 4. *Carry On Regardless* is not the best of the oeuvre by any judgement, but it passed a daft ninety minutes. I switched to BBC News at 5 o'clock and immediately regretted it. The leading story was a dismal re-run from Lemnos, another Greek island now bursting at the seams with refugees from Syria, Turkey and northern Africa. Euro MPs were working, once again, towards a monster fudge of an agreement to help, while solving a major humanitarian problem was actually the issue. And *Brexit* negotiations were back in the headlines – David Davies and Liam Fox, still on the arse end of 'no deal is better than a bad deal'; floundering in the shallows of reality, with talk of an uber-monstrous bill for the exit process, and chastised by opponents for still having no signs of a recognisable strategy.

At that point I decided a Chinese takeaway was likely to be more appetising fare than the rest of the news, found my wallet and walked the few hundred yards to the *Canton House* on Coldharbour Road.

Back home, I dawdled over the meal.

At 6.30, *Points West* was no less cheerful. The story of the stabbings headlined a litany of misery. And second up, standing in front of Police Headquarters in Portishead, the programme's political editor was in full flow...

In a massive U turn, the Police Commissioner and senior officers of Avon and Somerset Constabulary have reversed the Force's objection to the planned march through the city by the British Political Action Group. In spite of massive lobbying by Christian, Muslin and black community leaders, as well as residents along the route of the march, it will now take place as previously scheduled, a week on Saturday. BPAG leaders say they are delighted with the decision. The man in charge of making sure that everything runs smoothly is Assistant Chief Constable David Langley.

Cue the ACC, in formidable black uniform, scrambled egg fringed cap, polished buttons, black gloves and swagger stick, talking down to the TV audience in a style reminiscent of Maggie Thatcher. He confidently believed, he said, that everyone taking part in the march and those lining the route, would behave in a sober, democratic fashion; and allow the members of the BPAG to exercise the right they have to run an approved street event, with sense and restraint.

The last two elements are never much in evidence when the hard right takes to the streets, and given the current situation, they were unlikely to be absent from this gig.

Meanwhile, still no word from Danny Malone. So if I was going to do this...

* * *

I swung the car into Harriet Street twenty minutes later, located Thelma Turner's house and parked a few doors beyond it. The row of terraced cottages looks across the road to Brandon Hill and one of the city's landmarks, Cabot Tower. They have tiny front gardens, five or six paces deep. I tapped the knocker on the door of number 24. No one answered. I tapped a touch harder. Then banged it a couple of times. A middle-aged couple emerged from the house to my right, all dressed up and with somewhere to go. The man moved to the garden gate and opened it. The woman closed the front door, locked it, and paused to look at me.

"Do you want Thelma?" she asked.

"Mrs Turner, yes."

"I don't think she's at home. The postman left a parcel with us this morning. A man called around lunchtime, but left without getting into the house. I knocked half an hour ago, but there was still no reply."

"Do you know her daughter, Rachel?"

"No. Sorry."

She walked to the gate and caught up with her partner. I watched them move along the street. I stepped back a couple of paces and examined the face of the house. No sign of life anywhere. I left the garden, crossed the road, and walked into the park. Up to Cabot Tower on the brow of the hill.

I sat down on a cast iron framed wooden bench, stretched my legs out in front of me and gazed into the dusk settling over the city. The warm evening breeze was refreshing. The city spread out below me, like a maze invented by a man who'd lost track of the way to the centre. The noise of the traffic moving along Hotwell Road and over the Cumberland Basin reached up to me; a deep rumbling sound muffled by the closing of the day. I have lived in this town all my life, but, at that moment, the place seemed completely alien. Peopled by strangers controlled by forces greater than they could muster; sound and movement directed by the hours, minutes and seconds of the day; elements which fashioned a lifestyle that many could embrace, others could desire, and the remainder could only cope with as best they could.

And somewhere, lost in the un-caring confusion of it all, was the person who had killed Alfie Barnes. And right here, staring into the dusk, was an out-of-work detective who should be thinking more positively.

Two days ago, Joe Strummer and the Pogues had serenaded Alfie through his last few moments in this world. Danny Malone had proposed that I work for him in return for information un-gatherable anywhere else. His daughter had disappeared. I had no idea where his wife was either, or his mother-in-law. There was no pattern to any of it.

I decided I would make no progress raging at these frustrations while sitting on my arse and staring into the gathering gloom. I should call Chrissie and ask how she had survived her first day in school. I took my mobile out of a jacket pocket. Adam answered from the kitchen. He said Chrissie was in the study, took the receiver away from his mouth and called out to her.

The line clicked and echoed for a moment while both receivers were live.

"Dad," Chrissie said. Adam disconnected, the echo disappeared and Chrissie went on, "I had a fantastic day. A bit terrifying. God, I was so nervous at half eight this morning."

And she launched into a minute by minute narrative of the day. The story scrambled at times as she tried to talk about everything. Until she stopped and apologised.

"Sorry Dad, I'm rambling now. And I have lesson plans to check."

"I'm proud of you," I said.

"Yes," she said, "I know."

"We'll talk tomorrow," I said. "Sleep well."

"And you," she said.

I put the mobile back into my pocket, got to my feet and walked out of the park. The living room curtains in Thelma Turner's house were drawn closed, a low, diffused light seeping through. And there was light in the hall, shining through the transom window above the front door. I stepped up to the door and knocked. There was no response. I knocked again. This time there was a rustle of sound in the hall. A woman's voice spoke to me – elderly and uncertain.

"Who is it?"

I put my head close to the door. "Mrs Turner?"

"Wait a moment please."

I stepped back a pace. On the other side of the door, two bolts were pulled back and a Yale unlocked. The door opened on a chain and Mrs Turner peered through the gap between the door and the frame. I could see a forehead, two eyes, nose, mouth and chin.

"I'd like to talk with you Mrs Turner," I said. "My name is Jack Shepherd. I'm a private investigator."

She thought about that for a moment or two.

"Investigating what?" she asked.

"To tell you the truth I'm not sure. The brother of a friend of mine has been killed. And this may have some connection to your son-in-law. Who, in turn, tells me your granddaughter is missing."

"Are you here on his behalf? Because if you are you can -"

"No. He doesn't know I'm here." She looked at me steadfastly. "Please Mrs Turner, let me in. Just into the hall. I'll stay on the doormat."

"Move back towards the gate please."

She closed the door. I stepped back and waited. Five, ten, fifteen seconds. I couldn't hear anything happening inside the hall from that distance. Then the door swung open. Mrs Turner was silhouetted in the light from behind her. I walked towards the door.

"You say my son-in-law doesn't know you are here," she said.

"That's right."

"Slit your throat and hope to die."

I smiled at her. She stepped back a couple of paces.

"Come on in," she said.

I stepped into the hall.

"Close the door please."

I did so. She looked me up and down again, then led the way into the small living room. It was chintzy, homely and tidy. There was a cement tiled 1950s concrete fireplace, with a 60s gas fire standing on the hearth. It was lit, but burning low. One of the ceramic elements was broken. Thelma was seventy something, with just enough wrinkles to look older than Linda's parents, but not old. She had brown eyes and dimples in her cheeks and grey fly away hair. She pointed at the armchair to my right.

"Please sit down."

I did so. It was one of those soft cushioned chairs which sank and enveloped, and made it difficult for the sitter to get out of. She sat down on the sofa, her feet on the floor, her knees pressed together. She clasped her hands tightly in her lap. Still not at ease.

I waited. After what seemed to be due consideration, she unlocked her hands and spoke again.

"What can I do for you er... Jack?"

"I had a visit from your son-in-law over the weekend," I explained. "He says your granddaughter is missing."

Thelma nodded from the sofa. "Yes..."

"And you have no idea where she might be?"

She breathed in and took time to answer. "That's right."

"Has Amy gone missing before?"

"No."

"Do you think she might have had some sort of breakdown?"

"Why? She's got it all. A mother and grandmother who love her, talent to burn, fame and fortune, the next stop in her career films and Hollywood..."

"What about Amy's management. What do they know?"

"No more than us."

"So how many people are in the loop?"

Thelma shook her head, so I started counting. *The Causeway* producers, her agents, her mother, father, grandmother and me. A dozen people at most.

"It was a mistake telling my son-in-law," I heard Thelma say.

"Why do you think that?"

"He's nothing but trouble."

Most of those who knew him would offer a similar endorsement. The doorbell rang. It didn't seem to register with Thelma.

"Would you like me to answer that?"

She came back to me and nodded. "Please."

I got to my feet, walked into the hall, unlocked the door and pulled it back as far as the chain would allow.

A force outside hit the door like a battering ram, tore the chain out of the door frame and swung the door open. Danny Malone barrelled over the threshold and into the hall. I side-stepped. He couldn't stop, kept on going, and ran head first into the newel post at the bottom of the stairs. The scream of pain was loud enough to be heard by neighbours both sides. He dropped to his knees, clamped both hands to his forehead, rolled away from the stairwell and onto his back on the hall carpet. Blood began to seep through his fingers. Eyes closed, he gave a voice to the pain.

"Jesus Christ. Fuck, fuck, fuck."

Thelma stepped into the living room doorway and stared at her son-in-law with some malevolence.

"Do you think he's hurting?" she asked.

"I'm sure he is," I said.

"Good."

She turned and went back into the living room.

Blood seeped into Malone's left eye. He moved his left hand and gingerly wiped the socket. He took his hand away, opened the eye and looked up at me.

"You fucking -"

Another wave of pain put an end to the sentence.

"Not been the best of days has it, Danny?" I knelt down beside him. "Let me take a look."

"Don't you fucking touch me," he shouted.

55

"Take your hands away from your forehead."

He did. But only to reach up and grab me round the neck. I took hold of his wrists, prised them away from me and looked at his face. There was a vertical groove an inch and a half long, cut into the surface of his recently rearranged, considerably bruised forehead. He must have hit a corner of the newel post.

"The wound needs stitching," I suggested.

"Fuck that," he grunted.

I got to my feet. Malone dug a white handkerchief from a trouser pocket, balled it in his fist and clamped it onto the wound.

"Sit up," I said. "But that's all."

I called to Thelma, asked her if she could find a clean cloth, soak it in cold water and bring it to me. She appeared in the hall, turned away from us and moved into the kitchen. I heard a cupboard door shut, then a tap running. It stopped. Thelma reappeared and handed me the cloth. I gave it to Malone, who dropped his blood soaked hankie on the carpet and replaced it with the cloth. Thelma watched for a moment or two, then bent down, carefully picked up Malone's handkerchief with a thumb and forefinger and turned for the kitchen.

"Hey that's monogrammed," Malone said.

"It's going in the bin," Thelma said. She looked at me. "You've got blood on your shirt collar."

She moved back into the kitchen. I stood in front of the mirror at the foot of the stairs. Malone's blood was where his enormous hands had left it – on both sides of my neck. Not much of it, but grisly enough. Thelma called to me from the kitchen doorway.

"You need to take that shirt off right now and soak it in cold water. Give it to me."

I did as I was ordered. Thelma made another foray into the kitchen. I took a look at the edge of the front door. There was a chunk of wood missing where the chain had been ripped off, and a corresponding hole in the door frame. The rest was okay. I closed the door and locked the Yale. Malone had managed to prop himself upright against the newel post. He took the cloth away from his forehead and studied it. He searched for a non-bloody section. I dropped to my haunches in front of him. He looked at me and tried to focus.

"The bleeding's stopped," I said.

"No fucking thanks to you," he said.

"Stop sulking," I said. "You shouldered the door open."

He sulked a bit more. I suggested I take him to A&E.

"No. No hospital. I'll drive my car home."

"Not in that state."

"As soon as," he said. "I'm not staying with fucking Cruella de Vil in there."

I stood up again, and at that point it occurred to me to ask him where he had been all day. He told me that was none of my fucking business. I asked him why he had come calling. He told me he wanted to find out where Rachel was living. When she had called him three days ago, it was from an unlisted mobile. I asked how he was supposed to get in touch with her. Rachel had said that

57

her mother would act as a go between. He turned his head and glared balefully towards the kitchen.

"Only the fucking witch told me it would be over her dead body."

"So why are you here now?"

"Try to reason with her."

There was a novelty. Define reason Danny. His version would be light years away from any dictionary listing and probably involve a major degree of bodily harm to the reasonee.

I offered him a deal.

"I'll find Amy for you. And when I do, if you don't tell me what you know about Alfie's murder I'll go straight to the cops. The pain you're in right now will seem a minor discomfort come the moment of retribution. And I won't take your money. I'll do this on my pennies."

That made him look up at me once more. His brow furrowed as much as it was capable and he winced again.

"Nothing to do with feelings for you," I said. "I can't bring myself to dredge up any. We're not on the same side and never will be. I don't need your money, and it would make my stomach heave to take it."

Thelma appeared in the kitchen doorway.

"I've done the best I can with the shirt. I'll give it a spin in the dryer and iron it before you go home."

"Thank you," I said. Turned back to Malone. "And the other major condition is that you stay away from here, or any place where Thelma is. Disagreement is a deal breaker. Got that."

"Yes."

"Do you want me to help you up?"

"I'll do it myself."

It took him the best part of a minute. He swayed on his feet, reached for the newel post and hung on. I gave him another few seconds then stepped to the front door and opened it. Malone let go of the newel post and stayed upright.

"Be seeing you," I said.

Malone made it past me and out through the front door. He stopped at the gate and breathed deeply. He didn't bother to look back and say goodbye, simply took another step onto the pavement, turned left and inched painfully along the street. He weaved left and right a couple of times on the journey towards his car. I stepped back into the house.

Thelma phoned Rachel and gave her the story of the evening. She ended the call, sat down at the small bureau in the corner of the living room, wrote her daughter's address and phone number on a 'post it' note and gave it to me.

"Rachel says she will talk with you whenever you want."

She stood up again and hovered, looking a little short of purpose. I asked her if we had missed something.

"I'm not sure about this bit," she said. "Rachel says it's okay, but..."

I waited. She cleared her throat and went on.

"This information must stay between us. You and me and Rachel."

"Of course."

"Amy has a house on the Dorset coast. A village called Ewell. Just a tiny place looking out over Studland Bay. *Sands View*."

"How many people know about it?"

"Until this moment only Amy, Rachel and me. Now you know. It's a bolt hole, a secret place. She bought it a couple of months ago - early in July." Thelma, paused for a moment and then summed up. "Amy talks to my daughter, or me, every day or two. If the work load's heavy, twice a week. So no emails or phone calls for eight days, doesn't bode well. Rachel told me to give you my keys to the house."

She rustled them up from the bureau, then asked me what I charged for finding people.

"Expenses only, for friends," I said.

"Is that what we are?"

"Unless you're hiding something from me."

Thelma shook her head. "There isn't anything. I promise."

She handed me the keys.

I left the house in a cleaned and ironed shirt. Back in the Accord, I realised I had yet to drive the car in the dark. I turned the ignition key and the dashboard lit up like the city centre at Christmas. I tried switching on the lights and got the windscreen wipers. Reversed the process, tried another combination of buttons and got a roaring blast of cold wind as the air conditioning burst into life. I found the lights at the next attempt. The radio display blinked at me – I hadn't tuned it. Now wasn't the time.

I drove home.

CHAPTER FIVE

I called Rachel the following morning at 8.30. No live response and no message. Nonetheless, with a newly minted sense of purpose I slid into the Honda. I fished the road atlas out from under the passenger seat. You don't need a compass to find Studland from Bristol. The A37 takes you all the way to Dorchester. From there, it's barely twenty miles east to the Isle of Purbeck, then a little jig here and there gets you to the sea.

I clocked eighty-seven miles and made Studland in an hour and fifty minutes. The village of Ewell is a mile or two south, down a single track road. It's a peaceful little place, hanging on to the side of a hill above a semi-circle of coast. Half a dozen narrow streets slope gently down to the harbour. They meet the sea and stop at the harbour wall. Ewell's working community is housed in a cluster of buildings facing the sea; the old Harbour Master's office – now a pottery – a ship's chandlers, a small grocery shop, and a pub called, somewhat ominously, *The Last Cargo*.

I got out of the Accord and marvelled. The water trapped in the harbour sparkled in the sun, rippled and bounced in the enclosed space. A couple of lobster boats were moored together below me. A handful of ski boats lay tied to plastic buoys. And near the harbour mouth a handsomely expensive Sunseeker rode gently at anchor.

I looked at my watch. 10.35. So now what?...

The sound of an electric drill seeped into the peace and quiet. I located the source. At the far end of the western sea wall, a fishing coble had been hauled out of the water and on board, a fisherman was drilling holes in the deck. The man to talk to, clearly.

He stopped drilling as I arrived at his boat. He wished me a 'good morning'. I returned the compliments of the day and asked him if he knew where *Sands View* was. He pointed north across the harbour, beyond the Sunseeker.

"It's that way a bit. Towards Studland village. You can get to it in fifteen minutes if you walk along the beach."

"Thank you," I said.

Back at the Accord, I took off my jacket and left it on the rear seat. I fished an old pair of trainers out of the boot, swapped them for my shoes and socks, and set off along the beach.

Sands View wasn't big, but it was a handsome piece of architecture, an aspiring Frank Lloyd Wright sort of place. A single storey building hanging over the incline of the dunes with a deck in front, supported by heavy wooden pillars sunk into the sandstone below. A picture window stretched about two thirds of its width, framed by brown hardwood and double glazed against the wind from the sea. Steps dropped from the deck to the beach.

I climbed onto the deck, like any disrespectful tourist would do and moved to the window, skirting a pile of bricks and a lump hammer. I tapped gently on the glass; and then again, more heavily, with no response. I walked along the deck and round to the landward side of the house.

There was a turning circle in front of it and a track snaking back to the Studland-Swanage road. A battered Ford Fiesta was parked outside the front door, this an expensive piece of panelled mahogany set in a side-glassed frame. I stuck my forehead to the glass. The hall behind it, ran all the way back to the window overlooking the beach. I dug Thelma's keys out of a pocket, unlocked the door, pushed it open and stepped into the hall.

The first door on the left unveiled a cloakroom which housed three shelves of cleaning materials, a box of tools, a vacuum cleaner, an ironing board, two sets of waterproofs and a wet suit. The door on the opposite side of the hall opened into the bathroom – all mirrors and sky blue tiles and boasting his and hers washbasins. The third door gave me access to the bedroom. It was white all over and dominated by a king-size bed. The floor was covered in a long pile carpet, the sort that's murder to keep clean. You just can't get crumbs and marmalade stains out of a white shag pile. But then maybe Amy and her guests never had breakfast in bed. At the end of the hall, the living room, kitchen and dining room were separate parts of a *grande salle* overlooking the beach.

I stepped into the living area. More long pile carpet, this time a deep green, covered the whole floor. The furniture was straight out of the Heals catalogue – tan leather three-piece suite, oak and ash tables, designer art objects and a kind of small tapestry. On one side of the open fireplace was a big flat screen smart TV, on the other side, a sound system I would have to save up to pay for.

The interesting thing though, was that the long window looking on to the beach was now open. There was a bit of a commotion out on the deck and a man stepped into the room. Fair-haired, tall, skinny and shirtless, and wearing a pair of Bermuda shorts. He was holding the lump hammer.

I stared at him. He stared at me.

"Who the hell are you?"

"Jack Shepherd." I looked at the hammer. "Are you going to hit me with that?"

"What are you doing here?"

"I'm a private detective. I'm looking for Amy."

"Are you a friend of hers?"

"Are you?"

"Yes, I'm Neil Shore," he said. "S H O R E. I'm a writer."

"What do you write?" I asked.

"Screenplays. Amy and are working on a project together."

"You don't need a lump hammer for that."

He shrugged. "This is an isolated spot."

"Put it down."

He asked me how I knew about this house. I asked him if he knew where Amy was. He said he had absolutely no idea.

"I've been here since Thursday. I came to see her."

"Why?"

"I hadn't heard from her for a while."

"You do that, do you?"

"What?"

"Rush to her side in a perceived emergency."

"I called her mobile," he said. "It just goes to the voice message. So I…" The words drifted away. Then he focused again. "So I'll wait."

That seemed to be that. I suggested he put the hammer down. He looked at it. Felt the weight of it in his hand. Looked up at me again, like Walter Huston staring at Humphrey Bogart in *The Treasure of the Sierra Madre*, suspicion etched deep. The telephone sitting on a low oak table to my right, began to ring. I reached for it.

"Leave it," Shore said.

"It might be Amy," I suggested.

He waved me towards the kitchen. I didn't move. He became more agitated, upgrading his waving business to maximum. I crabbed away from the table. Shore grabbed the phone receiver and lifted it to his left ear.

"Amy?" he said. Then "Who?" Followed by "I don't know who you are."

He put the receiver back on its base. I waited for him to say or do something. He looked at me.

"Do you know someone called Rachel?"

I nodded at the phone. "Why didn't you hold on a bit longer? You might have learned something."

"Do you know who that was?"

"Give me the hammer."

Shore grimaced, and launched himself at me, hammer raised. I waited until he was within arm's length, ducked under the hammer, twisted away clockwise, swung round and jabbed my right elbow backwards into his ribs. Shore grunted and lost his balance. I completed a 360 degree turn, grabbed his right arm with my left hand, balled my right fist and chopped down hard on his forearm. He lost all feeling in his right hand and dropped the hammer. I reached for it. He bowed his head and lunged me. I straightened up enough to halt his progress. With him hanging on to me, arms round my waist, I swung through one hundred and eighty degrees. He lost his grip, overbalanced and fell backwards onto the oak table. He yelled out, rolled to his left and dropped face down into the shag pile. The phone rang again. I picked up the receiver.

"This is Jack Shepherd, Mrs Malone."

"Mr Shepherd," the lady said, her voice coated with distress.

"Hello," I said.

"Who did I just speak to?" she asked.

"Neil Shore. Spelled like Dinah not Bernard. He's looking for Amy too."

"What is he doing at the beach house?"

"Trying to work he says. He's a writer. He and Amy appear to be something of an item."

I looked at Shore. He rolled over onto his back, groaning. He opened his mouth to say something then closed it again.

"What is happening there?" Rachel asked.

"Nothing," I said. "We're just getting to know each other."

"Is Amy there?"

"No."

"Does that Shore person know where she is?"

"He says not. He showed up here last Thursday." There was a huge intake of breath down the line. "Rachel, leave this with me. Let me gather a bit more information. Then I'll call you back."

"Soon?"

"Yes. Later today."

"Please do. And thank you."

"My pleasure."

I waited for her to disconnect the line – always best to let the client do this, makes them feel they're in control of the conversation, not being cast adrift. I looked at Shore. He hadn't moved but he had stopped groaning. I picked up the hammer.

"I'll put this back on the deck and we can talk."

Shore ran the cold tap in the kitchen sink, dipped his head into the water, lifted it out again, then dried his face. I made us a couple of long cool drinks with some sort of fruit cordial and a couple of bottles of sparkling water I found in the fridge. Then we sat on the deck in sunshine for an hour or so, swapping biographies, talking about Amy and despite our introduction to each other, swiftly becoming 'Jack' and 'Neil'.

He and Amy had met at drama school three and a half years earlier. They became the star couple when she delivered a solo actor piece he had written. For Amy, that translated into being scooped up by a top agency, a year at the Old Vic and a swift migration to *The Causeway*. Neil's launch into the business proved considerably less successful. During two years of dogged attempts to prove he was an actor, he racked up twenty days of work and banked just a bit less than £5000. Then he wrote a couple of short dramas for television, which went out late at night and which few people saw. They failed to generate momentum. He wrote more, only to have producers and commissioning editors turn down his work. He hadn't earned anything in nine months.

"Amy and I are close," he said. "She bought this place back in July and a couple of weeks ago suggested I move in." He pointed along the deck. "I'm fixing some stone work around that side. And trying to write."

He stared down the beach. The tide was on the turn.

"So how did you miss Amy's mother when she paid a visit?" I asked.

He turned to face me. "When was that?"

"Day before yesterday."

"I could have been along the beach somewhere. Or in Ewell." He began massaging his forehead. "I've got a headache coming on."

I cut to the chase. "Amy hasn't been seen for ten days. Including Saturday and Sunday before last, she had a six-day break from filming and was supposed to be back at work on Thursday morning. She didn't show."

He took that on board, his face for a moment or two screwed up with child-like concentration. Then he shrugged and rubbed his forehead again, struggling with something a little more significant than a disappearance.

"She knew I was planning to visit," he said. "So if she had arrived and then for some reason decided she had to leave again, she would have sent me a text. Or left me a note. Unless..."

"She wasn't able to," I said.

That seemed to hit home. Neil got to his feet and began walking around the deck, circling my chair.

"Amy really is missing, isn't she?"

"Looks like it," I said. He was to my left now. "Where were you when you last spoke to her?"

"Sleeping on a mate's floor in Swindon."

"Did she sound stressed?"

Now he was behind me. "No."

"Did she give you any reason to suspect she wasn't okay?"

"No. I would have picked that up."

I twisted to my right. Neil stepped back into my line of vision and moved away, along the deck this time. So I brought up the one subject still un-aired.

"Why is this here, this whole Studland thing, being kept under wraps?"

Neil stopped moving. He swung round, his face blank, as if he missed the question. So I ploughed on.

"The only people who know Amy owns this house are you, me, her mother and her grandmother. Those who know she's gone AWOL are the production company execs, her agents, and us in the family loop. And apart from Rachel, none of those people know you exist."

He interrupted the flow. "Sadly... Especially the production execs and the agents." Then he looked a bit sheepish. "Sorry." He flapped his arms. "This, and me... Our two big ongoing secrets."

"Why?"

He looked out to sea. Moved to the edge of the deck. I raised my voice.

"For Christ's sake, sit down again, will you?"

He turned. Didn't come back to his chair, but at least he stayed still. Then, for the first time during this section of dialogue, displayed some annoyance.

"Nothing is allowed to get in the way of Amy's rise to stardom," he said. "She decided there were to be no personal complications. She told me this house was bought by her lawyers so that she didn't have to break cover."

"Does she have a PA or a team following her around?"

He shook his head. "No entourage whatsoever."

"Which means..."

I paused, to give the sentence some weight. Neil completed it.

"There is no one who can lead us to her," he said, and moved back to his chair. "My head hurts."

He grimaced. Stepped past me and into the lounge. I followed him. He swayed on his feet, managed to reach the sofa and dropped onto it. I asked him if he had any pain killers. He pointed towards the kitchen.

"There are some Cocodamol tablets in the drawer next to the sink."

I found them. Alongside a pack of throat sweets, anti-histamine tablets bottles of multi-vitamins, cod liver oil pills, garlic pills, charcoal capsules and Temazepam prescribed by a doctor in Swanage. And at the back of the drawer, two bottles of Dexadrine and Desoxyn and a couple of small bags of white, snowy stuff.

I took the Cocodamol tablets to Neil. He swallowed two of them, assisted by a hefty drink of water. I waved the bottle of bennies at him.

"Seen these before?"

"Yes," he said, demoralised again.

"In the kitchen drawer. Among with some ice crystal and a couple of 30 quid bags of coke."

"You don't understand..."

"All right," I said. "Explain it to me."

"Promise that what I tell you will stay in this room."

Those last three lines were straight from the script of a soap opera. I pointed back into the kitchen.

"Temazepam, amphetamines, methamphetamines, coke, Cocodamol by the hundred... You could grind up the contents of that drawer and knock out half of the parish."

Neil shuffled upright against the cushions. He had a choice. Play the nonsense out to the limit or 'fess up. After a long silence he chose the latter.

"Amy got to know about the up-coming Hollywood offer four or five months ago. She's always worried about her weight... But then Hollywood stars, female actors that is, are lean and long-limbed. It's a job specification perpetuated by all actors on the make, obsessed by the conviction that talent is not enough. She started taking Meridia, that's one of the iffy hydrochlorides, to reduce weight. It worked but she wouldn't believe it. I told her the scales didn't lie, and she accepted that for a while. Until she upped the doses. And then it rained side effects. She came off them, ran an extra mile a day, did extra work-outs at the gym. Then she was so full of adrenalin

71

she couldn't sleep. She took the Temazepam for that. And again, she was okay for a while, until her tolerance levels dropped and she found herself waking up at 4 o'clock in the morning. She went to work shagged out and took the coke at moments when she needed a hit before a take. From there it was a short step to methamphetamines, ice crystal and all that shite. Have you ever seen this before, Jack? Watched the decline into drug dependence?"

Far too often was the answer to that.

"Couldn't anybody see it happening?" I asked.

Maybe. But nobody said anything."

"Who is supplying her?"

"I don't know." He saw the look of disbelief on my face. "No really, I don't. It has to be someone local though. Bristol, Bath, Weston... She always has the stuff. Never runs out, never seems to go seeking it."

He grimaced, looked down at the carpet and shook his head sadly.

So we took a gentle, slow-paced walk along the beach. The receding tide had left a corridor of damp sand behind it. Our footprints sparkled in the sunshine.

"Do you think Amy is the addictive type?" I asked. "Has all this happened simply because of the pressures of work?"

"No she isn't," he said, "And yes, I would say it has."

"You know her that well?"

"I think so." Then a light came on somewhere. He reached for my shoulder and stopped walking. "If you can, I should check up on a bloke called Ridley something or other," he said.

I looked at him.

"Ring a bell?" he asked.

"No."

So he explained. "Amy and I had a row earlier in the year. When I thought she was seeing someone else. She had mentioned this Ridley bloke, once or twice, but when I pressed, she insisted he was just an old friend, nothing more. Does that help?"

I shook my head. "Still no."

"But worth looking in to. Yes?"

I nodded my head. "Yes, it is."

Neither of us said any more. Amy had built a fence of some substance around her. Which left the person she was most likely to confide in, and a detective she didn't know, standing side by side on a beach watching the tide go out.

* * *

Neil conceded there wasn't a great deal he could offer to help change the current circumstances. He agreed to stay at the beach house and call me if anyone showed up.

The sun was diamond-bright and the afternoon warm, in spite of the breeze blowing off the sea. I plodded back along the beach and by the time I reached my car I needed a long cold drink and some lunch.

A blackboard outside *The Last Cargo* boasted of the best crab sandwiches on the coast. I gave my order to the landlady and sat down in a corner, under a fishing net hung between two ceiling beams. I can't swear to the crab sandwiches being the best on the coast, but they were the best crab sandwiches I had tasted in a long while. When I stepped out of the pub an hour later I was feeling a lot better.

I strolled along the northeast wall to the harbour mouth, stuffed my hands deep into my pockets and looked out to sea. It was the sort of view you could stare at all day. Inshore, a ski boat sped from east to west, the skier up straight, leaning slightly back and well in control. Beyond the ski boat, a couple of yachts were tacking west to east and out on the horizon a container ship appeared to be sitting still, going nowhere at all. Brilliant sunshine, a soft sea breeze and a September afternoon. Surely all was right with the world... Well this bit of it anyway.

The fisherman I'd met earlier had disappeared. I walked back to the Accord, climbed in, started the engine and headed for the Swanage-Studland road.

* * *

I was sitting in a lay-by north of Shepton Mallet with a plastic beaker in my hand, drinking coffee I'd picked up at a petrol station, when my mobile rang.

"How are you, Jack?" George Hood asked.

I swallowed a mouthful of coffee before I answered.

"I'm fine. Congratulations on your promotion."

"Thank you. I need to ask you some questions."

I swallowed another mouthful of coffee. Hood took the pause from my end as a prelude to me being unhelpful. He made his first question simple.

"Do you remember Danny Malone?"

'There is no such thing as coincidence' has been a long held tenet of mine. It's still a shock, however, when something like one turns up. Hood asked me where I was.

74

"In a lay-by, drinking coffee," I said.

He asked me if I was busy later. I asked him how much later. He paused. A white van pulled past the Accord and parked five or six yards ahead. Hood came back to me.

"All right, no bollocks," he said. "We'd like to talk with you."

I decided if this concerned Danny Malone, I would need time to think.

"About what?" I asked.

Hood picked up the vibe.

"I want you to call on us at Trinity Road. Let's say tomorrow morning 9 o'clock. Does that give you enough time to come up with a story I'll believe?"

I rate George Hood. Like his one-time boss, he is a mightily experienced copper and difficult to outsmart. Able to read every implication in the smallest of details. He is always in the moment, however long or short or bizarre or devious. His best guess will always be right on the button.

He continued. "Special Crimes Unit, second floor."

"Okay. Scouts honour."

"We'll accept that then."

He disconnected the call before I could say anything else.

Danny Malone. The malignant bastard was all over me again. Like a dose of the flu.

I finished the coffee, got out of the car and dumped the plastic beaker in a rubbish bin. The sun had disappeared. I continued to walk the distance of the lay-by, then turned and walked back to the car. The sun came out again. I leaned against the passenger door and stared across the fields beyond the lay-by. I needed to come up with a story which put some distance between me and whatever this was about. But it had to be rehearsed, I couldn't just wing it.

* * *

I got home at 25 minutes to 6. Made some tea, talked myself out of watching the news, and instead, called Linda to ask how she was.

"Deep in work," she said. "Come over later, if you like."

"I can't, I'm busy too," I said. "Thinking."

"Oh well, that's something that'll take a while," she said. "See you tomorrow."

I de-frosted a ten inch pizza, cooked it and ate it all. Then I spent two hours arguing with myself over my position vis-a-vis Danny Malone. I came to the conclusion I would just wing it at Trinity Road after all.

I went to bed early, but the moment I lay down my brain stormed into overdrive. I was still awake, cursing Malone and punching the pillow, at 1 o'clock.

CHAPTER SIX

In the Special Crimes Unit squad room, a DS called Henson recognised me and nodded a greeting. At the far end of the room, George Hood stepped into his office doorway and waved at me. I joined him.

"It's good to see you, Jack."

"And you."

He invited me to sit down and got straight to the point. Asked if I was working for Danny Malone.

"What's he done?" I asked. "What's this all about?"

"At 2 o'clock yesterday morning," Hood said, "two uniforms from a patrol car found Malone face down on the concrete in Broadmead. He's in the BRI. It was a professional job. Just short of life threatening. He was thumped and kicked in every place it matters. All the broken bits will mend, but take a long time to do so and hurt every step of the way. Current thinking is that someone was giving him a warning."

More than a single someone, I thought. Anybody trying to take Danny Malone down would have to be mob-handed.

"Whoever did it, or ordered it to be done, meant business," Hood said. "Knew how many it would take to do the job. He wasn't mugged. His wallet was still with him. And a small pocket diary, with a dozen telephone numbers written on a notes page at the back. Guess what? One of them is yours."

He took a beat. Waited. Then continued.

"Now if I were to suggest that - "

I interrupted him. "Don't bother. Malone called on me a couple of days ago."

"For what reason?"

"He said I was the best detective he'd ever worked with."

Hood looked deep into my eyes.

"Two things," he said. "One... you will engender a better response from me if you don't try and be smart. And two... just answer the question I asked."

"That's what he said, George. Really and truly."

"Okay. I'll re-phrase. What did Malone want you to do for him?"

I took a moment. Hood decided I was stalling again.

"Isn't that question precise enough?"

"He asked me to find a relative," I said.

"What relative?"

"That's confidential information," I said.

"It's bollocks," he said. "There's no such thing in this office. Just you and me and the furniture and the truth."

"It is the truth," I insisted. "The person in question is a blood relative."

Hood rocked back in his chair and allowed me a few seconds to elaborate. I changed tack.

"Okay... I was forbidden to take any interest in the Alfie Barnes case. So I looked elsewhere for work. The offer was surprising, as you can imagine, but Mr Malone insisted."

"I don't see any evidence of violence on your person," Hood said.

"I outwitted him."

Hood grunted. "Yeah, well I guess that could do it." He leaned forwards and his chair rocked upright. He stared at the top of his desk for a couple of seconds, then looked up again. "So what can you can tell me about your client's unfortunate encounter in Broadmead?"

"Absolutely nothing. I have no idea what he is currently engaged in. I do know that he works as an enforcer for Gaghan Nash."

Hood cut the ground out from under me. "We know that, too. We've had a team on the firm for a while."

"Because?..."

Hood shifted in his chair "I can't tell you that."

So I offered a theory. "Maybe Malone met someone who didn't fall for his brand of sinister and got a couple of mates to help prove it."

"Maybe," he said, then took a pause to give what he was about to say some emphasis. "I guess we have enough confidence to trust both of our judgements in this. But you're on the radar, Jack. And if your association with Malone continues beyond a time I deem reasonable I will haul you back in here."

He meant that. So I tested another idea.

"Was he actually encountered in Broadmead do you think, or was he dumped there? I only ask because he's my client."

Hood sighed. "You know, I'd forgotten how this works. You dancing around and dodging my questions."

"I can't tell you anything, George," I said. "You've got a team on this, you must know a hell of a lot more about

Malone than me. Where the uniforms found him and why he was there, is the puzzling bit surely?"

Broadmead is part of one big open air shopping mall and it's no night time rendezvous - except for the multiplex. There are no pubs, clubs, or meeting places. The cafés and restaurants close early. So that begged a question. Did someone actually organise a meeting in Broadmead at a time when all sensible souls were at home in bed? Leaving Malone in the middle of the street was something of a dramatic statement. So what was that all about? Alternatively, if they kicked his insides out somewhere else, why did the perpetrators then drive him into Broadmead to dump him? He wasn't hidden. Certain to be found a lot earlier than if he was left in a ditch out on a road to somewhere. Maybe that was the idea.

"I'll tell you this much," Hood said. "We think Malone has been at full throttle for some months, at least."

"As an employee of Gaghan Nash?"

"Something to consider. Gerald Gaghan has a lot of clout. And behaves like it. No shrinking violet by any stretch of the imagination. So stay well out of his way, Jack,"

The phone on his desk rang. Hood picked up the receiver, listened for a second or two and then looked across his desk at me.

"Yes he is... Yes, I'll tell him."

He disconnected the call and put the receiver down.

"Superintendent Butler wants you to drop in for tea and biscuits."

"How did he know I was here?"

Hood shrugged. "Information, information, information." He stood up. "Go carefully, Jack."

We shook hands across the desk.

Two floors below, I walked past DS Mailer who said 'hello'. Inside his office Harvey waved me to a chair. I asked him if he monitored everybody coming into the building.

"We operate a preference service. The front desk has a list of people of interest to us. Sergeant McCann informed me of your presence. Something to do with Danny Malone, I understand."

I refrained from asking how he understood that. Instead, I asked him how Mailer's investigation into Alfie's death was going.

"The enquiry is progressing," he said.

"Oh come on," I said. "That's the sentence for journalists who irritate you."

Harvey grinned. "Okay. Cling on to the concept of 'irritate', and don't use up what little credit you have left with this department."

I tried to look hurt. "I was told you were inviting me for tea and biscuits?"

On cue, a young DC came into the office with two cups of tea and a plate of digestives. I thanked him, he said it was a pleasure and went out again. Harvey picked up a biscuit, dunked it in his tea and conveyed it to his mouth before it disintegrated. He polished off a second one then offered some information.

"We have found someone who saw Alfie on the 224 bus a time or two."

"And did this person tell you where he got on and off?"

"Indeed he did," Harvey said.

He paused. I waited, not too patiently, for him to go on.

He grinned again.

"Pisses one off doesn't it, lack of co-operation? Of course I can't stop you getting on a 224 bus at the stop nearest to Alfie's address and doing all the leg work we did, and hey... you could get lucky, might only take a week of double shift days."

Harvey was enjoying this. He had an axe buried in my head and was managing to grind it at the same time. Finally, he relented.

"He got off at a stop in Prince Street," he said. "Near the *Arnolfini* art gallery." He picked up the plate and offered me another biscuit. I said 'no thank you'. Then he got to his feet, suddenly as convivial as Mr Fezziwig.

"Go carefully, Jack," he said.

George Hood had said that, too. Perhaps it was in the manual. Harvey held out his right hand. I stood up and shook it.

* * *

I drove back across the city. Linda's office was locked. I sat down in mine and stared at the clock on the wall.

11.30.

So Alfie went to the *Arnolfini* three times a week, or somewhere nearby. Not altogether helpful. And Malone in hospital was a major blow. To the case that was. No doubt a subject for rejoicing in certain circles.

I switched on the laptop and updated the case notes. Read them back to myself. Stared at the pages, to no avail. I called Rachel, as I had promised, and updated her on stuff. She thanked me, but the way she spoke demonstrated she was on edge. The tone of her voice was resolute enough, but she really just wanted to say over and over 'Find Amy, Jack. Find her, find her, find her.'

In the meantime, a hospital visit beckoned. I left the office and walked to the floating harbour ferry stop outside the *Nova Scotia*.

The Bristol Channel has a tidal range of more than fourteen and a half metres. Which means boats of any reasonable draft can only get up the River Avon and into the city for a couple of hours either side of high tide. So, along with building his mighty steamships, bridging the Avon Gorge, and driving the Great Western Railway from Paddington to Bristol, Isambard Kingdom Brunel solved the tidal problem too. He built massive lock gates to capture the river at high tide and imprison it inside the harbour, so that business could go on round the clock. Now the wood yard, coal yard, warehouses, machine sheds and shipbuilders are gone. The floating harbour is the domain of leisure craft and the Ferry Service. The small yellow and blue wooden ferry boats run every day of the year.

The *Brigantia* arrived, its figurehead one of eighty giant Gromit sculptures decorated by, among others, Peter Blake, Gerald Scarfe and Disney Pixar. Fabulous additions to locations in the city during 2013; until in October of that year, when Tim Wonnacott took the auctioneer's hammer and knocked down the greatest dog show on earth for a cool £2.3 million, all of which went to the Bristol Children's Hospital Charity.

I climbed into the *Brigantia*, handed over £4.00 for a return ticket and sat out on the foredeck next to Gromit. Together, we slid gracefully over the water, past the waterfront apartments, the *SS Great Britain*, the old steam cranes, the moored yachts and motor cruisers. Fifteen minutes later I disembarked, crossed the centre and began walking up Colston Street towards the BRI.

"Are you a member of Mr Malone's family?" the nurse at Intensive Care Reception asked.

"We used to work together," I offered. "He has no close family."

The nurse looked down at her notes. "Yes, we have no record of next of kin." She looked up at me. "Let me see if I can find Doctor Alison." She motioned across the floor. "Please take a seat."

I took a seat and looked around me. I nodded to the only other waiting room visitor – a lady with sad eyes, pale cheeks and wearisome rounded shoulders. She nodded at me in return. The room was decorated in shades of cream, darker below the dado rail. The carpet was worn and the skirting boards were streaked with dark lines where the vacuum cleaners had rubbed the surface of the paint. I picked up an old copy of *Hello* and tried to get interested in the ranks of Z list celebs who, arm in arm and page after page, beamed into the camera from mega expensive, champagne fuelled gatherings on emerald lawns in front of mansions with white porticos. People

84

with aimlessly earned six figure salaries, who could stump up the cost for a new carpet and a new paint job in this room and not feel a thing.

Doctor Alison was obviously hard to chase up. I waited, shuffled in my seat, got up, walked about the reception area and sat down again. Ten minutes later, she hove to. Early 40s or thereabouts, tall, slim, fair haired; wearing a light blue shirt and light-grey chinos under the un-buttoned white coat.

"Mr Shepherd," she said. "I'm Margaret Alison. The ICU Registrar. Apologies for keeping you waiting, I was dealing with something a little tricky. Come with me and we'll find somewhere to talk."

She led the way along a corridor in the direction of the IC Ward, stopped outside a consulting room and knocked on the door. There was no response. She opened the door, checked inside the room, and asked me to join her. She closed the door, picked up a chair, placed it at the corner of the desk, and then sat down in the consultant's chair.

"Who are you, Mr Shepherd?" she began. "I have to ask."

I told her who I was and what I did and where I did it from. She seemed amused at first – which is better than hostile – and in the end genuinely interested. She asked me what I was doing for her patient. I told her I was trying to find someone who was missing and hoped she would understand why I couldn't say more than that. She said she understood absolutely, and was sure I would appreciate there was information she could not divulge either. We nodded at each other. We were two very understanding people.

"Mr Malone has not regained consciousness since he arrived here," she began. "We found serious injuries to his knees, his ribs and his head. Last night we put him into a controlled coma, so that we can begin to investigate how bad those injuries are. I can take you to see him, that's all. I'm sorry, but it's the best I can offer."

I followed her to a small room alongside the IC theatre. We looked at Malone through a window. He seemed to be hooked up to every piece of hardware available.

"How long is he likely to be this way?" I asked.

"Impossible to say. Perhaps as little as a few days, or as much as weeks, perhaps months." She turned to look at me. "Do you know any of his family?"

All of them was the answer to that question. I fudged a bit.

"His wife and daughter ran away from him some years ago."

"I see."

"And he doesn't know where they are."

"Do you?" she asked.

"Yes."

"Will you tell them about this?"

"Yes I will."

I refrained from saying they wouldn't give a toss.

"Good. Thank you." She retrieved a card from the breast pocket of her white coat and handed it to me. "That's a direct line to my office. My secretary is on station every weekday from 8.30 to 6.30. Please call her and leave a number for us to call you. And ask Mr Malone's wife to get in touch. Will she do that?"

"Probably not, but I will ask her."

I stared through the window at Malone. There was a time when I would have rejoiced to see him like this. Maybe even as recently as the day before yesterday. The man was big and tough and irredeemably rotten to the core. At least he had been, until persons unknown kicked the shit out of him in the shopping centre. Danny Malone was not a man to have compassion for. He didn't seek it, and nobody I knew had ever offered it to him. But here he was, in the hands of a team of strangers, who were doing all that was humanly and technologically possible to keep him alive. The beleaguered National Health Service cared about Danny Malone.

From miles away, I heard the Registrar asking me if I wanted to stay for a while. I said no. She led me back the way we had come, shook my hand again and reminded me to stay in touch. Then she went back to work and I went out of the building.

I bought a ham and cheese roll from *Subway* and walked to the ferry stop at the Castle Park jetty, pondering the state of play. Clearly, Danny Malone was now out of the picture. Because he knew something about the Alfie Barnes killing? Because those he was working for had decided he was a loose cannon? Because representatives of the legion of people he had threatened, bullied and beaten up during his unsavoury life had finally taken their revenge?

87

The *Independence* — sister ship to the *Brigantia* — arrived, and conveyed me back to the western end of the harbour. I ate the ham and cheese roll as we chugged along. And then a more alarming question surfaced. Was Danny Malone hooked up to machinery because he had talked to me? If so, then whatever I had got myself into wasn't just a matter of life and death, it was more important than that. I resolved to try not to dwell on the issue.

I stepped off the ferry and into the arms of two wide-shouldered, flat-nosed gentlemen in off-the-peg suits. One of them, a pasty-faced, mean looking, forty something; the other younger, black, heavier and altogether more impressive.

CHAPTER SEVEN

Gerald Gaghan lived above it all, in a 1970s ranch style bungalow on the edge of Leigh Woods, built in the grounds of what was once a Slave Trader's estate. From his terrace, he had a panoramic view of the Floating Harbour, the Cumberland Basin and the southwestern part of the city. The terrace and garden obviously soaked up the sun all day – the elements permitting. Currently, with summer lingering on, heat was bouncing off the brick terrace floor and the stone walls of the house. And five hundred watts of *Long Hard Times To Come* was reverbing around the place.

Gaghan was sitting in a lounger in front of a bank of lobelias, facing away from me and looking at the view. All I could see of him was the back of his head bobbing up and down. Another wide-shouldered type wearing a short, white jacket, was pouring drinks into glasses sitting on a low garden table by Gaghan's elbow. He said something which I presumed was 'thank you' and the drinks dispenser retreated into the house. The black guy to my left called out to his boss.

"Mr Gaghan, we've got Shepherd here."

Gaghan didn't move, other than to lift an arm and beckon me towards him. My escort melted away like the man in the white jacket had done. I stepped towards Gaghan, semi-circumnavigated the lounger and looked down at him. He raised his arms like a priest calling up to God.

"Gangsta Bluegrass. Got it on a loop. I fucking love it."

He was mid 50s at a guess, five feet nine or ten, greying temples, smooth unlined face, dark blue eyes. Wearing light brown cotton trousers and a white designer tee shirt with cream horizontal stripes. His face had the solid stone look of a man who is used to being disliked and is unshaken by displays of hostility. Neither of which precepts augured well.

"Makes your fucking bollocks tingle."

I looked back at the house. Another huge employee opened the French windows and lurked in the space. Gaghan waited for my attention to return to him. Then he waved to his employee. The music volume faded.

"Doesn't it cost you a fortune to feed them all?" I asked.

"It's not the food bill that's crippling," Gaghan said. "It's the rabies shots."

His south Bristol accent was as thick as milk chocolate. He pointed to the matching lounger on my side of the table.

"Sit down."

I looked at the lounger, then back at him. He responded by looking offended.

"All right. Please..."

I sat down on one side of the lounger, with the soles of my shoes on the terrace. Gaghan swung himself upright and did the same. We faced each other across the table, between us two generous measures of gin, an ice bucket, a bottle of tonic water and a plate of sliced limes. Gaghan stretched out a hand and slid one of the glasses to my side of the table.

"Help yourself to the ice and stuff."

He waited until that was done and the glass was halfway to my lips.

"Why'd you go and visit Danny Malone?"

I swallowed a mouthful of gin. Asked Gaghan if he was the person who had ordered Malone to be pounded into the concrete. He ignored the question, did the mixing business with his glass, raised it to his lips, drank from it, and asked another.

"How long is it since I offered you a job?" he asked.

"Does it matter?"

"Would you consider another offer?"

"Will it be better than previously?"

Gaghan sighed. "If this…" he pointed his right index finger at his chest, and then waggled it between us, "is to be all questions, we're not going to get anywhere."

"I don't have anywhere to go," I said. "And the afternoon's all mine."

Gaghan looked straight into my eyes. "You have a smart mouth, Jack."

"One of my failings," I said. "But I'm working on the problem."

"I'd hate it to get you into trouble," he said.

"Oh come on, Gaghan, you wouldn't mind any trouble I got into, especially if you had the controlling interest."

He thought about that, grinned and nodded.

"So… Are you working with, or for, Danny Malone?"

"I thought he worked for you."

"He's a contractor. You've met all the employees. Howard the white bloke and Maurice the black one who brought you here, my steward Harry, and Julian the man in the doorway." He called over his shoulder. "Julian, say hello to Jack Shepherd."

Julian bade me welcome from his position at the living room door and Gaghan returned to his first question. I told him I wasn't working for Malone and it would be a cold day in hell if I ever did so. I said I'd never enjoyed his company, even when we had occupied adjacent desks fifteen years ago.

Gaghan nodded his head again. "Yeah. Hard to like, isn't he? But he's useful. At least he was."

There was a pause in the dialogue, while we both swallowed some more gin. Then Gaghan shot me another steadfast look.

"So he came to you, not the other way around?"

"Yes."

"What about?"

I looked at him. "If this were the other way round, me in your seat and you with the thumb screws on, would you answer that?"

He sniffed and shrugged.

"You'd tough it out, of course," I said.

Gaghan called over his shoulder. "Julian..."

He was the tallest man I have ever seen. He ambled across the terrace from the living room door and stood behind me. I stared across the lobelias and attempted to admire the view. My host set about replenishing his glass. I could hear Julian breathing. Gaghan lifted his glass.

"A toast," he said.

"To what?" I asked.

"Plain sailing." He looked into my eyes again. "Just tell me what you are doing for Malone?"

"Nothing."

Which was absolutely true. It looked like Malone was never going be in any shape to talk about Alfie. And finding his daughter was another sphere of activity altogether. The response didn't impress Gaghan however. He nodded at Julian. From behind, I was wrapped into a full nelson and hauled to my feet. I began to choke. I waved my arms at Gaghan. He nodded again, Julian eased his grip a little and my feet regained contact with the floor.

"We had a contra deal," I managed to say. "Malone agreed to do something for me if I found somebody for him."

Gaghan pondered for a moment. Even at less than one hundred percent Julian had a grip stronger than superglue. My neck and shoulders were beginning to hurt. I struggled on.

"However, as he is no longer in command of his faculties, I now consider the contract null and void. He can't honour his side of it, so – "

Gaghan had run out of patience. He stood up and yelled at me.

"Who did Malone ask you to fucking find?"

Julian re-tightened the stranglehold and pulled me clear of the floor again. It hurt much more than the first time he did it. I managed to punch out a few words.

"Somebody who owed him money," I said. "I found that person... but he told me to piss off. I.." I tried to swallow. "I was about to relay the message to Malone..." I tried to breathe. "When persons unknown sent him to intensive care." I began to choke again. "Come on, Gaghan, get Mick McManus to unlock me?"

My plea fell on deaf ears.

"And what was he going to do for you?"

"Give me a couple of names," I said.

"In connection with what?"

He looked into my eyes and waited with all the patience in the world.

"It's a long story," I croaked. "And I'll be... in no position to tell you anything if... if Julian doesn't let go of me."

Gaghan considered this, then nodded at his minder. I was dumped back on to the lounger and released. I choked and gasped for as long as seemed plausible, and I managed to dredge up something so far-fetched it had to be believable; refining a 'get out of jail' story I'd used before, about two fourteen year old twins and a scam to defraud an insurance company. Always an empathetic narrative, as everybody's knee-jerk response is to hate insurance companies and to cheer when somebody sticks it to them.

It took me five minutes to get through this paean to a broken childhood and a brave defence against the might of corporate villainy. Maybe Gaghan believed me, or maybe he simply tired of trying to unpin all the elements of the melodrama. Whatever, the menace quotient dropped considerably and he motioned Julian back into the house. I reached for my glass of gin and Gaghan summed up.

"Howard and Maurice will take you back down the hill. But you're on the radar now, Jack, and I promise to make your life a fucking misery if you don't stay out of my business."

I was driven back to the *Nova Scotia* and politely evicted from the company Mercedes. I wandered back to the office building, lacking most of my sense of purpose, my throat still hurting.

The door to Linda's office was open. I knocked on it, gently. Linda looked up from behind her pc and smiled at me.

"Jack..."

I stepped through the doorway. Linda stood up, moved around her desk and into my arms. I held her close. I could feel her chest thumping.

"I hate this, Jack," she said. "Feeling like this."

"You're allowed to," I said.

"Maybe, but it doesn't help." She paused. I waited for her to go on. She stepped back from me and looked into my eyes. "Alfie was so much more than the sum of his parts. Not that any of us knew exactly what they were. We didn't really know how he worked. It was impossible to second guess him. I loved him to pieces, but there was so much about him I never got to grips with. Though he seemed to know all about me. And I miss him, Jack. Absolutely, profoundly."

The next move had to be mine. I resolved a long time ago never to get involved in open police cases. At least not knowingly, or deliberately, although sometimes what I take on ends up that way because of what I discover. Most of the work I do starts with being hired to find somebody; something that most detectives aren't interested in and aren't very good at. I am. But looking for Alfie's killer involved breaking the number one house rule and, in the process, pitching myself into conflict with the city's toughest and brightest copper. Harvey Butler couldn't stop me from working in the interests of my client, but he could throw me into jail for interfering in the course of a murder investigation.

Linda and I had kind of committed to each other. Her long-time partner, a funny and brilliant teacher and an early mentor of Chrissie's, was knocked down and killed by a drunken piss artist in a Nissan two years before Emily died. The Shepherds banded together to take care of Linda. The entire Barnes family repaid the debt, when we were left stricken by Emily's cancer. By the same reasoning, Alfie as part of this big extended family was just as important. His death was a reason for all of us to mourn. And for one of us to go looking for the truth.

I eased out of her arms.

"I'll do some digging," I said. "The police have some information which might lead somewhere."

"How do you know?"

"Harvey told me."

Linda looked perplexed. "He also told you to stay out of the way."

"Yes. But neither of us believed I would. That's why he handed me a morsel about Alfie's bus journeys. Which he is expecting me to follow up."

"Why?"

"Because I can work in ways he can't."

"You mean climb over walls and into places through windows," Linda said.

I offered her my best 'who me?' look. She rounded off the premise.

"And because he knows you won't let go."

Uncle Sid once told me that my old Scoutmaster had watched me learn how to tie a bowline round my waist, then attach the other end of the rope to a tree trunk, shuffle backwards to the edge of a fifteen foot ditch, abseil – sort of – down into it, then heave myself up and out again. I was eleven years old and I repeated the process over and over, until it was easy and I was fearless. Whereupon, according to Uncle Sid, the Scoutmaster turned to him and said, "That lad has stick-ability". It has become a kind of watchword with me, stick-ability. In homage to the man of extraordinary presence and stick-ability himself who bestowed it on me.

I asked Linda if she had a recent photograph of Alfie.

"There are one or two at home," she said.

I followed her to Portishead in the Accord.

We cooked and ate, and over brandy and coffee we talked. About Alfie, about Joanna and Patrick, about Chrissie and Adam and Sam, and about us. And we listened to Carole King and James Taylor.

The music was gentle, evocative and personal; the poetry of the lyrics custom made for an evening dedicated to the memory of someone close.

And we both knew we had a friend.

CHAPTER EIGHT

I struggled awake the next morning. Saturday. Linda was fast asleep. I turned my head on the pillow and looked at her. I felt lost and disconnected from something or other. I didn't know what. I didn't want to get out of bed either.

Some words of Samuel Taylor Coleridge began playing on a loop in my head.

I moved, and could not feel my limbs;
I was so light – almost
I thought I had died in sleep,
And was a blessed ghost.

I realised they were from *The Ancient Mariner*. And that brought back the memory of Lengthy, a red haired boy I knew at school. Nicknamed Lengthy because he was, and because his surname was Long. Lengthy Long... I tried to remember his first name, to no avail. And then I remembered he had learned the whole of Coleridge's masterwork. All 117 stanzas of it. Lengthy was dead letter perfect. And at break times, lunchtimes, in classroom down time, the gym changing rooms, on the bus home, he never passed up an opportunity to recite the work, no matter how many books, pencils, blackboard dusters or rugby boots we threw at him.

Amazing what slides into your head when you know the day in front of you is destined to be difficult and staying in bed seems the most desirable option. And unlike the Wedding Guest I wasn't about to rise *a sadder and a wiser man*. Suddenly more of the piece was coming back to me.

I slipped out of the house without waking Linda. I drove into the city, along the north bank of the river, then into the car park off Wapping Road. I walked from the car park towards Prince Street and the *Arnolfini*, intending to pound the pavements with Alfie's photograph. My mobile began ringing. I fished it out of a jacket pocket.

"Are you anywhere near a TV set?" Adam asked.

I told him no. He went on to tell me that the current *BBC News* segment was leading with an item about Amy and her face was all over the screen.

Word was out. Amy Turner was officially missing.

By lunchtime, the early edition of the *Evening Post* was in full conspiracy mode. The banner headline on the front page yelled out *Soap Superstar Disappears*. And another line at the head of the sidebar next to Amy's picture, *Suspicious Circumstances*, led two columns of half-arsed conjecture. I dug the mobile out of my pocket and rang Adam. His voice told me he wasn't there. I called Rachel, only to be told that she wasn't there, either. I called Thelma. The number was engaged. I disconnected the line and the phone rang before I could get it back into my pocket. Thelma said Rachel was with her, and Harriet Street was packed with members of the fourth estate.

I abandoned the Accord in a long stay car park at the bottom of Park Street and walked up to St George Street, intending to cut through to Thelma's house via one of the lanes which feeds deliveries into the rear of Park Street shops and restaurants. It wasn't the grade one idea I had hoped it might be. There was pandemonium on every pavement within a two hundred yard radius of Thelma's house. Paparazzi Volvos, Renault Espace news crew vehicles in the streets, ITV West Country and BBC remote trucks setting up in Brandon Hill Park across the road from their target's house. A dozen people around me had mobiles glued to the sides of their heads. I recced the lane behind the garden. Just as jammed as the front street. So I came up with another idea.

All the adjoining garden walls in the terrace were brick and around five feet high. From my end of the lane I had six garden walls to scale before I reached Thelma's. I was up and over the first three, before someone yelled to me from a kitchen window. I waved cheerily, stood on the lid of a convenient dustbin and vaulted into garden four. Only to have my trousers grabbed by an over excited Terrier of some sort. I dragged him across the garden with me and managed to shake him loose as I climbed onto another bin which smelled like a mature compost heap. I was spotted scaling the sixth wall by one of the photographers in the lane. Fortunately Thelma had padlocked the sculpted cast iron garden gate and he could do no more than wail at me through the bars.

I banged on the kitchen door several times, before I heard Thelma's enraged voice shout at me.

"It's Jack," I bellowed in return. "Let me in."

She opened the door and I stepped into the house.

"A studio rigger called Terry somebody leaked the story," she said. "He's been suspended apparently."

Thelma ushered me into the sitting room. Rachel was sitting on the sofa, there in body, but miles away in her head. I began by telling them both about Neil and what he thought was supposed to happen in Ewell.

Thelma asked the question. "And he has no idea where Amy is?"

"No."

Rachel stared into the fireplace. The silence was deafening. So I went back to basics. Asked Rachel if she would give me the names of Amy's close friends. Thelma interrupted by saying she could do that. I said okay, but wondered why she was a better source than Amy's mother. She sat at the bureau in the alcove to the left of the fireplace, found a sheet of paper and a pen, and began making a list. Rachel said nothing at all. I found another question to ask.

"Have you talked to the police?"

There was no response.

"Rachel."

She looked at me as if I'd dug her in the ribs. She sat up the chair.

"Sorry. I was miles away."

"Have you talked with the police?"

She nodded, then looked at the clock above the mantelpiece.

"An hour ago. A detective constable from some department at the Bridewell came round and asked a couple of questions. He didn't seem very interested in the answers."

He had called in because Amy was all over the breakfast news. If the missing person had been Thelma's next door neighbour, there would have been little response, an information logging exercise at best. I ploughed on.

"Do you know of anywhere, apart from the beach house, that Amy might have gone?"

Rachel shook her head. "No."

"Have you rung the beach house again?"

"Yes."

"Did anybody answer?"

"No."

I was trying to get blood out of a cairn of stones.

"Not even Neil?"

She seemed not to hear that question. I raised the volume a bit.

"Did you tell the DC from the Bridewell about the beach house?"

Thelma answered that from her station at the bureau.

"We only answered the questions he asked. As we know she's not at the beach house we didn't mention it. Amy insists we keep the place secret."

Rachel came out of the trance she was in and apologised again.

"I'm sorry, Jack. I'll try and get myself together."

Thelma showed me the list. I read it. Passed it to Rachel. She read it and gave it back to me. Said she didn't think anyone was missing from it. Three of the names belonged to local addresses - Thelma had already called there. Four others were actors from *The Causeway*. One was a director Thelma had been introduced to. The last two names belonged to Amy's representation. I added

103

Neil to the list. Not exactly standout suspects, any of them.

I stood up to leave. Rachel stood up too and looked at me as if the last thread in her unravelling cardigan was about to fall to the floor.

"I'll do what I can," I said.

"Thank you," she said. Then added a hurried afterthought, "We haven't made this business official, Jack. How much do you charge?"

"Nothing right now," I said. "I'll poke around for a couple of days and if I think I'm getting somewhere we'll talk about money then."

I left the house, navigated my way through the press corps in the street; through an onslaught of 'Who are you?', 'What are you doing here?', 'Who is in the house?', 'Is Mrs Turner worried about her daughter?' questions.

I walked back down Park Street to the Accord and drove to my office.

* * *

Which wasn't playing host to a barrel of laughs, either. Somebody had ransacked the place. And made no concessions to care or subtlety. The complete contents of the desk and filing cabinet drawers were strewn all over the carpet, the shelves had been prised out of their wall mountings, the cafetière, the mugs and the desk phone had been smashed with the proverbial blunt instrument.

Linda wasn't in her office next door. So I tried Ernest the philatelist on the other side. He said he hadn't heard a thing.

"But I was out for half an hour or so mid-morning," he said. He stared around the office. "What a mess."

A masterpiece of understatement that. But then he is a stamp collector.

Walter came up from the Security Desk, stepped across the threshold and stared, gobsmacked, into the room. He took a deep breath and blew out his cheeks.

"Jesus Christ..." he said. Then channelled Ernest. "What a mess." He looked back at the door frame and at the lock on the door. "Nothing wrong there. So, we're not looking at breaking and entering. Maybe just entering."

"Not without a key," I said. "I have the only one." I stared at him. "Apart from you."

Walter took that personally. "Surely you don't think I —"

"No I don't," I said.

He began shaking his head. "This kind of thing has never happened. Not in all the years I've been a security person. No building under my care has ever experienced this situation."

"Walter," I said. "Don't sulk. Let's go down to the Security Room and take a look at the CCTV disc for this corridor."

He cleared his throat. Then stared down at his face reflected in the polished toe caps of his boots.

"Yes we could do that..." he began, then cleared his throat again. "But I have to tell you that two engineers came to check the system mid-morning. It was off line for about twenty minutes."

"Two engineers?"

105

"Yes."

"With the proper ID?"

"Absolutely."

"From your firm?"

"Yes."

"Did you recognise them?"

"No…They said they were on contract, covering for two blokes who were sick."

"And they didn't know who those blokes were?"

"Well they wouldn't, would they?

"And did these blokes spend any of the twenty minutes on this floor, in this corridor?"

"I suppose so. We can still look at the disc," he said, trying to brighten up.

"But we won't find anything, will we?"

Walter looked downcast again. "Probably not."

"Then please go downstairs," I said. "And take a look at the spare key collection and the masters you have. See if they're all there."

He looked at me as if he was about to cry. "Yes of course. I'll do that."

He backed out of the room, swung to his right and set off along the landing. I moved behind my desk, picked up the desk drawers and slid them back into position, upturned my chair and sat down in it.

I'd never had my office burgled before. Then it occurred to me, maybe not this time either. Maybe somebody had simply come in to smash the room to bits. Difficult to assess with everything in the wrong place. The rationalisation kicked me into action. I'd never know until

I cleared up. I got up out of the chair. The noise of a hurried tread along the corridor produced the return of Walter holding a telephone base and receiver.

"No keys are missing, Mr Shepherd. None at all." He paused. I nodded at him. He thrust the phone at me across the desk. "You will need this until you purchase another one."

I said 'thank you' and took it from him. He looked around again.

"Well I'll erm... Leave you to it. I should erm..." he thumbed in the direction of the corridor. "I'll erm... Later."

He turned and left the office. I plugged the phone base into the wall socket, checked there was a dialling tone and put the receiver back in its cradle. Half an hour later I had all the pieces of paper back in the filing cabinet, probably fifty percent of them in the right folders. I was on my knees with a dustpan and brush sweeping up the broken glass when I had an idea.

I picked up the phone receiver and called Joe Locke. The only malefactor I have ever admired. A one-time safe cracker, head and shoulders above his peers; now supplementing his pension, appropriately, as a part-time locksmith. Joe's father, like his father before him, was a miner from Treorchy, his mother a dressmaker from Derry. She had named her only son after her favourite tenor Josef Locke, who began singing in churches in the Bogside at the age of seven. She tried to teach her husband and her son the great man's repertoire – *Galway Bay, Hear My Song, I'll Take you Home Again Kathleen* –

but she had picked the only two Welshmen in the valleys who were tone deaf. Joe said it had been the disappointment of her life. However, she lived to be ninety-three, ten years longer than Joe's father, and had many a day to enjoy berating her kin.

Joe answered the phone in his workshop.

"Joe the Lock."

I told him I had a job for him. I could picture the ironic grin on his face.

"And what would that be, Jack?"

"I want you to break in to my office. Or at least pick the lock."

"Why? Are you locked out?"

"Come round here and I'll explain."

He said he'd be with me in twenty minutes.

I pondered. Gerald Gaghan may have been motivated to send Howard and Maurice to do this. Reinforce the message to the gumshoe, remind him of the position he's in, and make it clear that breaking up the office is a minor incursion when compared to the range of measures at his disposal. Danny Malone might have done this, assuming he was fit and well. But right now, he was a heartbeat away from permanent immobility. I couldn't think of anyone else I'd recently stirred up. And speculating beyond that was an exercise in diminishing returns.

Joe arrived in my doorway. Sixty-eight years old, five feet seven, long white hair, alert blue eyes and a grin as seductive as marshmallow. We shook hands. He looked around.

"I see you've made some changes."

"Not all of them were my ideas."

He grinned at me. I told him what I wanted him to do.

"Whoever did this had less than twenty minutes to get in, smash the place up and get out again. The door wasn't forced, they didn't use a key. So..."

Joe finished the summary. "Somebody picked the lock."

I nodded. "Which is what I want you to do and see how long it takes."

It took him exactly nineteen seconds.

"Can anybody else do it that quickly?" I asked.

"Nobody I know," he said. "It's a good lock, but not difficult. An efficient amateur could pick it in a minute plus."

"So providing nobody sauntered along the corridor while he was at it, he had a good chance of getting in without being seen?"

"I'd say so, yes."

I thanked him. He said it was a pleasure to be allowed to get in some practice. I waved a twenty pound note at him. He refused to accept it.

"You can pay for lunch one day next week."

We shook hands on the deal.

"I'd offer you a drink if I had the means..."

Joe told me to take care and left the office.

I sat in my chair again and took stock. The shelves torn from the wall, the invasion of drawers and filing cabinets, the broken glassware and crockery... Somebody had left an impressive calling card. If he or they could get into the office so easily and create all this havoc, then there was clearly a host of other stuff they could accomplish as well. Stuff to do with crunching heads and breaking bones. In which case they were, in all probability, the contractors who had dealt so comprehensively with Danny Malone.

Most times I can talk myself out of an attack of glumness, but I was having difficulty on this occasion. It all changed with a telephone call.

"Mr Shepherd, my name is Val," the lady said.

"Val..."

"Alfie Barnes was a friend of mine."

I stayed as relaxed as I could.

"Okay," I said. "Then we should talk."

"Yes, we should."

"Name the time and the place," I said.

"I'm busy for most of the afternoon. So can we meet around 4.30?"

I said we could and asked her where.

"There's a bar on the dockside near the *Watershed*. You can't miss it. It's called *The Quay*. It's not busy late afternoon on Tuesday."

I told Val I knew it.

"See you then," she said and ended the call.

I listened to the line buzz for a second or two then disconnected my end. Put the receiver back in its cradle, stared at it, then picked it up again and dialled 1471. No number. Withheld, or maybe she had rung from a non-contract mobile. I rang Linda at home.

"A lady named Val just called me. She said she was a friend of Alfie."

There was the sound of cushions sighing and Linda sitting up straight.

"I don't know her."

"Are you sure? Alfie never mentioned her?"

"No. Friends weren't an item in Alfie's life." Then the tone of her voice changed. "Was she a close friend? I mean was she?..." Linda slipped into silence.

"She didn't say. Didn't say much at all in fact. Just ask me to meet her."

"Where and when?"

"No, no. I do this. I'll tell you about it later."

Linda sighed and muttered for a while, but realised that was all I was going to impart. She came up with something else.

"Why has she come to you?"

"I'll ask her that question," I said.

"Why hasn't she been to the police?"

"I'll ask her that, too."

I spent the next couple of hours completing my attempt to restore order in the office. I borrowed a mug and a spoonful of coffee from Ernest, drank it black, took the mug to the kitchen along the landing, washed it and returned it to him. Blagged the key to the cleaner's cupboard out of Walter and Henry'd the room carpet. The place looked tidy again, except for the broken shelves piled in a corner.

The clock on the wall said 4.14.

I put on my jacket, took the lift downstairs, handed the cleaners key back to Walter and left for my rendezvous with Val.

CHAPTER NINE

She was sitting in one of those silver-grey, pretend steel chairs so beloved of quayside haunts, beside a matching table. Mixed race. Light brown skin. Black shoulder length hair, dark eyes, slim hips and as far as I could assess, great legs. When she stood up to greet me, I could see that they were. There was nobody else drinking alfresco. We shook hands.

"Val," I said.

"Short for Valiqa," she said.

"I'm Jack."

"Do you mind if we talk out here?" she asked.

I told her not at all and asked what she would like to drink. She said it was a bit early so she'd like a lime and soda. She sat down again and I walked into the bar. It was sparsely populated, as Val had said it would be. There were patrons at most of the tables, couples and singles, save for the Wild Bill Hickock table in the corner – the one from where you could see the whole room. It was stacked with bottles of lager, most of them empty, drunk by the four men around it. They were in their 30s, maybe younger, a bunch of well-oiled cronies. There was no one at the bar except the barman; a five feet six, fifty something, one time second storey man called Mickey Balfour. I'd known him for twenty years.

"Jack Shepherd, as I live and breathe."

"Good to see you, Mickey."

"What are you doing here?" he asked.

"That same question occurred to me."

112

"The job prospects for ex-cons aren't bright," he said. "It pays the rent. Besides, I'm a stayer. Good at that. I hold on and wait out the rough patches." Then a morsel of suspicion crept into his eyes. "Is this a business visit?"

"No. I'm buying a drink for a lady sitting outside."

Mickey relaxed and went into action.

"Let me introduce you to the house cocktail," he said.

He set about making a 'Breaktimer' from a range of bottles on the shelf behind him. I didn't follow this closely, cocktails aren't my thing. He did a passable imitation of Tom Cruise doing his barman routine and ended up pouring a dark blue liquid out of the shaker, cloudy and scummy. I stared at it.

"Wait," he said. "And watch."

I did so and within moments the liquid cleared, pure as crystal, and began to sparkle under the bar lighting.

"Try it now," Mickey said. "Go on."

So I tried it. It was some time before I was able to speak. Mickey grinned.

"Want to know what's in it?"

"No."

There was a loud roar from the gamblers' table, followed by a bellow of laughter. I turned away from Mickey and looked across the room. The man in the Bill Hickock seat – who had obviously said or done something of comic weight – leaned backwards, tilting his chair and expecting the wall to take its weight. The chair had too far to go, tipped beyond the fulcrum, hit the wall and slid down it. For a moment Bill Hickock was horizontal and then suddenly he was on the floor, flat on his back as the chair slid out from under him. All of which was immensely entertaining to his mates, two of whom got to their feet and attempted to extricate the joker from under the table.

I looked back at Mickey who was staring into the corner as if he'd just seen someone take a piss into the miniature tree in the doorway.

"Ridley fucking Gaghan," he muttered.

He could smell trouble on the way. He moved to a phone sitting on the end of the bar. He lifted the receiver, thumbed a couple of digits, said a dozen words, replaced the receiver and came back to me.

I wanted to make sure I'd had heard what he said.

"Ridley Gaghan?"

He nodded. "What will the lady have?"

I told him. He poured a generous portion of lime into a highball glass, took the top off a bottle of soda and set it down in front of me. He looked across the room again.

"Not one of nature's noblemen," he said. "Even a pain in his father's arse. He's kind of running his own riot. Doesn't work for a living. As far as I can tell."

"Because his Daddy's rich?"

"Maybe. Or maybe, because he's making his money some other way."

Ridley Gaghan. Amy Turner's supplier? What a prospect… Thinking about it though, Ridley had all the qualifications needed for the job. Money to buy and deal, and unperturbed by notions of right and wrong. I moved the premise on.

"Do you think he'll talk to me if provoked?"

"There's no telling what he'll do if provoked," Mickey said. "And in this mode, nothing can calm him down. I've seen him like this before. Drinking too much, raging on about everything... his broken dreams, his father, his need to be his own man, his father again. And about getting revenge."

"On whom?"

"Fuck knows. Seems like everybody, when he's in the mood. His Dad owns the place. Banned his son from coming in here. Not that it's enforceable. Keeping tabs on the kid is a thankless task, he's a major prick. I just called the two blokes who keep him out of trouble."

"Close by are they?"

"In the *Spinnaker*, the other side of the Plaza."

"His Dad owns that too?"

Mickey nodded again.

"Along with that new drinking den on the far side of the floating harbour," he said. He looked back at the carousing four. "Word has it Ridley started behaving like a twat after his mother died."

"Has he got a record?"

"Not so far."

Ridley was hauled back into his upright seat. One of his mates sneered and said something. Ridley heaved the table up and over. The two men sitting opposite collapsed under the onslaught of glass bottles and beer. The couple nearest to the action stood up and left. The man at the table next to the couple, drained his glass and did the same. Sneerer stepped into Ridley's line of sight and head-butted him. Ridley's head snapped back and the rest of him followed until all of him met the wall again. The bald man to Sneerer's left wrapped his arms around Sneerer's shoulders and heaved him away from the table.

I looked at Mickey. He shook his head.

"Leave them to it."

The dozen drinkers still in the place got off their seats in unison and aimed themselves in the direction of the door. Baldie released Sneerer, spun him round and aimed one of the best right hooks I'd seen in a while. I could hear the crack of knuckles hitting cheek bone from where I stood. Sneerer's head completed the spin, his body followed, he went over another table and crashed to the floor. In the gamblers' corner, the fourth man was attempting to keep Ridley at arms' length. Sneerer raised himself on to his elbows. Baldie did a Jackie Pallo special. Suddenly he was in the air, horizontal. Sneerer looked up in terror. Baldie landed on his chest with some force – an old fashioned body press which squeezed all the breath from Sneerer, just before the back of his head hit the floor.

At which point the cavalry arrived, in the shape of Howard and Maurice. They went straight to the corner. Maurice unglued Ridley's hands from the neck of his assailant and swung him away. Ridley opened his mouth to protest. Maurice, at least six inches taller than him, grabbed the whole of Ridley's chin in one huge hand, lifted his arm and pushed. Ridley stretched up onto his toes, choking and trying to swallow.

"Enough now, there's a good boy," Maurice said.

He released Ridley who dropped his chin and leaned back against the wall. Maurice looked round. Howard had the last miscreant up against the wall a couple of yards away, his forearm across the man's throat.

"Don't move," Howard said. "Not so much as a fucking twitch."

Maurice stared down at Baldie, now sitting on the floor. "All right?"

Baldie nodded. Sneerer was groaning.

"So piss off. At the double," Maurice said. He pointed at Sneerer. "And take him with you."

Howard stepped back from his prisoner. Gestured over his shoulder.

"Go and help him."

And suddenly, all was calm. Sneerer was hauled to his feet and dragged out of the bar. Ridley was standing in the corner of the room with a look on his face which said 'Oh shit.'

Maurice turned to me. "Good afternoon, Mr Shepherd. A thousand apologies for this unpleasantness." And to Mickey, "You all right Bra?"

"Sure Mo."

I had a swift moment of admiration for Howard and Maurice as they escorted Ridley out of the bar. I ordered a beer, told Mickey I'd be back to collect it, picked up the highball glass and the soda bottle and stepped outside.

Maurice was sitting in the chair Val had occupied. She was nowhere to be seen. He nodded at the drink in my hands.

"For me?"

I put the lime and soda on to the table and asked him if he had seen a lady as he entered or left the bar.

"What lady?"

I wasn't sure if the question was genuine. He supplied the answer notwithstanding.

"Nobody here when I arrived and nobody when I came out."

I changed the subject. "Where's Howard?"

"He's taken Ridley away to put him straight on a couple of things. Something that has to happen every now and again." He looked at the drink. "Lime and soda yeah?... Just right, when you're working."

"Why are you sitting here?" I asked.

"Waiting for Howard to come back," he said. "And it's nice to relax for a short while. I don't usually get the chance to do that on a Tuesday afternoon."

Back in the bar Mickey was righting the last couple of chairs. He pointed in the direction of my beer.

"The lady still outside?" he asked.

"No."

He muttered something about that hardly being a surprise, surveyed his handiwork, deemed it satisfactory and stepped back to the bar. I picked up my glass of beer.

"Ridley's the bloke to hire to clear a room," I suggested.

"He's a fucking menace. As for his mates, if I wanted customers to dribble in the peanuts I'd bring in my sister's Spaniel."

"Can you tell me anything else about him?"

Mickey glanced at the door. "Not here."

"Can I talk with you later? Tomorrow? Your place if you like."

He took the half empty liqueur glass and put it in the sink. I waited. He turned back to me, his mind made up.

"Okay, Jack. What do you want to know?"

"The answers to a few questions that's all. Then I'll get out of your way."

He gave me his address. "But not tomorrow, I'm here all day. Thursday morning. About ten." He picked up a half pint glass, filled it from the lemonade squirter and raised it. "Cheers."

We both drank in silence. He finished his glass a couple of seconds before I did. He asked me if I wanted the other half. I told him I had to go. He reached across the bar, extending his right arm. I shook his hand. He smiled at me.

"Take care, Jack."

Maurice was still sitting outside. He had drunk the lime and soda.

"Enjoy the rest of your week, Mr Shepherd," he said.

My mobile rang as I got into the Honda. A man named Wooller calling me from his office. He spoke in soft, conspiratorial tones, as if the whole of the third floor was listening. His wife was being unfaithful to him, he said, and could I follow her? Where? I asked. He said if he knew that he wouldn't have called me. I told him I was busy with another case and I didn't have time to follow anybody anywhere. He put the phone down as if I'd kicked him in the teeth.

I spent the rest of the drive home wondering where Val was. Did she have a change of mind at witnessing the unpleasantness in the bar? Was she frightened off by the company she had found herself in? By the time I reached my front door I'd convinced myself she was another someone I had to worry about.

I called Adam. Asked him if he could liberate all the information there was in the *Post* files about Ridley Gaghan and his father. I talked with Chrissie for a while. Told her I had found and lost Val. Which was followed by a moment's silence and an invitation to supper. I chose the line of least resistance and politely declined. I called Linda.

"How did the date go?" she asked.

I repeated the story I had given to Chrissie.

"And you've no idea where Val is?"

"No. She may be in trouble. I'm sure her connection to Alfie will prove helpful, but until I can find her again..."

I had no more to say. And it seemed Linda had slipped into the same mode. I suggested I drive over to Portishead. She said she'd rather be by herself and anyway she wasn't in any sort of convivial mood. She'd only put a damper on things. Unlikely, it seemed to me. I thought I was already fully dampered out.

I went to bed early.

When I finally got to sleep, I dreamt I was in a room getting smaller by the second. A young man with no face was laughing at me somewhere in the darkness. But not naturally, fluently. Instead, like the end of a movie, where the actors ho ho energetically as the camera cranes up and back before the picture freezes and the end credits roll. The face morphed into vision - a 17 year old, out of his mind on angel dust, standing in a garbage strewn alley, astride a bloody corpse, a meat cleaver in his hand. The cleaver flashed in broken neon light, the .38 revolver in my hand roared and spat out flame. The pictures distorted and mixed and re-mixed. Bodies dissolved into garbage, meat cleavers into handguns, flashes of flame into a close up of a 17 year old with murder in his eyes.

I woke up at dawn exhausted, demoralised, trying to remember what day it was. The dream returns less than it used to, but each time it does I recall a conversation I had with a young George Hood fifteen years ago.

"Harvey Butler says you're leaving the force. And it's not because you're a bolshie bastard."

"What would you say?" I asked him.

"I'd say… you didn't join the force to shoot anybody, but sometimes it happens."

"Not to me. At least never again."

"He was just another street kid. And soon he'll be just another statistic."

"Nobody's ever 'just' anything." I said.

CHAPTER TEN

"You look terrible," Auntie Joyce said from her kitchen in Suffolk.

I glanced at the insert picture of me on the screen. Given that on *skype* everyone looks like they have a hangover, I thought I was just about presentable. But Auntie Joyce is a wizard at reading faces and body language.

"I had a bad night," I said. "That's all".

"Several by the look of things. Are you working?"

I updated her on the Alfie investigation. She listened without moving in her chair.

"How is Linda?"

"Not doing well."

"And her parents?"

"I haven't seen them since the funeral."

"Do you think they'd appreciate an email from Sid and me?"

"Yes. I'm sure they would."

There was a noise off screen. Uncle Sid hove into view with two mugs of coffee. He stared at the screen.

"You're looking better than when I last saw you," he offered.

Auntie Joyce looked at Uncle Sid with some scorn, then gave up her chair to him.

"Make sure he hands you back to me before you disconnect. I haven't finished this conversation."

Uncle Sid took up the screen space.

"Are you in trouble again?" he asked.

"Apparently."

"You know where it comes from, this concern."

Yes I do. And I strive never to abuse it. My parents died in a car crash on the Mendips, four days into my first ever week in school. Auntie Joyce and Uncle Sid gathered up a frightened little boy, folded him in their arms and gave him all the love in the world. All the best bits of my life since I was five years old I owe to them.

"I promise you I'm okay," I said.

I told him about Linda, too. He listened without interrupting. Seemed not to breathe until the end, when he said simply, "We're always with you, Jack. And anyone else who's at your side."

"I know."

And suddenly we both cheered up. I asked him how his work was going. He told me he had a bursary. A bursary?

"Yes," he grinned. "At the age of 67. From the University of East Anglia. Twice a week I go and talk to the students. Me. And they listen to me. It's amazing."

"No it's not," I said. "It's an acknowledgement of the man you are. And so richly deserved."

"Thank you, Jack," he said. He looked to his left. "Oh oh, she's back. Talk again soon."

He gave up the seat and disappeared from the picture. Auntie Joyce sat down.

"I heard those words about Sid," she said.

"I meant them," I said.

"I know. And thank you. He'll be chuffed to pieces. He's not just my husband and your uncle, he's one of the

123

wisest men in the world. There's nobody better in a crisis. And it looks like there's one on the way."

She threw the last sentence away and I almost missed it. I went back to the sentence before.

"What do you mean by crisis?"

Auntie Joyce took a moment or two to rehearse before she answered. "Sid may be getting Alzheimer's," she said. "He's... beginning to... drift a bit. There are tests to be done."

The immediate reaction to news like this, is to be fatuous out of concern.

"It may not be Alzheimer's at all," I said. "He's getting older could be all it is. And he's never been able to remember names. Has he forgotten yours?"

She shook her head.

"Or the Prime Minister's?"

"No one in a confused state," she said, "however advanced, could forget the person who recently stepped into number 10 with a mission to make the rest of us suffer for her misdeeds."

I grinned and she smiled at me. The smile that had always swept up sorrows and magic'd them away. Suddenly both of us felt a little better. She went on.

"Sid has more hospital tests next week. When we get the results, we'll talk about what has to be done. There could be a hard road ahead."

'Little better' slipped a notch or two. Auntie Joyce wound up the conversation before I could dredge up another something about nothing.

"We'll be fine. Give my love to the Clevedon set. And we'll talk soon."

"As soon as you know any more," I managed to say.

"Of course. Bye, Jack."

There was a bleep and the screen went dark. I switched off the pc. Suddenly I was back with Coleridge again... *I could not feel my limbs...*

* * *

So I did what I do on weekday mornings when I'm un-motivated. Walked the hundred yards to my newsagent and bought a copy of the *Guardian*. But back home, I couldn't find the energy to read it. Not even beginning with the sport section.

Adam rang as I was making another pot of coffee.

"Good morning," he said. "How are you?"

"Not as resolute as I might be."

"Oh dear..."

He paused a beat or two, waiting to see if I intended to elaborate. When I didn't he moved on.

"About the Gaghans," he said. "Let's meet. Halfway. There's a Coffee House on the Clevedon to Nailsea road."

So, twenty minutes later, Adam and I were drinking coffee with a plate of mini fairy cakes on the table between us.

"Did you know Trevor Swanley?" he asked.

I didn't have to think about that. "No. Never heard of him."

"Well he was a reporter. An arrogant bastard and a gigantic pain in the arse, thought he was Woodward and

Bernstein. But he could write. And he was on Gerald Gaghan's case for over eighteen months."

"Was?"

"Died in January last year. The police called it an overdose and the coroner recorded 'death by misadventure'."

"If that's what they're calling it, it probably was."

Adam shook his head. "No. Trevor wasn't a user. I'm one hundred percent certain of that. His body was a temple. He didn't drink. And he worked out twice a week."

"What happened to his research?"

"Nobody knows. He didn't store anything on the Post database. His wife Angie let me search his office at home. There were no files to do with Gaghan on his Mac, no hard copy in his cupboards or filing cabinet. No record on his back up discs either. I had our hi-tech boffin at the *Post* go through everything. Then Angie remembered an old laptop he used from time to time. Missing she said. No one found it."

He took a drink of coffee. I waited for him to continue.

"But here's the thing… Three days before he died, he told me he was working on a connection between Gaghan and a Belgian hard right outfit called *Action Politique*. I looked them up. The website is more alarming than evil – in that it appears no more raucous than your average right wing outfit. An article by a *Daily Mirror* journalist I know had a sentence or two about the organisation. I talked with him. He mentioned a guy called Yanis Mertens, but like Trevor, he had no intention of giving away what he thought was going to be a big story. I spent an hour or two checking on Mertens – he has overnighted in police cells in Antwerp and Ghent. Then I got involved in something else and…"

He shrugged. Returned to the main subject on the agenda.

"You will realise, I've no doubt, that good old Gerry is a player."

"You mean he thinks he is," I said.

"No I don't. He *is* a player. A bit more than the owner of two clubs and three pubs. He made several column inches in the local press two months ago, when he announced his support for a project to re-vamp the city's infrastructure, hailed by the Mayor as truly revolutionary. He's up for re-election soon and has Gaghan Nash money to fund his campaign."

"Is that causing any raised eyebrows?"

"Of course not. However…" Adam paused to give his next sentence weight. "Gerald Gaghan's current headline act is making him more money than he's collected in the whole of his egregious life so far. He buys debts. Or rather, takes them over with a little help from his Neanderthal henchmen. Has the debtors picked up one at a time, informs them of the now prevailing situation and hikes up the interest payments. Which leaves the poor sods with two choices. Sign the new agreement and see a major reduction in the comforts of life. Or stand up in defiance and face the prospect of not much of a life at all. He is aided and abetted in this inglorious business by the High Court Enforcers on his books, who go about their work supported by officers from the Avon and Somerset Constabulary. And only the insiders know which exercise is court-sanctioned and which is simply good old-fashioned extortion." He changed tack. "The constant irritation in Gaghan's life however, is Ridley. He's the boil on the heel of progress."

"Yes, I can see that."

"Basically... Ridley grew up disconnected from all that was moral and decent. He was indulged by both parents in the beginning, then punished by Gaghan père for his flagrant disregard of the house rules and embraced by his mother who regularly told him she understood his fears and failings. Driven to drink by the constant warring between the husband she grew to hate and the son she doted on, she committed suicide. Jumped off the suspension bridge when Ridley was fourteen years old. His father staged the grandest funeral this city has ever seen. Front page news and Gerry showered with condolences. While young Ridley, holding his father responsible for his mother's death, embarked on a so far undiminished commitment to feeding his resentment and sticking it to his old man at every available opportunity."

I regaled Adam with the story of yesterday afternoon's moment of melodrama in the *Quay*. Didn't surprise him at all.

Then I ended by asking him about Peter Nash.

"He's the brains of the outfit, clearly," Adam said. "And he keeps a very low profile. Never gets his name in the papers. He's rarely interviewed. Spends a lot of his time out of the city on business trips round the EU –

something that's going to change radically soon I imagine. I don't know anybody who's had reason to look into any of his activities. No pain, shame or blame attached to him or anything he has done."

"So they're an odd combination, Gaghan and Nash," I said.

"Exactly the right combination I would say, in business terms. It's probably fair to imagine they don't enjoy each other's company and don't socialise much. But Nash appears to run a very tight ship, with Gaghan as first mate."

He emptied the last of the coffee pot into his cup.

"I have two things going here," I said. "One... I'm looking into the circumstances surrounding the death of Alfie, but I'm just treading water. And two... Gerald Gaghan had me hauled in to see him after he thought I was working with the currently hospitalised Danny Malone. Which means he may also have some connection with the disappearance of Amy Turner."

He looked at me. I couldn't tell if the expression on his face was one of admiration or despair. He nodded at the plate between us.

"Do you want the last fairy cake?"

It was raining when we left the coffee shop. I sat in the Accord waiting for the temperature control inside the car to clear the screen and the windows. I called Linda. She was with Joanna and Patrick.

"How are you? All of you."

"Tired," she said. "Still a bit lost. I don't have any drive or resolution to get on with stuff. Mum is kind of closing down, like she's running out of energy. Dad constantly tries to lift her spirits, but his batteries are low too."

I knew exactly how she felt. I could recognise the same wasteland Chrissie and I slipped into when Emily died. One moment she was with us and the next she was gone. Forever. There was no shape in the space where she used to be. No trace of a look, a smile or a whisper. The house was as she left it. But of Emily, there was simply nothing.

"Take care, Jack," Linda said.

I drove home to Redland. Spent the afternoon updating my notes on the case. Drank lots of tea. Got round to reading the *Guardian*. Watched the news at 6 o'clock. The Clifton bomber had been identified as a radicalised student called Kamil Nasri. Born in Bristol, he didn't have a passport and he had never been across the channel, let alone to North Africa, the Middle East or Pakistan. His parents were in no state to talk to reporters. Neighbours and friends said he was a devout Muslim, charming and quietly spoken and they were deeply shocked by what had happened.

I found some vegetables in the fridge just beyond their 'consume by' date and cooked up a stir fry. BBC4 was offering the pilot episode of a French TV series about a detective in Paris in 1792, working for Robespierre's Committee of Public Safety. Created for history buffs and TV savvy viewers, it seemed, but I got hooked and stayed with it, subtitles and all. I retired to bed after the 10 o'clock news.

CHAPTER ELEVEN

Oh sleep! It is a gentle thing,
Beloved from pole to pole.

I couldn't get the Ancient Mariner out of my head now. Remembering more bits of it and being assailed as much as the wedding guest. I had another bad night. I drifted in and out of sleep, checking the time with the bedside clock twice an hour it seemed.

I got out of bed just after 7 o'clock, showered, shaved and caught up with the breakfast news headlines. Afterwards, I sat down in the living room and considered the trip to Mickey's place – a studio flat in Stokes Croft on the fringe of St Paul's. I decided to eliminate the problems of parking and took the bus. Crossing the city on the top deck offers a whole new perspective on the world. From the Bus Station I walked up Gloucester Road.

Studio flat was a somewhat fanciful description of Mickey's home. It was a bed sit with a bathroom really. It needed a coat of paint and a couple of cracked window panes replacing. Stud walls left and right connected the place to the rest of the rooms on the top floor.

"The couple that way, cook a lot and bang pots and pans about," Mickey said, then pointed in the opposite direction. "And that wall is so thin, you can hear the guy on the other side farting. Fortunately he's out most of every night."

"Doing what?"

"Fuck knows. Something not to pry into I imagine."

He waved me to the only armchair available, passed me a mug of coffee and sat on the edge of the bed.

"The place is anonymous enough. It's cheap. And the probation officer's just a five-minute walk away."

I asked how he long he'd been in the flat. Since he came out of Pucklechurch seven months ago he said, and this time he was going to stay out. Mickey had resolved such on a number of occasions during his career, but this time he had a job. I wanted to believe him.

"Ridley Gaghan..." I began.

Mickey sipped from his mug, then moved things along.

"I'm not going to waste my time telling you what you're getting into here," he said. "So I'll just advise you to pack a bag and take a holiday. Anything to do with either Gaghan can only end in tears."

"I appreciate the advice Mickey," I said. "And I don't ignore it lightly. But I've long since passed the point of no return."

He looked steadfastly at me. I tried to look as steadfast in return. He grinned.

"You're a stubborn bastard so I'll say no more on that."

"Thank you."

He put his mug down on the bedside table, shuffled backwards across the bed and propped his back against the wall alongside it.

"So what do you want to know?"

"Just how explosive is the relationship between the Gaghans?"

Mickey pondered for a moment or two.

"Dynamite, with a very short fuse. And it'll take only the smallest dose of stupidity to light it. As far as I can see from my place behind the bar, it could happen any time."

"Surely Gerald would hate to be responsible for doing that?"

"He might have no choice. If Ridley keeps on rampaging around the city, his dad will eventually do something serious to stop him." He paused and considered something else. I waited. Then Mickey went on. "I think old man Gaghan has political ambitions."

I stared at him. Gaghan was an equal opportunity offender. Fixer, bully, threatener and extortionist, dealer in all sorts of unpleasantness, briber of all classes and creeds and bender of all rules. But Gerald Gaghan politician...

"Why bother with local politics?" I asked. "He has the mayor in his pocket and the company has enough clout to get the man re-elected. He doesn't need to concern himself with all the dicking about that goes on in the council chamber."

"I think this is more than local politics. He's up to something on a much grander scale. He's raising money hand over fist. I've run the bar for a number of shindigs he's had in some influential places during the last four or five months, with peers and honourables as his guests. I've watched him work the room. He's very good at it. He can be charming when he needs to be. But when he wants to make a point, he produces this look that chills you to the marrow."

I told him I'd seen it.

Mickey picked up his coffee mug and looked into it, as if seeking inspiration in the dregs. He drained it, put it on the bedside table again, picked up a packet of cigarettes, took one out, put it back. Then he looked at me, arrow straight.

"He's also very good at dealing with people who get in his way," he said, genuine concern in his eyes. "What more I can I tell you?"

I stood up to go, handing him my coffee mug.

"Thanks, Mickey. I'll be in touch."

"When this is all over, Jack, if you don't mind."

"Sure."

I took the bus back to my office. Had it a door knocker with a face like Jacob Marley, it could not have been more unwelcome. Inside, the story was depressingly familiar too. No phone messages, no mail, the broken shelves still piled in the corner. And a detective with loads of information and no leads.

* * *

So I did something about the chaos. I took the shelves along the lane by the river to the spot where two men in battered coats and nowhere to go had a fire lit. I donated the shelves to their pile of wood. They said 'thank you'. I said 'don't mention it' and walked back to the Accord. Then I drove along Winterstoke Road to Sainsbury's and bought some milk, some ground coffee, a new cafetière, replacement mugs and glassware. On the way back, I called in at Wickes. Bought four six feet lengths of new shelving, shelf brackets, brass screws, rawplugs and some filler, and hired a cordless drill for a half day rate.

I set to work. Filled the holes in the walls, drilled new ones and screwed the shelf brackets into place. I borrowed a pin hammer and some oval nails from Walter, pinned the shelves on to the brackets and stood back to admire my work. I returned the drill just before six.

I was about to leave Wickes car park when a voice inside me said 'phone'... I decided I ought to give Walter his loaner back.

Currys' south Bristol store is not much more than a hundred yards from Wickes. So in I plunged, and found myself confronted by a row of television sets, all featuring a close up of Marine Le Pen at a *Front National* rally, in purple skin, pink skin, bronze or sepia, depending on the colour tuning. She's a disconcerting presence at the best of times, but on a 56 inch screen, sporting a deep azure dress and a maroon face she looked terrifying. An eager salesperson moved to my shoulder.

"May I assist you, Sir?"

I was about to ask him why he didn't get somebody to tune the TV sets, when maroon Marine disappeared and a graphic mixed onto the screen, charting the rise and rise of hard right European organisations since the waves of refugees hit the shores of the Greek Islands, Sicily, France and Spain. *Action Politique* in Belgium, *Lega Nord* in Italy, National Freedom Parties in Poland, Austria and the Netherlands. It wasn't clear what colours they nailed to their mastheads because the TV pictures were giving me a headache. The sales assistant also – he was rubbing his eyes.

I went searching for a phone.

At 6.25 I was back at my desk, two fingers of malt whisky in the glass sitting on it. Thirty minutes and another glass of whisky later, I was still sitting there, with a list of questions longer then the M4. Which were, in order of appearance...

Who killed Alfie Barnes?

Why was he killed?

Does Danny Malone really know something about it?

Why has Amy Turner disappeared?

Why are there gaps in Alfie's diary?

Where did he go when he got off the bus?

Is Neil Shore a help or a hindrance to the investigation?

Was Malone hospitalised courtesy of Gerald Gaghan?

How did Val find me?

Where does she live?

Where is she now?

Do I pursue a murder investigation or a missing persons case? Or both?

Is the threat to my life and limbs real or just Gaghan taking the piss?

Is *Puff the Magic Dragon* a dope song?

Does God exist?

What is the meaning of life...?

The telephone rang, stabbing through the ambient sound in the office. I sat bolt upright and spilled the remains of my drink down my shirt.

Linda was calling from around the corner.

"Are you okay?"

"Yes fine."

"Are you sure?" she asked. "You sound... confused."

"It may seem that way."

"I've just finished the day's business. Would you like a drink?"

I looked the now empty glass sitting on the desk top. Then at the clock on the wall. 6.58.

"Yes."

"Good. I'll pick you up in couple of minutes."

I put the phone receiver back in its base and realised the whisky was seeping through my shirt onto my chest. I got up out of the chair, walked along the corridor to the kitchen, found a dishcloth and was back in the office dabbing at my shirt front when Linda walked in.

"I'm not going to buy you drink if you're going to throw it down your shirt."

"Not entirely my fault. I was taken by surprise. You look terrific."

She did too. In a light grey two piece, with the skirt ending a couple of inches above her great knees.

"Thank you," she said. Then she picked up the half empty Laphroaig bottle and waved it at me.

"One drink that's all," I said. "I refuse to include the one I spilled."

"Well that's a relief," she said.

"Not your concern," I said. "You're my accountant, not my doctor."

"It's not your liver I'm worried about," she said. "It's this drinking alone in your office at..." She looked at her watch. "7 o'clock."

That wasn't something we should examine too closely, so I resolved to move on. The phone on the desk rang and changed everyone's plans.

"Two things," Neil Shore began. Then he mumbled, "Oh shit... Listen. I'm not sure but... Are you listening?"

I told him I was listening. Glanced at Linda. She opened her arms body width and raised her eyebrows. I mouthed an apology across the desk.

"I think there's somebody here," Neil said. "I mean not actually in here... but around here. And erm..." I could feel him shaking all the way down the line. "Listen," he said again. A kind of hissed stage whisper. "I've found something. A usb stick. A copy of Amy's vlog."

"Amy's what?"

"Vlog," he repeated, impatience getting the better of him. "You know, video blog, video diary."

"Have you played it?"

"Started to, but I heard something... someone... outside."

I looked at the clock on the wall. 7.03.

"Hide the stick. Make sure all the doors are locked."

"You're coming straight away? Yes?"

"Yes. Just stay calm."

"Easy for you to say."

"So get off the line and hunker down."

"Don't be long. Please."

The line clicked and I was left with the dialling tone. I put the receiver back in the base and got to my feet. Linda had waited patiently throughout that rigmarole, so an explanation was in order.

"Remember Neil Shore?" I said. She nodded. "That was him. Scared stiff. I'm going to see him."

Linda grimaced. "In Dorset? Now?"

"At this time of day I can be there in an hour and half."

"I'll come with you," Linda offered.

I shook my head. "No, you don't do this sort of stuff. I'll call you when I get there. And if all goes well, I'll be back before eleven."

"All going well, being the key to the plan."

I walked around the desk. Linda made space for me to step into her arms.

"Just you take care," she said into my left ear.

"I always do," I said.

She stepped back and offered me the look that sentence deserved.

It was the greyest of grey weather. The world was sliding into darkness much too swiftly for a September evening. Once out on the A37, I pressed a couple of buttons on the steering wheel and the CD stacker contents appeared in lights on the dashboard. Before I could read them the CD already in play mode slipped into life. Tony Christie was singing *Drive Safely Darling*. Linda had already said that and the song ends in tears, so I pressed the button again. Shania Twain. Not right now. I pressed again and was offered a Blue Oyster Cult album

139

from 1983, *Revolution By Night* – a loaner from somebody years ago which I had never returned. The rest of the stacker was deserted. So I sought refuge in FM radio and finally unearthed a local station which was playing non-stop R&B. That is, until the programme dredged up an execrable phone-in segment on safe sex.

I switched off the entertainment and stared ahead into the darkness. Just as it began to rain. In a moment all was extra dismal. The night became darker along with my mood and, encouraged by this, the rain began to hammer down on the roof of the car. The A37 became a skid pad. Visibility was reduced to yards. The de-mister on full power, the rhythmical clunk and swish of wiper blades and water on the windscreen, at first irritating, became mesmeric. After an hour and a quarter on the road, I gave up trying to progress, pulled into the yard of a pub called *The Rain Lashed Gate* and sought refuge.

It was 8.45 and the kitchen was closing. The best the chef could offer was egg and chips, and that was all right with me. I was clearing my plate when he arrived at my table with a monster slice of coffee cake and a jug of cream.

"I decided I had to do better than egg and chips," he said. "Have this on the house."

At twelve minutes past nine I stepped outside into a different world altogether. The rain had stopped, a banana moon was shining and the sky was pocked with stars. Morale soared to at least seventy-five percent. I fished my mobile out of the glove compartment and called the beach house landline. No response.

Half an hour later I was driving towards the house on the lane leading from the Swanage road. There were no lights on – at least not on the landward side. Neil's car was parked by the front door as it had been on my last visit. I eased out of the Accord, stood still for a moment or two and listened to the night. Nothing to hear but the sound of waves on the other side of the house. I decided not to use the keys I had, stepped around the side of the house and walked towards the beach. A glow of light from some source on the seaward side seeped from the left. I turned and stepped onto the deck.

At the far end, face down, his waist across the threshold, his head and torso pointing towards the beach, Neil Shore lay still.

CHAPTER TWELVE

I knelt down by Neil's body. He was lying with his right cheek on the deck, eyes closed. There was glass from the door around and underneath him. I felt for the carotid artery in his neck. There was a pulse. There were cuts and bruises on the part of his forehead I could see and on his left cheek. There was a dark coloured swelling around the base of his left eye and a lump growing behind his left ear. But no blood stains on the back of his shirt. I rolled him, as gently as I could, onto his back. The left side of his mouth was damaged and bloody, although the wound had dried up. I put my hands under his armpits and pulled him clear of the threshold.

I counted back. I had taken two minutes to drive along the lane from the Swanage road. A minute or so to move around the house. Maybe forty-five seconds to convince myself no one else was here and another minute to check how Neil was. A total of five minutes maybe. If I had just missed the visitors and they had left straight after clouting Neil, he could have been unconscious for less than six or seven minutes. On the other hand he could have been out of it for much longer, possibly as far back as the end of his telephone call.

Neil opened his eyes, moved his head and looked up at me.

"Jack," he said and tried to smile. "You got here."

"Too late however," I said. I looked at my watch. "It's quarter to ten. Have you any idea how long you've been unconscious?"

He made some effort to answer the question, but the pathways in his brain weren't connecting well enough for him to do simple maths. He gave up the struggle. I fished the mobile out of my jacket to dial 999. Neil said 'No don't bother'. I asked him if he could sit up. He said he would give it a try. His head hurt during the process and he favoured the left side of his rib cage. He said he felt sick, leaned to his right and threw up over a green hose coiled on the deck.

That seemed to help. He shifted his weight in the opposite direction and got himself onto his hands and knees. He stared down at the deck for a long time, then took a number of deep breaths. Each one seemed to be an effort and his reward was an assessment of his condition.

"Help me up please, Jack."

I stood behind him, and trying to avoid squeezing his rib cage I wrapped him in a sort of bear hug, and shuffling backwards hauled him to his feet. I asked him if he wanted me to let go. He said, not yet. So we stood and swayed in this curious embrace for three or four minutes. Then suddenly he wasn't swaying any more. He suggested I let go. I did. Stepped back and gave him some room. He turned slowly, heavy footed, like the archetypal zombie, and grinned at me.

"Right," he said.

I looked into the living room. "Can you make it to the sofa?"

I stepped to his left and he moved past me, assisted by the frame of the open French windows. He dropped back into the sofa cushions, winced in pain and felt the left hand side of his rib case. I trawled round the room switching lights on. In the kitchen I filled a glass of water and took it back to the sofa. His right hand shook as he took the glass from me. He cupped his left hand and used it to help steady the glass. He tilted his head and attempted to drink out of one side of his mouth. He dribbled some down his shirt, but he managed to rev up a bit. I asked him if he remembered when he last looked at the time. He struggled with that.

"No. At some point I woke up. I think the man was gone. Then I must have passed out again."

"Did you know him?"

"Never saw him before."

"What did he want?"

"To know where Amy is... was, is..."

He slopped another drink of water. I asked him when he last ate. He said it was probably four or five hours ago. I moved into the kitchen. There were some eggs in a bowl next to the hob. I located some mushrooms in the fridge. I waved the bag at him.

"How long have you had these?"

"Bought them yesterday," he said. "There's some ham there too."

I filled the water reservoir in the coffee maker, spooned four large portions of Columbian dark roast into the filter and switched the machine on. Then I made Neil a ham and mushroom omelette, sat him down at the breakfast bar and watched him eat. Slowly, he came back together. He finished the omelette and pushed the plate to his right. I filled his coffee cup. He did the head tilting slopping thing again, this time with more success.

"Why did that man want Amy?" Neil asked. "Was it a drugs thing?"

"How did he know about this place is the question you should be asking," I said. "As to why, I guess he wanted to muscle his way to the front of the queue. There's a long line of people desperate to find Amy. You and me, her mother and grandmother, good guys and bad guys, her father – currently hooked up to several millions-worth of hospital machinery. And a bunch of less than altruistic TV producers, worried about their ratings."

I waited for him to respond. He stared down into his coffee mug.

"Amy insisted she needed to go cold turkey," he said.

"When did she insist that?"

"A couple of weeks ago. She was running out of time; Hollywood was beckoning." He looked straight into my eyes. "Amy had a break from *The Causeway*. I didn't want her to be alone down here. I had no idea what I was going to do, I just… oh shit… I hoped I could help." His voice faded for a moment or two, then he yelled at me. "But it didn't fucking matter anyway because she wasn't fucking here."

He picked up his mug and hurled it away from him. Coffee sprayed out of it and plumed across the space. The mug hit the pvc frame of the deck window and bounced back into the room in pieces. None of that improved matters, but the shock of the action re-bounded and calmed him a little.

"I love her, Jack," he said.

He slid off his stool intending to pick up the pieces of broken pottery. I ordered him to sit down on the sofa. He did and watched me collect the bits of the mug, tried to work up some interest in what he ought to tell me next, then gave up, defeat stencilled across his face.

"Okay... So, this man who visited you earlier..." I said.

"He wasn't in the best of sorts when he arrived. Seemed to blame me for getting the gig. Grumbled a lot about having to come down to Dorset on a wet night. He turned up around -"

I interrupted Neil. "Hang on. This is important. Are you sure he said 'having to come down'?"

"Yes."

"He didn't say 'being sent down'?"

"No." He made the connection. "Oh I see... 'being sent down' indicates under orders, 'having to come down' might mean he decided on the visit by himself. He didn't explain a thing, just persisted in asking me where Amy was. I told him I didn't know. I think he believed me in the end, because he stopped hitting me."

I asked him what the man looked like. He described Julian.

"He works for a man called Gerald Gaghan," I said. "Ever heard of him?"

"No."

"He's the father of the recently discussed Ridley. You mentioned him during my last visit."

He took that on board, opened his mouth to say something, moved his position on the sofa and winced again.

"You might have a cracked rib," I said. "Let's get you to the nearest A&E."

Neil waved that away. "No no. That's probably somewhere in Poole. Besides..."

He got to his feet, swayed for a moment, regained his balance, breathed in and blew out his cheeks, walked unsteadily past me into the kitchen and opened the fridge. He dug among the vegetables and produced the usb stick.

"I hid it in the crisper." He moved back to the breakfast bar. Pointed across the room towards the TV set. "My laptop's in the corner"

* * *

An hour later we had watched the last four weeks of Amy's video log. Or at least, as much as we could stomach. The depressing slide from getting by, into out of control, had begun two months earlier. During the last month, Amy had attempted to record three times every day. After waking up in the morning, getting her head straight and taking the first amphetamine of the day. Then during mid-afternoon, in her dressing room between scenes, her stress levels on the limit and her capacity to concentrate slipping, sniffing one or more lines of coke. And finally, late in the evening, shaking and desperate for sleep, waiting for the Temazepam to kick in.

I asked Neil why she was making this diary.

147

"It's almost as if she's keeping a record for the day when she will have to do something about the state she's in," he offered. "She's organised, even in the mess."

So why didn't anybody know about this?

Answer, her fellow actors and the TV audience only saw the Amy who was up and ready and firing on all cylinders. She was skilful, aware, and right on the button when the director called 'Action'. That's what the broadcaster paid thirty thousand a week for. So what about in the make-up chair at 7.30 in the morning?

"Who looks their best at that time of day?" Neil said. "Besides, the make-up room is the holy of holies. Secrets are kept. And the face that goes into make-up is never the face that comes out."

The clock on the wall said 11.18. I called Linda and told her I wasn't driving home. She said she had expected that. I apologised. Told her I would be back in Bristol by 9 o'clock the next morning.

I asked Neil where I could sleep.

"The guest room," he said. "The bed's made up."

CHAPTER THIRTEEN

I left the house the following morning just after 7 o'clock. Neil was still asleep. Traffic was light on the A37, at least for most of the journey. I walked into the office building ahead of Linda.

I came up with a pro-active idea. I called Amy's agent, Celia Brown. Got her PA, Imogen, who was immediately sympathetic when I explained who I was and what I was doing. She said Celia was expected in soon, suggested a skype conversation would be a good idea and promised she would get her boss to call me straight away. I thanked her and decided coffee was next.

I was walking back along the corridor from the kitchen, a mug in one hand the cafetière in the other, as Linda stepped out of the lift. She paused, framed by the doorway. The doors closed behind her. She walked towards me, in blue jeans and a maroon jacket over a white tee shirt.

"Good morning," she said.

The skype ring tone burbled from inside my office. She gestured in the direction of the doorway.

"Come in," I said. "You're welcome to hear this conversation."

She sat in one of my client chairs. I sat behind my desk and took the call. Celia Brown appeared on screen. Sitting in a much higher spec office than mine. But then top agents earn 15 percent of every top dollar.

"Mr Shepherd," she said.

"Jack, please," I said.

Celia was dark haired and in her mid-50s I guessed, a good looking woman with a comfortable smile and complementary body language. But the news she offered wasn't what I expected to hear.

"I was sacked by Amy ten days ago," she said.

"Why?"

"I told her this was not the time to go to Hollywood."

"And she didn't agree."

"Amy is twenty-two, Jack. Yes she's a UK soap superstar. She's bright and extremely talented, probably one of the best young actors in the trade. But she needs another couple of years paying her dues here, keeping her feet on the ground, and maybe experiencing a moment or two when things don't go right for her. Hollywood is a massive step into the unknown. Littered with the egos and the sanity of many a burgeoning star. When you're working there's nowhere else to be, but when you're not it's hell on speed. And even if you arrive feted, the story can still have the wrong ending. The words 'Jack Shepherd, just the guy', produce a chauffeured limo to the current head honcho's office and dinner on Rodeo Drive. But the words 'Jack Shepherd? Oh Christ, the guy in last year's turkey', buy you a taxi ride to the pictures to watch some other actor in the role you know you could have aced. The second and third time you deal with the disappointment, but the fourth, fifth and sixth time this happens, you begin to think it's probably better to have a real dose of leprosy. So I told Amy I thought Hollywood should wait."

"And she yelled at you?"

"Way out of character, but yes."

Maybe. If she was on an even keel. I took a deep breath and asked Celia if she knew Amy had a drug problem. It was a hell of a blow.

"No I didn't," she managed to say.

I told her what I had found in the beach house. .

"The coke might explain why she got so angry," I said.

Celia shook her head sadly. "I didn't know."

"She could have been so down she didn't want to listen," I ventured. "Or so high after snorting a line or two she felt the world was hers to rule."

Celia leaned back in her chair. Both of us sat staring at our respective screens as if we had all the time in the world. She broke the silence.

"Do you think you can find her?"

"Maybe. I don't know."

"Does anyone else know about the drugs business?"

"Apart from her dealer, only her boyfriend Neil Shore. Do you know him?"

Celia nodded. "Yes he's a good guy. Needs a break though."

"You know about the house in Dorset?" I asked.

"Yes. I was allowed into that loop."

"Neil's there. Waiting for her to show up. He's trying to help."

Celia looked down at her desk, pondering for a second or two. Then she looked at the screen again.

"Are you being paid for this investigation, Jack?"

"Not exactly."

"Then let me do it," she said.

"Why?"

She took time over her response.

"I set up this agency twenty years ago. With a handful of artists. They were not just clients, they were friends. And the other artists we have gathered down the years, like Amy, have become friends too. We don't simply send them to meetings and auditions and then screw the biggest fee possible out of producers. We guide their careers... I want to pay for this because I would like to, because I can afford to, and because Amy's mother and grandmother might not be able to." She took a long deep breath. "And because I didn't help ten days ago when Amy stormed out. It is the least I can do."

She offered me enough money to cover a week's retainer. I gave her my bank details and closed the conversation.

"And I'll email you all my contact details," she said. "Phone any time, day or night. Meanwhile, take this name and number. Jonathan Taylor is the series line producer. Probably the best person working on *The Causeway* to talk with."

Celia said goodbye, and quit skype. I sat back in my chair and closed my eyes. Linda spoke from miles away.

"I'm sorry, Jack."

I opened my eyes and looked at her.

"I should have given you more room to do your job."

"Don't think about it. We're one big extended family the Barnes and the Shepherds. All of us committed to one another. Some tough things have happened over the last six years. We all know how crushing the pain of loss is.

152

Alfie was special. And the hurt is unbearable. I wish I could take it away from you. I can't do that, so I promise I will help find out why he was killed. But I need to find Amy Turner as well."

"The outlook for both endeavours is pretty dismal," Linda said.

"And maybe with Val, too," I said.

This was one of those rallying call moments when something has to be dragged from some dark corner to lift morale. Even in the absence of ideas, theories and leads. Just because there seems no detecting a detective can do, doesn't mean the detective can stop attempting to detect. So, belt and braces. I switched on the laptop and googled 'Valiqa'. There were 6,645 results. Sites to do with Muslim names, Middle East companies, Syrian politicians, Indonesian shopping outlets and on and on. Linda came up with a suggestion.

"Perhaps the police can help."

"If she's on the database," I said. "Checking might be constructive."

Linda left for her own office. I called Trinity Road. Asked for the Murder Investigation Team and DS Mailer.

"Good morning, Jack," she said.

"And to you," I said.

"Is this a call offering information, or do you need our help?"

Harvey Butler's mantra, George Hood's, and now that of Liz Mailer. I could, however, answer the question without my conscience troubling me.

"Both."

"A compromise of sorts," she said. "Perhaps we can work with that."

"I think I found a lady who has information about Alfie Barnes."

"You think you found her, or you think she has information?"

"Both."

"And you know where she is?"

"No. I lost her. Which is the reason for this call."

"Her name?" she asked.

"The deal first," I said.

There was bit of low volume line buzz, then Mailer came back to me.

"All right, Jack, go on."

"If she's in the city, I'd like to be with you when you knock on her door."

This was the tricky bit. As soon as I gave up Val's name, this ploy would be out of my control. I could be dismissed and left out of the loop.

"I need your word on this, Liz."

"Okay," she said, "The name..."

"Valiqa." I spelled it.

"Valiqa what?"

"That I don't know. But we've met. And if she's logged on your local database I can find her picture."

There was silence down the line. I persisted.

"There can't be too many Valiqa somethings."

She came back to me.

"Okay... I'll get DC Frayne to check and print out some pictures. Come over here in an hour," she said and ended the call.

* * *

Frayne sat me down at the empty DC's desk next to his and dropped nine photographs in front of me.

"People who are known to us, people we have brought in for questioning, arrested, or managed to convict," he said. "Two people are not in the collection. Both currently incarcerated. Enjoy..."

I recognised Val in photograph number six.

"This is her. Valiqa Harroun."

Frayne logged into the database, making sure I was glued to my seat and not able to see over his shoulder. Then he sat back in his chair.

"The lady is here because she's a translator. She speaks three or four European languages and several versions of Arabic. Born in Libya. She's called in to Trinity Road when interviews and evidence statements need an interpreter. Or at least she used to be. Apparently, she's been off the radar for a while. The address on the database looks to be one of those serviced apartments in Tyndalls Park."

Frayne picked up the phone receiver on his desk, looked at the screen again and punched some phone buttons. He waited. Then introduced himself and asked whoever was on the other end of the line if Valiqa Harroun still lived in the apartment block. The reply was short and sweet. He asked if there was a forwarding address. Again a swift reply. Val was clearly long gone.

Frayne thanked his interlocutor and ended the call. I pointed at the pc monitor.

"Can I have a copy of Val's picture?"

"Sure. The best of luck. I'll have to report all this to DI Mailer of course."

We stood up together. I thanked him and he escorted me into the corridor.

* * *

Linda said she had never met the lady in the photograph. I asked her how Alfie was on languages. She said he spoke German well and that he used to count in Russian. Something he had started doing a couple of years ago.

'A-deen' 'dva' 'tree' 'chye-tir-ye' – that's 4, I think."

"You mean he just recited the numbers?" I asked.

"No. He used Russian whenever he needed to count."

"Which he might have learned courtesy of Val Harroun," I suggested.

"Does that help?" Linda asked.

I looked across the office. Found myself staring at the cafetière. Linda sensed a moment of revelation and waited for clarity.

"Has anything in Alfie's room been cleared out?" I asked. "Anything thrown away?"

"No. My parents and I started going through his stuff, but we weren't having a good time so... we gave up."

"Good. Do you think we could search the room again?"

CHAPTER FOURTEEN

"What are you looking for?" Joanna asked. "What did the police miss?"

It was early afternoon. Linda and I were in the Barnes' dining room. Joanna and Patrick had looked at Val's photograph and shaken their heads. We had interrupted lunch and turned down an invitation to eat.

"Maybe nothing," I said. "This may be a fruitless exercise, but I think it's worth a try."

"It's just that..."

Joanna paused. I waited. Patrick intervened.

"I think what Jan is trying to say is – "

She interrupted. "No, Jack. Go on, look around. It won't seem like such an invasion with you." She turned to Linda. "Perhaps you could..."

Linda escorted me out of the dining room. We crossed the hall and began to climb the stairs.

"Is this what you'd call a hunch?" Linda asked.

"Something to do with Val Harroun's job," I said.

"How do you know that? I mean one moment you were staring into the cafetière glass, like Madame Rosa into her crystal ball, and the next moment we were up and out of the office."

I paused on the landing. Linda caught up. We moved to Alfie's bedroom door and Linda's requirement to be with me faltered.

"I don't want to do this after all," she said. "Do you mind if I just let you..." She didn't finish the sentence.

"Sure," I said. "I don't want any of you to be concerned about this."

Linda stepped past me, walked back along the landing and set off down the stairs. I opened Alfie's bedroom door.

It was the tidiest room I have ever been in. Approximately fifteen by ten, it held the minimum of furniture. A small desk on which sat Alfie's pc, returned by MIT, with a wickerwork armchair in front of it and three lengths of shelving rising up to ceiling height on the wall above it. The books were stacked upright and bookended with solid lumps of carved slate. A five foot bed with the duvet cover hanging over the edges of the mattress by the same margin at each side – the end of it over the foot of the bed running parallel to the carpet across its width. Two walnut bedside cabinets, lovingly polished. And an old pine wardrobe, six feet wide and eighteen inches deep; fitted with shelves on the right hand side, occupied by Alfie's boxer shorts, his vests, his sweaters, his socks. All neatly folded and carefully placed, with each pair of socks rolled up into a neat ball and enclosed by one of the pair folded back. His jackets, trousers and shirts, whites, blues and creams in collective order, were hung on identical wooden hangers. His footwear was laid in a precise row along the floor of the wardrobe; from left to right, two pairs of sneakers, one pair of brown soft soled shoes with a space where a second pair would have been, and two pairs of black shoes polished with great care. The curtains at the big sash window were carefully pleated and dropped dead straight towards the floor. A small, flat

158

screen TV sat on a plinth in one corner of the room, a Blu-Ray player underneath it.

Being in the room did feel like an invasion of a profoundly personal space. There was no ambient sound, no underscore from the garden outside. I realised I was holding my breath and let it out slowly.

There were few novels on the shelves and most of them were popular airport lounge stuff. Stephen King, Stieg Larsson, Bernard Cornwell... No female novelists and no classics. Lots of poetry though. Browning, Elizabeth Barrett Browning, Keats and Byron, all of which get my vote. And Milton who I never liked, and Gerard Manley Hopkins who I could never fathom - a man so lost in the power of his own imagery that he did nothing but irritate. But then poetry is personal. There were a lot of books on twentieth century European history, and a complete shelf of biography and autobiography. Then an odd collection of sociological and philosophical works by Diderot, Rousseau, Voltaire, Marx and Engels and Huxley. Along with Adolf Hitler's grotesque blueprint for the Thousand Year Reich, *Mein Kampf*.

I picked it off the shelf. It was a recent edition, published in November 2015, annotated with appendices galore. And with a foreward by some American professor who maintained that in light of current political fractures, it was now time to review this work as a significant historical document.

I flicked back to the front pages. There, in 12 point New Roman was the name of the translator. Valiqa Harroun.

I checked the other European books. Val had translated some of Diderot's essays during 2006, and a 2010 publication titled *Evidence from the Gulags* by a Russian journalist born in Novosibirsk now living in Paris.

I wondered if Joanna and Patrick knew what their son had been reading. Maybe not. At fourteen years old I managed to keep my copy of *Last Exit to Brooklyn* secret from Auntie Joyce and Uncle Sid. The Barnes weren't likely to enjoy being re-introduced to Hitler's brutal nonsense. Diderot, the French philosopher, playwright and art critic, and a major force during the Enlightenment, was a man after my own heart but never likely to be prescribed reading. He is responsible for the world's most emphatic view of revolutions, saying they would never work until the last Aristocrat was flogged to death with the entrails of the last Priest. Not that Diderot was a fan of revolutions per se, he simply saw deeper into the reality than anyone else. The Gulags book wouldn't be a barrel of laughs either, although it would probably turn out to be the least strident of the three.

I took the books downstairs and we all assembled in the living room, like the leading characters in an Agatha Christie dénouement. Patrick was as shocked as I'd expected him to be when presented with Adolf's struggle, Joanna less so. Linda said she had never read it. None of them knew anything about Diderot. The testament from the Gulags created some minor interest.

"Why are you showing us these books?" Patrick asked. "Are you saying we should have monitored what our son was reading? Because if that's the case - "

I jumped in. "No no no." I handed the books over. "Look at the author page. And the name further down."

Linda was the first to respond. "Alfie's Val Harroun?"

Joanna looked at me. "How does this help?"

"The new *Mein Kampf* edition was published two years ago. Which means it is probably still in print and the publishers still in contact with Ms Harroun. They might know where she is, and better still, tell us."

I borrowed the phone in the study, rang McEwan & Plater and asked for the PR department. From there I was transferred to a lady called Heather, with a dusky contralto voice. She asked me if she could be of service. I told her I wanted a contact number for Val Harroun. Heather said that wasn't the sort of information they dispensed to strangers. I explained that it was an emergency and some friends of hers were desperate to get in touch. Heather suggested I tell her what this was all about and she would ring on my behalf. She returned my call three minutes later.

"Something of a snag, Mr Shepherd," she said. "I rang the number I have and got a voice message from a gentleman called Roland Humphrey. I presume he lives in the flat." She paused for a moment or two then continued. "Which means, I suggest, that Val no longer does."

"When did you last ring her on this number?"

"A month or so ago. We had some work to offer her. She didn't respond to our emails either, so we passed it on to another translator. A pity. Her translation skills are highly valued here."

161

"If she has sub-let her flat to Mr Humphrey," I suggested, "perhaps he knows where she's gone."

"In which case I shall give you the number. On the understanding that if you do find Val you let me know."

Back in the living room I told the Barnes family what I'd found.

"This is good news," Patrick said, and looked round at the rest of us. "Isn't it?"

Joanna looked at him. "Do you know what? I don't care. I don't give a toss about someone we don't know." She got to her feet. "Whatever she tells us... whatever... is not going to bring Alfie back." Her eyes filled with tears. "It won't mean a damn thing."

She headed out of the room. Patrick watched her go, then rose to his feet.

"I'm sorry about that." He shuffled his weight from left to right. Gestured towards the living room door. "I should go and see if she's okay. No it's stupid to say that. She's not okay and won't be for a long, long time." He looked at me. "Thank you for what you're doing, Jack. It's much appreciated. I know Joanna would say that too if she..." His voice dropped away and came back again. "If she was... herself."

Linda stood up and moved into his outstretched arms. They held on to each other.

"I know Dad," Linda said softly. "I know, I know..."

There was nothing I could do at this precise moment. The second time in half an hour I had felt like an intruder. I walked out of the room across the hall, opened the front door and stepped out into the porch.

Three or four minutes later, Linda joined me.

"I think I'll stay overnight," she said. "You don't mind do you?"

"Of course not."

She kissed me, stepped back into the hall and closed the front door.

Back in the office, now armed with her full name, I googled Valiqa Harroun. The half dozen entries revealed no more than I already knew. So I switched endeavours and called Jonathan Taylor. He said he would be happy to see me.

* * *

The Causeway studio lot is enormous. Two sound stages, the workshop and the scene dock have been created inside the original sorting centre. The offices once used by managers, the works foremen and admin staff are now dressing rooms, make up rooms and a green room. In orbit around the building are pre-fabricated offices for the producers, directors, writers, editors, floor managers, assistants and assistants to assistants, the design office, props and electrics stores.

Jonathan gave me a tour of the exterior sets, then conducted me to an empty dressing room.

"Best to talk away from the madding crowd," he said.

We sat down in two armchairs, opposite the wall with the worktop and the mirrors.

"What is the real news about Amy?" he asked.

That was an uncomfortable opener. In order to avoid answering the question I asked if Amy was a friend of his.

"I'd say so."

"Do you spend time with her? Socially I mean."

"A bit of social time yes. Drinks, sometimes an evening out."

"Is that all?"

"Yes. The work schedule is punishing. And the line producer's job is to make every day go smoothly. We're fairly close in that situation."

"Does Amy have any enemies among all this?"

He blinked. "Enemies? Good God, no."

"How many people work here?"

"One hundred and thirty plus," he said.

"So is there anyone she doesn't get along with? I mean not all of one hundred and thirty people can adore each other all of the time."

He took time to respond.

"Okay… This place is a hothouse of egos. Actors earning a lot of money, directors on the rise devoted to creating an impressive CV, producers who need to show who's bossing the outfit. But that's normal."

He noticed my look of surprise.

"It is, I assure you. That's the working environment. Everything is just more supercharged than other places of endeavour."

"How much socialising goes on here?"

He looked at me warily. "Erm… I'm not sure what you mean?"

"Yes you do. How close do people get?"

He chose to answer carefully again. "Some get very close. Others just pitch up, do the day's work then go home again. Nothing extraordinary happens here. No drinking, no flamboyant behaviour, no orgies..." He paused for a second or two. "Some secret screwing in dressing rooms I've no doubt, but..."

"That's all part of the working environment as well," I suggested.

"We're a close-knit group," he said. "All of us pretending twelve hours a day. Emotions at large all over the set. Everyone needs to unwind, at times."

"And Amy?"

"She is calm, organised, focused," he insisted. "Always ready for the moment in front of the cameras. We've both been here since the soap began and I can't recall her once throwing a tantrum."

"Has she come to work recently in the wrong frame of mind? Unprepared? Nervous, out of joint?"

Jonathan shook his head. "Not that I've noticed."

"Is this the party line you're giving me?"

"No. Certainly not. Amy is a bloody good actor. She's talented and very disciplined. Comes to work prepared and gets on with the job. She's destined for great things."

I wasn't going to get any more from this conversation. I fished into the inside pocket of my jacket and found a business card.

"If anything comes up, good news or bad, if you hear anything from Amy, or about Amy, please let me know."

He took the card from me.

"I will." He looked at his watch. "Would you like some lunch?"

I politely declined the offer. Jonathan escorted me back to my car.

Back in my office, I made notes on my conversation with Jonathan, then rang Celia and relayed them to her. She thanked me and reminded me to keep in touch. I ate the sandwiches I'd bought on the way back from *The Causeway* lot.

I switched jobs again. Called Roland Humphrey's number. His answering machine told me he wasn't in, but he was delighted I had called and requested that I kindly do so again later, or leave a message. Maybe I could catch Roland at breakfast next day.

The clock on the office wall said it was 3.45. I shrugged into my jacket, rode the lift to the ground floor and took myself for a walk. Over the ancient cast iron footbridge which spanned the river and into the park – a small well of quiet in the midst of traffic moving in four different directions. It was the sort of September day which encourages you to think that summer is far from over. A warm afternoon sun, not a single fallen leaf on the grass, and in spite of the muted sound of traffic, nobody going anywhere in a hurry.

I sat on a re-furbished, cast iron bench, as a five year old burst into my eye line on the end of a dog lead. The beast was nearly as tall as she was and much stronger. She tripped, let go of the lead and fell face downwards onto the grass. Her mother rushed up to the girl as she struggled into a sitting position, none the worse for the experience. She pointed in the dog's direction and yelled 'Bertie!!' The dog bounded his way back to her, she opened her arms, Bertie leapt into them, she fell

166

backwards, grabbed hold of him and they barrel-rolled across the grass. The mother grabbed them both, and managed to untangle the lead from Bertie's choke chain. The dog scrambled away, cantered over to the shrubbery bordering the river and lifted his right leg. He then sniffed around a bit, to ensure he had left a substantial enough calling card, and jogged back to the girl.

I watched all three of them play together. Even got in on the action at one point, when Bertie's frisbee sailed in my direction. It landed four feet in front of me. The pursuing Bertie back-peddled himself to a stop. He stood stock still, panting and nodding alternately at me and the frisbee on the grass. Then he sank back on all fours and waited for the next explosion of action. I picked up the frisbee and swung in the direction from which it had arrived. Bertie executed a seamless 180 and hared after it.

Then I stumbled across an idea.

I went back to the office and called Chrissie. She was at home. I asked about her day. She said things got better and better with every new challenge. It was good to listen to a teacher, feisty and excited, not yet ground down by government edicts and interference. I once asked my local MP if he would like me to spend my days telling him how useless he was at his job and how to do it properly. He mumbled some shite about his situation being different. I've long passed the point where I mind politicians lying to me, I expect no less. But what I do take offence at is their patronising expectation that I will believe what they say. Like Big Daddy, I too can smell the odour of mendacity.

Chrissie had read Russian and French Studies at university. I jogged her memory. Asked if she had come across Valiqua Harroun.

"Yes," Chrissie said. "Eight years ahead of me at university, but something of a star in the department. Got a publishing contract while she was still a student. She still lives in Bristol I think."

"But you don't know where?

"What's this all about, Dad? She's not in trouble is she?"

"No. She's gone to ground somewhere and I'm trying to find her."

Chrissie read between the lines.

"Gone to ground as in fleeing from the pack, or simply to get away from the crowds?"

"Honestly," I said, "I don't know."

Chrissie took that with a hefty pinch of salt. "Okay, are you in trouble?"

"No more than usual."

"In your terms that's simply a question of degree," she said. "It's like one of those irregular verbs. *I am a little concerned, you have a problem, he is deep in the clarts*."

She invited me to dinner. I apologised and told her I was busy. We wished each other a 'good evening' and ended the call. I sat back in my chair and stared at the crack in the wall above the office door, which I'm constantly reminding myself to tell Walter about.

I'd had enough of the day. I locked the office and went home. To an evening of solitude. I didn't want to disturb Linda. Or rage at the TV news, or dig into the woeful two hours between 7 o'clock and 9 o'clock, which no broadcaster can decide is either juvenile or grown up time and usually fills with antique hunts, 'celebrity' game shows, faux reality shows and cooking competitions. And 'let's go back a few hundred years' programmes, in which 21st century families, deprived of all comforts and communication systems, try to live in huts or holes in the ground and attempt to enjoy catching and cooking squirrels and making their own clothes out of animal skins and straw.

A root around in the DVD library produced *Hot Fuzz* which is always worth a look. I watched the film considerably cheered, and then went to bed.

CHAPTER FIFTEEN

I slept better and woke with a clearer head. Another Saturday morning. A week into the case.

I rang Roland Humphrey's doorbell at 5 minutes to 8.

He was clearly out of bed, because he answered the door before I rang a second time. Shorter and thinner than me and probably in his early 40s, he was wearing a long white woollen bathrobe over blue and red striped pyjamas. He was overwhelmingly cheerful for a man whose privacy had been invaded so early in the day. I told him I only needed a couple minutes of his time. He looked disappointed.

I asked him if he knew Val Harroun. He asked me who that was. I told him. 'Ah yes,' he said, and suggested I drop in on Parker's the estate agents, from whom the flat was rented. He gave me the address. And as he reached out to close the door he left me with, "Oh, you could try the lady across the hall. She might be more help."

A brunette with a second hand tan and a lumpy face, told me she had no idea where Val had gone. Not exactly a gregarious sort of person the brunette said. They had a drink together now and again, but always early in the evenings. Val seemed to have a regular something to do after 9 o'clock. She could only imagine what that might be. There was a shout from inside the flat. The brunette looked pained. A face crusted with beard stubble and narrow eyed suspicion poked itself round the door from behind her.

"What the hell is this?" The face glared at me. "Fuck off!!"

"Wrong address," I said to the brunette. "Sorry to bother you."

She smiled 'thank you'. The face disappeared. The brunette followed and the door slammed shut. I heard the sounds of an argument beginning as I walked away along the corridor.

Parker's Estate Agency is in Clifton village, where rents for one bedroom flats peak at around £950 per calendar month. I couldn't find anywhere to park. Eventually I thought 'what the hell', and in defiance of the Mayor's *Space in the Streets* crusade I squeezed the car into a 'residents only' parking space.

There were half a dozen work stations inside Parker's, laid out in the obligatory herringbone pattern along the length of the room. A comfortably curvy, streaked blonde in a smart navy blue two piece looked up from behind the first pc screen on the right and asked if she could be of assistance. I asked if could speak to someone about Val Harroun. The lady looked discomforted, glanced to her right along the herringbone pattern row and then back at me.

"Excuse me for a moment," she said.

She walked the length of the room, leant over the side of the last desk in the row and began a whispered conversation with a brunette, who listened, nodded her head, looked in my direction, then got to her feet, smoothed the skirt of her grey two piece down over her hips and walked towards me. She had the same graceful legs as Val Harroun. Which was no longer surprising when she introduced herself.

"I'm Terri James," she said. "Val's sister, well half-sister."

She held out her right hand. I shook it, not altogether up to speed.

"Jack Shepherd," I said.

She smiled at me with all thirty teeth.

"May I buy you a cup of coffee?"

"Yes," I said, grinning foolishly. "Thank you."

Five minutes later we were sitting on the terrace of the Avon Gorge Hotel – the place from where you get a great front stalls view of Brunel's suspension bridge – drinking the coffee and eating chocolate bourbon biscuits. Terri listened to my account of the meeting with her sister without saying a word. When I finished she answered the first question I would have asked.

"Val never talked to me about Alfie Barnes. Sorry."

"Tell me about her," I said.

"Our father was from Libya. An engineer. Val was born there, in 1984. Her mother was killed by Gaddafi's soldiers when Val was two, during one of his cleansing operations. Dad left the country twelve months later. He and Val came here. He married my mother in 1989. He died three years ago. Cancer."

She told all that efficiently. As though she'd had practice. I sat still, absorbing it all. Terri moved on.

"You would like to know where Val is, yes?"

"Yes I would."

"So would I," she said.

I stared at her and tried to frame the next question. Terri cut straight to the explanation.

"Two weeks ago, Val told me she was moving. Temporarily she said. She asked me if I could sub-let the flat for a short period, with a couple of months' cancellation notice on either side. I did that, to Mr Humphrey, a week later. And Val moved out."

"Where did she go?"

"I don't know. She didn't say. Not altogether unusual in Val's case. She's a knee jerk mover. You say 'Been here a long time', she says, 'I'm on my way'. She'll turn up again in a few months."

"What does she do during these periods?"

"Drifts, visits friends, goes on holiday..."

I let this information trundle around my brain for a moment.

"How does she afford to do it? Doesn't she have work commitments?"

"Nothing she can't work around," Terri said. "It's always been that way. Translation work she can do in any hotel room, on any terrace, in any garden..."

"Are you concerned for her?"

"No."

She smiled at me. I must have looked perplexed.

"You're bothered by this, I can see," she said.

"Don't you think she disappeared in"... I searched for the most useful phrase. "Less than regular circumstances?"

Terri shrugged. "Would you hang around a bar while a bunch of people were smashing it up?"

I thought about that. "Maybe not."

Terri gave way to a little impatience.

"Okay, it's not always convenient. I usually end up with her problems on my desk. Some are small, irritating, more than anything else, but now and again she leaves with something hanging."

"Like what?"

"Like you coming to visit and asking where she is."

"Have you a mobile number for your sister?" I asked.

"Yes. But you'll need a little more to convince me I should give it to you."

"Okay," I said. "You will no doubt have heard of Gerald Gaghan."

"Of course. Most people in business hereabouts have."

"Well I've come up against a trio of his enforcers and I can still feel the bruises. Gaghan may have something to do with the death of Alfie Barnes and your sister's disappearance. Is that enough?"

Terri was sitting up straight. The colour had all but drained from her cheeks. I repeated the question. She nodded.

"Yes it's enough."

She produced a tiny notebook and a pen from a jacket pocket. Wrote the information down, tore the page out of the book and handed it to me.

* * *

Back in the office I called the mobile number. Val's voice mail answered. I left an eleven word message. *This is Jack Shepherd. Call me as soon as you can.* I made some coffee and then some more which I let go cold. Suddenly I was pissed off. With the day, the case, the confusion and the not knowing.

I had always assumed it was impossible to disappear completely. Buster Edwards and Ronnie Biggs hadn't managed it and all they were up against was Skipper of the Yard. I'd covered all the bases I could think of. This investigation was eight days old. But that was no better than eight weeks... months.

The private eye with a feel for the streets and the beat of the city; an insider in the real world, with his own take on the nature of the human condition informed by a hefty dose of cynicism, may be the stock in trade of noir writers, but it has never driven the way I do things. I've never been a loner. I always had Emily. And Chrissie, although I'd driven her to distraction most of the time and left it to Emily to broker the peace deals.

Emily had always been there, more often than not to pick up the pieces. Although she had never knowingly settled for anything less than the best she could make of any situation, she had deserved better. I owed her so much. My very life probably. And now I was out of my comfort zone and out of ideas. Sulking and feeling sorry for myself and being exactly the sort of person she would have despised.

In times past, and on sunny days like today, I'd polish the Healey put the top down, drive up onto the Mendips and tail gate along the lanes for a while. The best I could do in the Accord was to roll the glass roof back.

So I drove out of the city on the A38 and headed northwest to the Severn.

A couple of miles downstream from Berkeley, a narrow track leads to the river. It ends at the waterside behind the embankment on the eastern shore, once studded by terraces of eel putches, the long conical shaped wicker baskets which gave local families a living. Now the eels and the putches and the reason for being on the riverbank have gone. It's not the sort of place you fall in love with, not these days. But standing on the bank at high tide, with the two mighty Severn crossings downstream to the left, the Forest of Dean half a mile away on the opposite shore and to the right Sharpness, and beyond that Westbury on Severn and Gloucester, you can feel the river's power and purpose. Here you meet total strangers, ramblers, dog walkers and one time boat people, and there is always a moment for conversation. About the weather, the view, the time and the tide and 'how you are today?'

There is room for three cars to park at the end of the lane. I was the only visitor. I got out of the Accord into a world of silence, underscored by bird song, the sound of the moving river and the distant rumble of traffic on the bridges. I locked the car and climbed the half dozen steps up to the track along the embankment. All the archetypal stuff closed in and embraced me. The 360 degree view of South Gloucestershire, the sunshine, the peace and quiet, and a skylark.

The bank side which slopes to the water's edge is mostly grey soil, stones and shingle. Above it, the embankment begins as a kind of raised beach flattened along the top into a path by millions of feet over the years. The tide was high but on the ebb, and the Severn had taken charge, pushing the salt water back, slapping at the embankment as it moved towards the Bristol Channel. I walked northeast for half an hour. Stopped when Berkeley Castle crept into view. I sat down on the grass and watched the river slip by. No visitors, ramblers or dog walkers today. I lay back, squinted up into the sunshine and closed my eyes.

I dozed for a while, then opened my eyes again. Something was blocking out the light.

Someone it turned out. The person from Porlock.

Julian grinned down at me and said 'hello'. He stepped away to my right. The sun flooded back into my eyes. I blinked, sat up and focused on him again.

"Don't move any further," he said.

I told him I wouldn't dream of it.

"We've been keeping an eye on you," he went on. "And on a couple of other folk too. My shift today. And this is a fine place to talk."

"Talk?"

"I hope so. I don't want our first private get together to descend into any kind of commotion. On the other hand..."

He took hold of the right lapel of his jacket and pulled it away from his body. A lightweight revolver sat in a holster below his armpit. Which meant he was left handed I thought, although how that was going to be useful during the next few minutes I had no idea.

Julian got straight to the point. "Where is Val Harroun?"

I feigned my best feigned surprise. "Who?"

Julian sighed. "So obstructive straight away."

"I've no idea who you're talking about," I said.

"Mr Gaghan is not a patient man," Julian said. "I, on the other hand, don't mind a little banter, and in most cases I'm content to give those I approach a short length of rope. I appreciate you came here to chill a bit, given that it's a lovely day, but if you don't mind, we'll get on with things."

I tried out a question.

"How long have you worked for Gaghan?"

"Long enough to be trusted," he said.

Emboldened, I tried another.

"Why are you looking for Val Harroun? I thought Howard and Maurice had spirited her away."

Julian read everything implicit in that sentence. I had a moment to consider stuff too. And it dawned on me that maybe neither of us knew as much as the other expected. And if Gaghan genuinely didn't know where Val was, then she was safe. For the moment anyway. Julian seemed to be coming to the same view as me. Both of us, if not in the dark, were in the shadows at least.

"You were the last to see her," he suggested.

"Maybe," I said. "But you are trying to find her."

"So are you. Along with Amy Turner."

I looked straight into his eyes and moved on

"Did your boss have you and Howard and Maurice beat up Danny Malone?"

That question wasn't on Julian's agenda. Suddenly he lost patience. He'd had enough of the banter and the lovely day. He reached inside his jacket and pulled the revolver from its holster. A short barrelled .32. He pointed it at my chest.

"This location isn't private enough," he said. "Stand up."

It seemed close enough to the middle of nowhere to me. Still, I wasn't going to argue. He gestured to his right.

"Back to the car."

"That's a mile and a half," I said.

"And I shall be behind you all the way," he said.

So we set off in silence and in tandem, like two of the three wise men. Julian with all the gold, me with the myrrh. I consoled myself with the notion that I had thirty minutes or so to figure a way out of the situation. But when you settle down with the purpose of doing some thinking, you invariably come up with nothing. Ideas need to arise and fester for a while. And half an hour wasn't much festering time. As we arrived at the steps from the embankment down to the lane I had no plans, A or B or otherwise.

"Hold it," Julian said from behind me. "Turn around."

I did that. He was seven or eight feet away. He looked down the steps.

"We'll leave your car here and take mine. You can drive."

He fished the Mercedes car key out of a jacket pocket and lobbed it towards me. I caught it. And came up with a plan, barmy though it was, in that instant. The river was a

179

dozen yards to my left. I swung my right hand like a fielder on the boundary and the key sailed into space, rising all the way to the river's edge, and then arcing its way gracefully downwards into the water.

I didn't wait to see the end of its flight. Julian on the other hand was transfixed. By the time the key hit the surface of the water, I had closed the space between us. He turned and thumbed the hammer of the .32.

I ducked my head, twisted my neck to the right and hit the ground with my right shoulder. My legs followed, turning my body like a propeller shaft. I was on my back when the bullet scorched over my chest and beyond. Julian's face came into view directly above me and for a split second I stared up into his eyes. Then the propeller did another revolution and I slammed into his shins. His feet left the ground, he hung in the air for a moment then dropped onto his face.

He lost the .32 trying to break his fall. Momentarily confused, he rolled in the wrong direction - away from the gun instead of over it. I reached it as he scrambled to his feet and I pulled the trigger. The gun kicked in my hand. I heard Julian grunt in pain, a moment before his body crashed down on top of mine. My head snapped back into a stone embedded in the path, the sunlight flashed white hot then slipped through grey into blackness.

My return to the light of day may have been only moments later, but it was sudden and painful. I propped myself on my elbows and tried to sit up. It took some time.

From my right I heard Julian say, "For Christ's sake come and help me."

He was sitting a couple of yards away, his left hand covering his right, both of them pressing down hard on the inside of his left thigh. Blood was staining his trousers around the wound.

"I need... help with this," he said. "A tourniquet... There's a first aid kit in my car. The boot."

"We don't have a key," I said.

"Just smash a window for fuck's sake."

You've seen how the hero does that in the movies. Bends his arm and elbows the glass in. That doesn't work, all you get is bursitis. You need something long and tough and pointed. I got the tyre lever out of the Accord boot and jabbed the business end at the Mercedes driver's side window. The alarm went off instantly, a great howling noise which hit the embankment and bounced back down the lane. The second jab smashed a hole in the glass. I switched my grip, and swung the handle end of the lever at the window. It shattered and sent shards of glass in all directions. I unlocked the car door, opened it and pressed the boot release button at the base of the driver's seat. I grabbed the first aid kit out of the Mercedes boot – a green metal box the size of a briefcase – slammed the lid, moved to the Honda, unlocked it, grabbed my phone from the tray in the driver's door, kicked the door shut and went up the embankment steps three at a time.

I dropped to my knees next to Julian. His face was the colour of parchment. His grip on his thigh had loosened but the flow of blood appeared to have slowed nonetheless. I opened the first aid box and found some large pads for binding on to wounds. I reached for Julian's collar. He flinched.

"I just want your tie," I said. "And don't pass out yet, we're both needed for the next bit."

I relieved him of his tie, tore the paper covers off the pads, grabbed the scissors from the green box, and cut his trousers away from the wound, which was clean at least. I piled a thick cushion of pads onto the bullet hole and told him to press again. Slid one end of his tie under his leg and pulled it back over the top, took hold of both ends, did the first left over right of the knot, until it had almost trapped his hands, told Julian to take his hands clear of the knot, and pulled the tie tight. He yelled in pain. I told him to put his hands back and keep the tie in place. He yelled again when I completed the knot. And then he passed out.

The primitive tourniquet I had made actually worked. I called 999, yelling above the wail of the Mercedes alarm. Then I got to my feet and looked for the revolver. I found it and dropped it into the inside pocket of my jacket.

Julian woke up, groaned and gulped in great chunks of air.

"Christ my fucking leg hurts," he said.

I shouted at him. "The emergency services are on their way."

He attempted to prop himself up on his elbows. His right arm slid away from him, he fell back and yelled again.

At which point, the Mercedes alarm stopped. The silence returned like a blessing. I checked Julian's tourniquet. The knot was tight and the bleeding appeared to have stopped. I asked him how he was feeling.

"Terrible," he said.

That was all right by me. And it looked unlikely he'd die. I stood up again and stepped to the edge of the embankment, leaned forward and plunged my hands into the river.

The car alarm stabbed onto the soundtrack again. An ambulance siren faded up and began to do battle with the alarm. Enough was enough. I returned to the Mercedes, found a couple of spanners, and disconnected the battery. The ambulance came to a halt as I slammed the bonnet down. The driver switched off the siren. The paramedic in the passenger seat jumped out, introduced himself as Ben and asked me if I was the person who had called 999. The driver joined us. Told me her name was Suzy.

I led the two medics to Julian, who was sitting propped up on his elbows and contemplating the pros and cons of trying to get onto his feet. Ben and Suzy set to work. I moved away. Looked downstream towards the Channel. The third siren of the morning announced the arrival of a police patrol car.

I met the two uniformed PCs at the head of the embankment steps.

"I'm PC Donaldson," the taller of the two said. "And this is PC Walcott."

We nodded at each other.

"Are you the person who made the call?" PC Walcott asked.

"Yes."

"So you can tell us all about the incident."

I gave them chapter and verse and handed over the revolver.

"There are still five bullets in the chamber. The missing one is in the thigh of the man the medics are treating."

Walcott nodded at Donaldson, who walked towards the trio.

"Stay with me, Sir, if you don't mind," Walcott said.

* * *

I went through the saga again, at Dursley Police Station. I'd been in trouble with Gloucestershire Constabulary before. In particular with a uniformed officer called Heather Renshaw. She was now a DC, based in Stroud. She dropped a grey folder onto the table between us.

"Another shooting incident, Mr Shepherd," she said.

"Good afternoon," I said.

"The other one a bit less than three years ago. Which wasn't your fault either as I recall."

I asked her how she was. She smiled at me.

"Jack, may I call you Jack?"

"What do I call you?"

"DC Renshaw," she said. "You've committed a host of firearms felonies, Jack. Then there's grievous wounding and maybe attempted murder."

"You don't mean any of that DC Renshaw."

184

"However... Your old friend in the Avon and Somerset Special Crimes Unit, DI George Hood, has asked that I spare your blushes. If only because of a major investigation he is leading into issues which may be affected by you having taken the law into your own hands."

"Hardly that," I suggested.

"Apparently you know the man you shot."

I didn't say anything.

"He works for a man with some clout in Bristol," Renshaw persisted. "Who will, no doubt, take it amiss."

"No doubt."

"Although speculation, apparently, has it that this man with some clout, is in turn unlikely to want the incident noised abroad. Therefore a low profile from every guest at this party is requested and strongly advised. So, in the interest of cross border co-operation, the Gloucestershire Constabulary has agreed that you should be allowed to return to Bristol. Providing you report immediately on your arrival, to the aforementioned DI Hood. That last bit is an order, Jack. Are we clear?"

"As crystal."

She stared at me to add emphasis. The uniform stationed by the door did too. Then Renshaw summarised.

"So, by the book this. Your car is in the car park. PC Donaldson will drive it to Bristol. You will follow, along with PC Walcott and another uniformed constable, in a patrol car. Let me see you to the door."

CHAPTER SIXTEEN

"Must I take away your driving licence and have you tagged?" George Hood growled.

I opened my mouth to reply. Hood held up his right hand.

"That question was rhetorical." He dropped his hand. "I can keep you here for twenty-four hours. And that can generate another twenty-four or forty-eight hours, as soon as the nearest magistrate or judge hears the words 'hand gun' and 'shooting'."

I offered him my best 'unrepentant' stare. He persisted.

"You say that Julian Farrar was looking for people, on behalf of his boss Gerald Gaghan?"

"Yes."

"And those people are being sought by you also?"

"That is correct."

"But you are not inclined to tell me who those people are?"

"I'd rather not."

Hood got to his feet. "Sorry, Jack." He moved to his office door and called to the nearest detective. DS Henson arrived and looked at me.

"Jack..."

"Never mind that," Hood said. "Take Mr Shepherd downstairs, have him processed by the Custody Sergeant and detained for twenty-four hours." He glared at me. "Which means until 4.23 tomorrow afternoon."

I did my best to look undefeated.

DS Henson escorted me from the office. I was allowed the famous one phone call. Actually two. The Custody Sergeant Tommy Morris and I had been on the beat together twenty-five years ago. I called Chrissie and got Adam. Told him I was busy and would be out of communication until at least this time tomorrow. He took the news with a hefty dose of cynicism but asked no questions and said he would pass the message on to Chrissie. I called Linda at home and dispensed the same information to her answering machine.

"Lucky with that last call, Jack," Tommy Morris said.

I said it was a pity he and I didn't have time to talk. He said he'd pop along to the cell with a cup of tea before he went off duty and we could catch up then.

"At least we don't have to take away your belt and shoelaces," he said.

The police cell looked like it had been made from a pre-moulded kit and dropped into place. The tiling looked like tiling but it wasn't. It was a resin of some sort, tough and stronger than a stone wall. The bunk bed, made of the same material, rose out of the floor without any apparent jointing — no nuts and bolts, seemingly super-glued to the floor and the wall behind it. The only movable thing in the room was the blue, plastic covered length of foam which served as a mattress. And maybe the loo, providing you had the tools to unscrew it, or lever it up from the floor. The cell was warm however. The heating came in via a vent low down in the wall to the right of the door; daylight through a window high in the wall opposite. A single light shone down from the centre of the ceiling, and like the window, eight or nine feet up and too high to reach. Even the most desperate inmate would have to be extraordinarily inventive to take his own life in this room.

I'd been lying on the bed staring up at the ceiling for half an hour, when the window in the door slid back and the Tommy announced I had a visitor. Harvey Butler stepped into the cell.

He looked at me, shoved his hands deep into his trouser pockets then stared at me. He moved his elbows outwards, then backwards and forwards like a vulture exercising. He seemed to be fighting an overwhelming desire to take his hands out of his pockets and fasten them around my neck. Instead, he stepped into the centre of the room and looked down at me.

"I'm amazed this is only your first overnight," he said.

"Is this visit part of a 'welcome to the cells' policy?" I asked.

"You see," he grunted, "you're incapable of being civil. Even in here."

I had to admit that was probably a joke too far and apologised.

He pointed at the bed. "Shift along."

I sat up and shifted and he sat down next to me.

"George Hood is in no mood to be lenient. Which is a pity, since he's always been on your side. More so than I, as you probably appreciate. He's all for leaving you here to rot. So..." He paused to enhance the drama. "On behalf of all those in the station who know you're here – some of whom are rejoicing I have to say – I'm simply going to ask... Why don't you answer the man's questions, save us all an unnecessary twenty-four hours of fucking about, and unchain the poor sod along the corridor from the paperwork he is having to do."

I needed twenty-four hours to make up my mind. Val Harroun had connections to both sides of this investigation. I had to be certain, if push came to shove, which side she would favour.

"I'll sleep on it," I said.

"You do that," Harvey said and stood up again. "You can be out of here in the time it takes to sign a statement. Do yourself a good turn. It doesn't have to be the hard way every time."

"Maybe it does," I said. "As I recall, you never take the easy way out. We both believe in right and wrong and law and order. It's just that the principles line up on your side differently from those on mine."

Harvey shook his head. "I have a sign on my door which reads 'Superintendent'. And there's only one right and legal way to get things done. You, on the other hand, have a complete disregard for that ethic."

"Principle."

"What?"

"Not an ethic."

Harvey looked as if he was losing patience. I explained.

"Wrongs have to be righted, Harvey. And sometimes you have to interpret the rules in a different way to accomplish that."

"No one with a badge and an ID card in his or her pocket can afford that luxury. There's no such thing as natural justice. Not here, not in this place."

"And that goes for all crimes and felonies?"

"Yes."

"For wife beaters and sociopaths and people traffickers and paedophiles?"

"Them, too."

"Don't you ever wish you could go through the back door once in a while and surprise the bastards at it?"

"We do that."

"Laden with warrants and rules of engagement."

"That's the way it must be, Jack".

We'd had this conversation more times than I could recall. And we will have it again, and again probably. Until the time comes when we will both be too tired to bother. I stood up and offered Harvey my right hand. He took it.

"See you in the morning, Harvey," I said.

He let go of my hand, walked across the cell and banged on the door. Tommy Morris opened it.

"Sleep well, and sensibly, Jack."

He stepped out of the cell and the door shut behind him. I lay down on the plastic covered foam and stared up at the ceiling.

* * *

Jack Shepherd's first night in jail. In a police cell, ten by eight. Something of an event. Or rather a non-event, as there was nothing to do.

At twenty minutes to six, Tommy Morris returned, as promised, with tea and chocolate Hobnobs.

"From our secret horde," he said. "You don't get an evening meal until half seven. And then it's not much."

We sat on opposite ends of the bed, the tea and biscuits between us. He asked me why I was here. I told him I had shot Gerald Gaghan's chief enforcer.

"They ought to give you a medal. Did you kill him?"

"No."

"Oh well. Maybe some other bloke will have more success."

He grinned at me. I asked him why he did this job when he might have risen to greater heights in another department. He said he was long past the time when ambition held him in thrall. He'd tried other departments but he liked the better hours this job offered. The shifts were user friendly. Checking the miscreants once in a while was no chore.

"I get to spend time with the wife and kids," he said. "Like all proper fathers should." He looked at his watch and got to his feet. "Finish the biscuits. I won't see you in the morning, there'll be another bloke on then. So I'll just wish you good luck."

He left with the smile of a holiday landlord who had just shown me round the cottage I'd rented for the weekend. I decided I could handle one night, but two or three would be overdoing it somewhat. George Hood was on a roll and I couldn't do any sleuthing locked up.

The screen covering the hole in the door slid back. A face I didn't recognise filled the window.

"May I come in," the face asked.

'Come in'? Whose property was this? I told the face to be my guest. It disappeared for a second or two, the lock rattled, the door swung open, and the swing shift Custody Sergeant stepped into the cell.

"I'm Sergeant Atkins," he said.

I nodded a greeting. "Sergeant."

"Sergeant Morris told me to introduce myself and ask if you wanted anything."

I asked him what was for supper.

"Ham, egg and chips," he said. "Which will arrive around 7.30."

"I don't suppose there's a comedian next door," I said. "Not that I'm complaining you understand, the service is cordial enough. But it could benefit from a little entertainment."

The sergeant grinned. "No comics in the corridor, sir. And you wouldn't want to spend time with the joker next door. He's a little... odd."

"I don't mind odd," I said.

"In his case you do, believe me."

"Can you lay your hands on something to read?"

Sergeant Atkins reflected for a moment. "I called at the library on my way here. Got a couple of books in the car. Mystery stories. Probably just the ticket for a man in your line of work. I'll send Constable Smythe to get them. Won't be long."

He left the cell. Constable Smythe pitched up with the books five minutes later.

"There you are, Mr Shepherd. Have a pleasant evening."

He retreated, locked the door and the slid the viewing porthole closed.

Two books from two different writers. *Secrets and Broken Dreams*, a mystery romance by a middle aged lady who gave up serving in Morrisons when her first book *The Body in the Ha Ha* sold a hundred thousand copies. And *The Rusted Blade* written by an ex-copper from Barnsley. From Morrisons to mainstream author at the stroke of a pen, had to be favourite.

I spent the next hour devising how I was going to tackle the combined force of George Hood and Harvey Butler. Whereupon my evening meal arrived on cue.

I ate it, then settled down to read.

CHAPTER SEVENTEEN

"Books?" George Hood said.

I told him I had friends in the building and they had been most courteous. He looked at the plastic covered foam and asked me if I had slept well. I told him not well enough. He offered me a choice.

"We can talk here and now. However, if I have reason to believe you are going to be co-operative, I'm sure we'd both be more comfortable in my office."

I caught Sergeant Atkins just before he went off duty and gave him his library books. Hood invited the duty DC to join us in his office.

"Write down every single bloody word he says."

During my pre-supper debate with myself the previous evening, I had resolved to make this encounter as precise as possible. I gave Hood an unabridged version of the Val Harroun story. The phone call, the rendezvous, the fracas and the disappearance. I edited the bit about the publishing connection I had made and jumped to the encounter by the river.

"And that's the lot is it?" Hood asked when I had finished.

"Yes."

"Anything not there that should be there?"

"No."

Answering specifically, that was true. The conversation with McEwan & Plater had no bearing whatsoever on the rendezvous with Julian; in the sense that he had followed me without knowing anything about it. And to the questions which were about to come, I could respond with the clear and unvarnished truth.

"Why did Val Harroun ask for a meeting?"

"She said she wanted to talk with me."

"About what?"

"Something to do with Alfie Barnes."

"And you didn't discover what that was?"

"No."

"How did she get to you in the first place?"

"That would have been my first question."

"And what is her connection to Gerald Gaghan?"

"I have absolutely no idea."

Hood took a deep breath. Decided he was as satisfied as he could be.

"Get that typed up," he said to the DC. "And get Sherlock to sign it before he leaves."

In the car park I pointed the key fob at the Accord driver's door, as Harvey Butler climbed out of his Volvo. I asked him what he was doing at Trinity Road on a Sunday morning. He replied with a question of his own.

"Are you still on the case?"

"Where else would I be?"

Harvey was substantially not pleased, but he took it well.

"That's that then."

He pointed his gizmo at his car door. It beeped. He walked away across the car park.

I watched him go. I had managed to get myself tangled up with two police departments and two very formidable coppers. George Hood and Special Crimes

195

wanted Gerald Gaghan, Harvey Butler and MIT wanted Alfie Barnes' killer. And Val Harroun seemed to be stuck somewhere in between.

Back in the office, frustration and tiredness gave way to a major bout of unreason. I didn't want to continue searching for an over-indulged, well paid actress, whose grasp on the day to day problems which afflict ordinary mortals was slippery at best, and who despite her addictions was living a life to which ninety-nine percent of her fans could never hope to aspire. On the other hand, I was seriously concerned about Val. Finding her had to be a priority. Gaghan wanted her, and if his enforcers located her before I did, then, in all probability, the link to Alfie would disappear along with her. I am supposed to be good at finding people. It's one of the bullet points in my sales pitch. But the people who hide in plain sight are the ones you miss. Val Harroun hadn't gone to ground, she was simply not visible.

I drove home, picking up *The Observer* on the way. A shower and a change of clothes later, I sat down to read it.

My mobile rang.

"Val has just called me," Terri said. "I told her you were looking for her. She said she would meet you."

"Where?"

"She said you could choose the place, bearing in mind that neither of you wants to be followed."

I did some thinking. Terri waited. I came up with an idea.

"The Park and Ride in Long Ashton. Do you know it?"

"Yes of course."

"It's perfect camouflage. Two more cars among several hundred."

Terri pondered for a moment. "So how will you find each other?"

"Tell Val to start with Area D and work outwards, away from the bus stop. If D is full, go on to E and F and so on. But park as soon as she comes across a spare bay or two. Understand?"

"Yes. That's clever."

"Only if we don't get caught. Tell her we'll communicate with mobiles."

"Fine. She has three."

Terri ended the conversation. I looked at my watch. 9.16. I looked at the clock on the wall. 9.17. Close enough. A minute either way shouldn't matter. I sat for another four minutes, my heart rate rising as the seconds ticked by. My mobile rang again.

"Mr Shepherd?"

"Val..."

"When do you want to do this?"

I looked at my watch. Twenty-two minutes past nine.

"Are you close to the Park and Ride?"

"I'll need fifteen minutes to get there."

I looked at the clock again and suggested we rendezvous at 9.45. She said that was fine and recited her car registration number.

It occurred to me that with Julian out of action, Gaghan might have deputised someone else to keep tabs on me. I picked up the Accord and drove back towards the office, underneath the Cumberland Basin flyover, onto Cumberland Road and headed for the car park beyond Brunel's *Great Britain*. The place is on the quayside, ground level only, and anyone driving in and out can be seen.

I parked as far away from the entrance as I could get and waited. Nothing unusual happened. An old Morris Minor Traveller trundled into the car park, burning oil and blowing dark fumes out of the exhaust pipe. Hardly the vehicle to chase people around in. A man got out and sauntered over to the water's edge. A dark blue Golf arrived. A couple eased out of the front seats and three children tumbled out of the back. The man locked the car. The woman assembled the offspring and led them off in the direction of the *Great Britain* dock. The man followed. Five cyclists, clad in lycra shorts and replica *Tour de France* tee shirts, swung into the car park line astern and dismounted. They pushed their bikes towards a couple of quayside benches. All human life was here, clearly, but Gaghan wasn't having me followed. At least not today.

Five minutes later I drove into the Park and Ride. Areas D and E were full. There were adjacent empty places in F. I found Val, parked with a white Transit van to her left and two empty bays to her right. I nosed the Accord into the one next to the Vectra. Inside, Val nodded hello and gestured to me to join her. I did.

She looked as good as I remembered, wearing tight grey corduroy trousers and a matching silk blouse. But her hair was different; cut short and dyed a lighter colour.

And she was wearing an expensive pair of glasses with designer frames. She realised I was scrutinising her face.

"Sometimes I wear these instead of lenses," she explained.

"The look works," I said.

"Thank you. I figure that if I need to, I can dress down, wear something long and loose, change the specs for another pair, and I might have a chance to pass unnoticed. At least to those who have only seen me once or twice."

She glanced around the car, as though checking that no one was sitting in the back seat.

"And thanks for meeting me," she said.

"Saved me putting the thumb screws on your sister," I said.

"I mean it. I want to help. I want to tell you about Alfie."

I needed to get two questions done with first.

One. "How did you find me?"

"Alfie talked about you now and again. When I asked him how his family was doing, you featured also. And even these days, you can still find the answer to anything in the *Yellow Pages*. All you have to know is the question."

Two. "Were you Alfie's partner?"

She smiled in response. Then looked at me with some indulgence, rather than berating me for assuming something so unlikely.

"No. But we were close," she said

"How did you get together?"

"We met in the library. In the Foreign Languages section. We walked around opposite sides of the end of a row of books and bumped into each other. I dropped the books I was carrying, he picked them up, fussed a lot, checked the books one by one, looked down and around to see if he had them all, fussed a lot more, and insisted on buying me coffee."

"When was this?" I asked.

"Eighteen months ago," she said.

"Sorry, that was the wrong question. I should have asked what day of the week it was."

Val smiled. "Of course. It was a Wednesday afternoon."

For a moment or two we sat in silence. There wasn't a sound in the car. In the distance, traffic hummed along the Ashton Bypass. I set the conversation going again.

"Why did you pick *The Quay* for our meeting? Is it a regular haunt?"

"I've been there half a dozen times."

I tried the other big question.

"Do you know Gerald Gaghan?"

"No. At least not personally."

"So why is he looking for you?"

"Is he?" Deadpan. She was irritatingly good at this stuff.

"His son Ridley was inside *The Quay* the afternoon we met. He was responsible for the commotion. Do you know him?"

"No."

"Or either of the two men who arrived to sort out the nonsense?"

She shook her head. "I must have gone by then."

Not exactly advancing the plot, this dialogue. Val was sharp and cool and right on the ball. Maybe you needed those attributes to be a translator. However, all that 'stickablility' training made me persistent.

"So why did you leave when the unpleasantness began?"

"Why? Patrons fleeing the place. Alone amongst a bunch of strangers taking chunks out of each other..."

That seemed a realistic response. We were still a degree or two away from Alfie however. I changed tack.

"Why do you use three mobiles?"

She acknowledged the swerve without looking uncomfortable.

"I need to be organised," she said, as if that was enough.

I filled the pause which followed by leaning back in my seat.

"Sorry," she said. "One is for work, one was for Alfie and one for other personal stuff. Everyone gets filed, as it were, in the right place. No one cross connects."

"So which phone are you using to call me?"

"Currently, the business number."

"And is that where I'll stay?"

"I don't know yet."

"The Alfie mobile," I said. "Was it used for contacting anyone else?"

"No."

201

Then for the first time in the conversation she betrayed some emotion.

"It's in a safe place. I er... deleted the call logs... in and out... all the texts and the voice messages. Now that Alfie's..." She paused again. "It was personal stuff and not needed any more."

I changed tack. "Why didn't you go to his funeral?"

"We were a secret," she said. "Or at least his time with me was. It was the way Alfie wanted it to be and I felt no need to ask why. He was embracing the relationship. It was something he didn't have to put out there for explanation. I went to visit the crematorium Garden of Rest a couple of days later."

Then she moved to item one on her agenda.

"I assume the police have all the papers Alfie kept at home."

"Including his diaries," I said. "Which have regular blank spaces in them. Friday evenings for example."

She smiled, for the first time in the conversation.

"That was my time. Alfie came to me every Friday evening at 6 o'clock. He stayed until 9 o'clock, when he left."

"Even during times you were moving around?"

"I've always had a second address. We met there."

"Where?"

She smiled and shook her head. "Not yet."

I tried another tack. "He never missed a date?"

"Never."

I could see how that would work for Alfie but not for Val. She explained.

"I gave him a key. And if I wasn't there he'd let himself in and stay for his customary three hours anyway. He left me the same note every time he spent the evening alone. Just two words. 'Thank You'."

"And how often did this happen?" I asked.

"I was there more often than not. But a girl has to work. And Alfie understood… I'm in Brussels a lot. Translating, some interpreting, for people in the city on business. All of us now wading through the slurry of the Brexit nonsense."

"And how is all that?"

"The same thing only different. The same bureaucrats, politicians, journalists, trade delegates. The same cast as before really, except that the closet right wingers are now in full cry. Racism hasn't been so in vogue since the *Empire Windrush* docked in 1948. Did you know the boat was a re-named Nazi cruiser? Flew a swastika at the masthead from 1933 to 1945…" She looked at me without blinking. "Some irony there don't you think?"

She didn't expect an answer so I sat still and waited.

"So here we are now, with a legitimised far right. Marine Le Pen's *Front National* was once the home for displaced World War 2 colonels, enemies of De Gaulle, mad bastards and malcontents. Now she has millions of poor whites, clinging to her coat tails, furious and aiming their malice at immigrants. And Le Pen and the sceptics are new best mates."

She took a beat rest, then moved on.

"In Brussels and Strasbourg, most MEPs are in a state of terminal confusion. It was thus long before the current schadenfreude. Hell it's no surprise. Contrived diplomacy is no business for the honest among us." She looked into my eyes. "Does that sound cynical?"

"Somewhat."

"I like the EU, Jack. And Europe needs it. The problem is finding people who are wise enough to recognise that and to represent it. Who was it said that politics was too important to be left in the hands of politicians?"

She was warming to her subject. I let her go on.

"You know that Bristol is twinned with Bordeaux, right? Well, last autumn, there was a big jamboree in the Gironde valley, funded by the EU."

"Yes I remember," I said. "Lots of satire about the Mayor being on a jolly with a bunch of local worthies he was grooming to help support his re-election."

"There was a bit of that, but there were actually all sorts of people in Bordeaux besides the self-servers and the chancers. Community organisations, local government representatives, law enforcement agencies, companies who do lots of business in Europe, a group of genuinely interested persons and the odd agitator. Believe me, Jack, the cause is just. *'One for All and All for One'* need not be an idle boast."

She held my gaze for some time, then leaned back in her seat, turned her head and stared through the windscreen.

"Back in the Spring I was on Lemnos, an island in the Aegean. The farthest refugees have attempted to travel from Turkey. A glorious day. Hot, dry. The beach was full of French, German, Italian and English tourists. We

204

watched two leaking and listing Turkish fishing boats packed with refugees drift into the shallows. An overwhelmed Greek policeman tried to marshal a group of tourists who had waded into the water to drag frightened and exhausted migrants on to the sand. The boats had sailed from Edrimit on the Turkish coast, north west one hundred and forty kilometres across the Aegean. A long and perilous voyage. But when people would rather die than live in their homeland, the odds on triumph over death shorten. In their imagination at least." She paused for a second, shook her head and went on. "Meanwhile, the cries of 'Stop them coming' echo around Europe, voiced by people who have no insight into the problem at all. 'Immigration is the big problem' say millions of people, latching on to the coat tails of politicians who know how to stoke the flames of suspicion and ignorance to get themselves and their bonkers ideology onto the front pages of the tabloids. I mean, for Christ's sake, nobody gives all they have in the world to a trafficker, then with toddler in arms, risks life and limb on a desperate voyage with no likelihood of salvation at the other end, because they think it's an adventure..."

She turned back to me, eyes blazing with anger.

"I speak some Arabic, but no one on that beach needed an interpreter to tell them what the boat people were screaming. Anguish, despair and fear are recognisable in any language. One woman in particular, was yelling in frenzied gasps and pointing out to sea. An Italian I had met a couple of days earlier, offered me a pair of binoculars. 'Something out there,' he said. 'What do you think it is?' Something red was floating on the surface of the water. I took the binoculars away from my eyes and looked at the man. He had kicked off his sneakers and was standing on one leg removing his jeans. He said 'If we form a chain in the water, it won't be difficult to get back to the beach.' I handed the binoculars to a German who had joined me. 'It's a child,' he said, 'in a red life jacket.' I followed him into the sea, until the water was waist high. The Italian passed the child to the German who held the tiny bundle close to his chest and back stroked towards me. I scooped the dead little boy into my arms, turned and waded back to the beach. The mother who had reached us, grabbed her son, wrapped him in her arms, buried his face in the folds of her coat and sank to her knees overwhelmed by grief. I don't want to witness anything like that again, Jack. Ever."

The anger had left her eyes. She sat back in the seat, switched on the ignition, pressed a button on the console between us, and the driver's window rolled down. A breeze drifted into the car. She breathed slowly.

"Those tourists ran into the water to rescue men, women, toddlers and babies in arms. No one took so much as a second to think. An instinctive surge of humanity took over, like the power was switched on. People on holiday. They ran into the sea."

"As ninety-nine people out of hundred would do," I suggested.

"Yes. There's something... I don't know... ordinary and un-heroic about that. Dragging someone out of the sea is easy, emotionally. The aim is simple. Save a human being's life. However, when you're asked to take him home with you, that's another thing altogether."

That conjured up a flashback. A black comic from Barnsley, called Charlie Williams. He topped the bill on the variety circuit during the 1970s and 80s. He always opened his act with "*If you don't laugh I'll come and live next door to you.*"

Val turned to face me again.

"The truth is, Jack, that in everything a bit difficult, governments are refusing to nail their colours to the mast. Remember last weekend's big story? Close to seven thousand people from Syria drifted onto a Sicilian beach over two days. Sixteen fishing boats and twelve inflatables with just enough fuel to get within range of the Italian coast. Seven thousand people, Jack. Including twins, born on the journey. Can you imagine that? The politicians and the 'border sovereignty' obsessives can't. Just look at the tip of the iceberg... IS on a mission, Syria a charnel house, hundreds of thousands of people fleeing for their lives from Pakistan, the Middle East and Africa, paralysis in the EU, the UN and NATO, British politicians being accused, not without substance, of anti-Semitism, boatloads of people drowning in the Aegean..."

She took another deep breath, then wound up.

"And millions here in the UK, bleating on about sovereignty and migrants and all the other world phobic shit."

She sat back in her seat and softened a little.

"It's far too easy, Jack, to put stuff into the 'hard to do' box and lock it away."

We were miles from where we had begun, but Val dug more out of the locker.

"And something else… Gerald Gaghan was at the jamboree in Bordeaux. Beaming his nuclear powered smile at all and sundry. During the four days, he had at least half a dozen meetings in small rooms, with a couple of hefty blokes stationed outside in the corridors."

"What were they about?"

"I don't know, precisely. The contracted interpreters weren't given the gigs, but we did speculate about what might be going on." She looked me straight in the eyes. "Consensus was, the meetings were something to do with financing right wing politics throughout the EU."

A hell of a rationalisation. And my turn to stare through the windscreen.

"That's all I know about Gaghan, Jack. And the only occasion I've seen him in the flesh." She cleared her throat. "However…"

I looked back at her.

"I believe… that someone is looking for me."

"Gaghan is. His main man Julian was very clear about that."

"Would that be the man who called in at Parkers?"

"Yes."

"Where is he now, do you know?"

"Probably still in hospital," I said. "I shot him."

She sat upright, as though somebody had electrified her seat.

I told her the story. She rewarded me by returning to the point of this rendezvous. As if I had finally passed muster.

"I have some stuff Alfie gave me. Some things to have and to hold and some things he asked me to keep for him. Increasingly I'm given to wonder what I should do with those. Do you want to see them?"

"Yes."

"Okay," she said. "If you'd like to follow me..."

I got out of the Vectra.

CHAPTER EIGHTEEN

I followed Val into the heart of Clifton and to the car park behind Chancellors Hotel. A brochure would call the place a 'boutique' hotel. If there were a brochure. This up-market hostelry doesn't advertise. It has twenty-three rooms for discerning guests and a policy of absolute discretion. I visited once, in my early days as a private investigator, at the behest of a potential client who wanted to find the man who had just left him and the apartment they had shared for six years. He was distraught, and desperate to ensure that the secrets of his relationship be kept just that. Three days later, I found the man hanging from the ceiling beam of a cheap top floor flat in Weston Super Mare. My memories of Chancellors weren't great.

Val picked her handbag off the back seat of the Vectra and got out of the car. I sat in the Accord and waited. Pressed the button in the door arm rest and the window slid down. Val reached the car, dropped her head and looked in at me. I suggested they wouldn't let her and me into a place like this.

"I live here," she said. "I spend a lot of time in hotels. I've had a room in this place for a while."

I got out of the Accord.

"I assume we can continue talking in confidence," she said.

I told her we could, and believing in my un-impeachability she led the way to the rear service entrance. We rode the lift to the top floor. Actually a very posh attic conversion into two suites. Val led the way past the first door and unlocked the second. She stepped to one side and with an extravagant wave swept me into the hall.

The bathroom to the right of the hall was expensive and stylish, with everything white, including the ceiling, the walls and the floor. Two brightly coloured towels, and a matching striped bathrobe hanging on the door, stamped their authority on the room as the only pieces of colour. The hall opened out into a heavily 60s living room, dominated by two six feet sofas in an orange coloured chunky corduroy fabric with chrome feet and leather belt arms. A circular, glass-topped coffee table sat between the sofas. A highly polished, acrylic finished, sideboard stood against the wall separating this suite from the next one. An Eames chair with footstool and a low drinks table sat by the big sash windows overlooking Portland Square. A door in the wall opposite led into the bedroom.

Val read my mind.

"I don't pay for this," she said. "I live here rent free. Sit down."

I sat on one of the sofas. She stepped to the window and looked out of it.

"I need your word, Jack. You can give it unconditionally because the story doesn't affect anything about my relationship with Alfie."

She turned round to look at me.

I nodded. "Okay."

She took a deep breath.

"I have two er... careers, you could say. You know about the interpreting, translating stuff, of course..."

She looked steadfastly in my direction. I didn't say anything. She pointed across the room and got right down to it.

"The man who occupies the suite next door owns the hotel. He's a bit like King Lear. He divided his fortune between his three daughters, sold his big house, but rather than living with one of them, or all three in turn, he moved in here. I look after his sexual needs. I have nothing to fear from him. And for this service, I get this suite rent free."

"How old is he?" I asked. "Forgive me but er..."

"You're interested, but not pruriently." She grinned at my discomfort. "He is 66. Almost exactly twice my age. The only job condition imposed is that, unless one of us is out of town, or out of the country, I be here and available every evening at 9 o'clock." She stopped and waited for a reaction. I dredged one up.

"That explains something your ex-neighbour said. The lady across the hall. Whenever you went out together you called time on the fun at 9 o'clock. It also chimes with Alfie's visits. Always over by nine."

Val was two sentences behind and betraying some concern.

"How was she? Lucy, across the hall."

"Not altogether happy. Our conversation was interrupted by an ugly, ill-tempered heavyweight, who shut the door in my face."

212

"Lucy's been with him something like eighteen months. As long as I've lived in the building. She won't leave him. And, I swear, the relationship grows more and more brutal."

They always do. And eighteen months is a short time in many of them. In the end things do fall to bits. But sometimes not soon enough, and sometimes too late for the people who can help solve the problem. I've worked with police officers who can't prove partner violence and have to let stuff go. There are teachers who know they're sending kids home to violent parents and can't get anyone to take up the case. Doctors who see evidence of physical abuse, but whose patients won't talk to them. Victims and witnesses are silenced, juries tampered with. And lawyers, defenders of evil people and unable to bring their own moral compass to work, fail to help courts get at the truth. Innocent until proven guilty is written in stone – it must be – but it's an imperfect system, hiding truckloads of deep seated passions and terrors.

Val's voice seeped back into my head.

"Alfie kept a few things here."

I looked at her. She continued.

"An alarm clock he used to set, in case he lost track of time. A scarf and a black woolly hat in the bedroom chest of drawers. Photographs of me in Brussels and in Strasbourg. And a notebook, which you ought to take a look at."

She moved away from the window and across the room to three rows of bookshelves on the wall above the sideboard. The notebook lay on top of some books on the middle shelf. She collected it and moved back to me.

"Alfie was found by, or offered his services to, Gaghan Nash," she said. "It's all in here."

That news produced a moment's pause.

"To do what?" I asked

"I'm not sure," she said. "A lot of the information seems designed to confuse people not in the know and most of the rest is in shorthand."

"Pitman's shorthand? The stuff people went to secretarial college to learn?"

"Yes. I never mastered it. But I guess Alfie could have done so in no time at all, given his power to concentrate."

I stared at her. She sat down and went on.

"I know what you're thinking. You can't write shorthand on a QWERTY keyboard. Well, Alfie wrote in short longhand first, then scanned the pages into his notebook." She waited for the expression on my face to change. "And now you're asking, why the hell would he do that? The answer is, because he could. The same logic would be applied to a job offer from Gaghan Nash. If Alfie thought it was something stimulating, he would do it. And he would stick to it."

"Regardless of right and wrong?"

Val nodded. "Perhaps. If the job was clever enough, he would get totally involved and moral judgements wouldn't crop up."

"Until he got fed up, or until Gaghan Nash had no more use for him."

"Yes. Doesn't sound edifying, does it? You see, Alfie had a system through which he worked day by day. The purpose was singular, the attention exclusive. There was no deviation at any point. I once asked an educational psychologist for a lay person's explanation. He said it was best explained by the story of the boy and the shopping. He's arrived home with his Mum. They're in the kitchen and she says to him 'Go and get the bags out of the car.' So he does exactly that. He takes every item out of the bags, leaves the shopping in the boot, and takes the bags into the house." She summed up. "So Gaghan could have understood enough to realise where Alfie was coming from. And Alfie could have been attracted by Gaghan's approach and locked onto something about it which interested him?"

"Okay," I said. "But how could he pop up on the Gaghan Nash radar?"

"Alfie was an Imagineer. You know that right?"

"Yes."

"Paid by games industry majors to come up with brand new ideas, and once the designers have got to grips with them, to write the codes... Have you seen his website?"

"Yes, it's a bit wierd."

"It's more than that, it's brilliant," she said. "I think Gaghan, or Nash, came across it or were directed to it. Nash in particular would have realised Alfie had all the things he wanted in an employee. Attention to detail, microscopic care for what he was doing and a one hundred percent ability to see a scheme through."

"Did you ever bring this idea up with Alfie?"

She shook her head.

"If I had mentioned it, Alfie wouldn't have understood where I was coming from. He would have rejected it, and the conversation would have been closed."

"Nonetheless," I said. "Whoever killed him would need to cover his, or her, tracks. And if that person made the connection to you and became disposed to believe you might know something..."

I left the sentence unfinished. Val looked gloomy.

We sat in silence for a while. Then she spoke again.

"All right, how's this? Gaghan's fringe meetings in Bordeaux were important. And secret enough to have wide shouldered guys on the doors. None of us could get in. So we began to believe he had some sort of outreach programme going, checking on whoever was showing the slightest interest in his business. Perhaps he did discover my relationship with Alfie."

"Okay. How might he have done that?"

Val sighed and stared down at the carpet. "Hell, I don't know." She shook her head as if trying to clear it.

"Yes," I said. "It's a bit of a reach isn't it?"

She sat down next to me, put the notebook on the coffee table and fired it up. The notebook asked for a password. She slid it along the table top towards me.

"You do this. Type capital CH... okay, then in lower case d v a t s a t... the number 2... and in lower case again s h e s t."

I studied the password. *CHdvast2shest*. I asked her if she had any idea what that meant. She grinned.

216

"CH is this hotel. And the rest is his age, 26, spelled phonetically in English. I taught him to count in Russian."

"Why?"

"He asked me to. And he picked it up far more quickly than I did in the beginning."

I clicked 'documents'. There were six folders.

"Start with *Mon-Wed-Thurs*," she said.

Inside were a number of files dedicated to work he was doing for Gaghan Nash. At least, so it seemed. 'G' and 'N' appeared regularly. The empty afternoons in his diaries were detailed in the note book. Dated and timed. He recorded his arrival at an office somewhere, and at the end of the document, the time of his departure. The shorthand notes were in between.

"Some work needed there," Val suggested, then pointed at the screen. "*GN-YM* however. No secrets in this file. I printed the pages."

She stood up, stepped to the sideboard, opened a drawer and took out two white A4 size envelopes. She handed me one of them.

"Take a look."

I did. At hard copies of emails. Communications between a Belgian called Yanis Mertens and Gaghan Nash over a period of sixteen months. Swopping details of proposed action, organisation, histories of demos, plans for subversive action, and confirming a schedule of meetings organised for later in the year between Gaghan and the leaders of *Action Politique*. Mertens' emails were written in crisp, clear English. The kind of English penned by a foreigner who is taking great care not to make any mistakes or create any confusion.

"I know Yanis Mertens," she said. "At least I've seen him. Twice in a café in Brussels. And eighteen months ago in Paris. I was translating international reports for *Paris Soir* at the time of the shootings at *Charlie Hebdo*. He was interviewed by a TV journalist. I was given a transcript of the piece to edit. Which, incidentally, was never aired or published. Somebody pulled it."

"So who is Mertens?"

She sat down next to me again.

"A man consumed with anger. He has a shaved head, a chain of swastikas tattooed around his neck and a thirst for confrontation which is unquenchable. There's not much he likes about the world, but then the part of it he was brought up in is broken and unfixable. A no-go area for calm and reason. A suburb of Antwerp with 55,000 inhabitants, representing something close to forty different nationalities. The majority of them migrants from North African and Muslim states, who had made their homes in the old Flemish neighbourhoods. Mertens was four years old when his father was killed – stoned to death by an Arab street gang. His mother left the family eighteen months later, and he and his younger sister were handed over to the neighbours. He grew up without much concern for the difference between right and wrong. And now, his world view doesn't stretch beyond the white Flanders community which made him what he is. A committed racist. And it was this which drove him to Sint-Jans-Molenbeek back in the spring. He muscled the rest of his compatriots from *Action Politique* into a march through the streets protesting against moves by the regional government to allow more migrants into the district. In the Cour de Commerce, they were confronted by a group of African Muslims. The police weighed in with water cannon, tears gas and tasers. Sixteen people were taken to hospital with injuries minor and serious. One of them died on the way, another, twelve hours later in intensive care."

She paused for a second or two, then wound up the biography.

"Mertens is probably the most vicious, xenophobic leader of the Belgian hard right. A grade one, gold-plated neo-Nazi."

And Alfie was hooked up with this man. If this was the connection Danny Malone was keeping secret, he couldn't give it away on anything less than a dead cert. It was probably knowing about it which got him broken into bits.

"Difficult to believe isn't it?" Val said. "Alfie, our Alfie." She stood up again and walked back to the window. "What was it Sherlock Holmes said? When you eliminate something, whatever you're left with is erm…something else…"

"He said, *When you eliminate the impossible, whatever remains, however implausible, must be the truth.*"

"But Alfie…" She turned round, rubbed her eyes with ends of her fingers, then pointed at the notebook again.

"Look at the next folder."

I opened it. All the documents were written in German. She pointed at the second white envelope.

"I translated them."

To no avail. The English was no clearer than the German. The first page I picked began with... *Mode A. Strategy 7. Arrangements no change. Wolfgang 1. Franz 2.* Then a number of complete sentences followed, the only fathomable one a series of directions. The other eight pages were written in the same way – modes, strategies, more about Franz and Wolfgang and some of it introducing Jacomo, Richard, Hector, Dmitry and Fred.

"I've had time to think about the names," Val said. "They're all composers. Liszt, Mozart, Puccini..."

"Who is Hector?" I asked

"Berlioz."

"Dmitry?"

"Shostakovitch. Richard could be Strauss."

"More likely to be Wagner," I suggested. "Given the people we're dealing with."

"Who's left?" Val asked.

"Fred. Chopin."

"Or Haydn. Fred was his middle name."

"A joke of sorts, I suppose."

"Do you think these people crack jokes?"

"Probably not."

"Alfie did. He liked jokes. Although he tended to tell the same half dozen over and over. He'd scream with laughter nonetheless."

I dropped the sheets of paper onto the table in front of me. Val waited for me to offer something to improve the shining hour. All I came up with was another question.

"So why was Alfie sending coded messages to neo-Nazis around Europe?"

"Perhaps, simply, because he could," Val said.

I thought about that… Alfie had always done stuff because he could.

"Did you notice they're not emails?" she said.

"So how did he send them?"

"Not as attachments," she suggested. "Hardly secure these days."

"Are there any responses in the files?"

"No," she said. "But there must have been acknowledgements from the composers. How else could Gaghan and Nash be sure the messages had been received?"

"Mobiles maybe."

"If that's so, then why aren't they in Alfie's notes?" Val asked. "He copied or logged everything else."

"Maybe the acknowledgements by-passed him. Half a dozen words which went straight to his employers. They wouldn't need Alfie for that."

We both lapsed into silence, neither of us convinced we were improving the shining hour. We sat still, pondering the predicament for ages. In the end, Val pointed at the notebook.

"I read all that stuff a few hours after I learned Alfie was dead. "I thought about it for days. Then I called you. I wouldn't have arranged to meet at *The Quay* if I had known it was owned by Gerald Gaghan."

Another silence.

"So..." I said. A kind of reflex, not meaning anything.

"I'm glad you talked with Terri," Val said. "And I'm glad you found me."

The situation was completely surreal. In a suite on the top floor of an up-market hotel, with if not the most deadly news in the world, something close to that. And a white supremacist in Leigh Woods threatening both our lives. That had to be a first, surely.

Val ordered sandwiches and beer from the hotel kitchen. We didn't have a plan to cover what should happen next, except to keep a low profile and endeavour not to antagonise Gerald Gaghan if at all possible. We decided to meet again after I'd found someone to read Alfie's shorthand.

She gave me the phone number she had reserved for Alfie. Now for me and me alone. We agreed on a series of code words to put in front of all messages we had to leave. If they weren't there we would know that someone had hi-jacked the line. We would change them when we felt they had been used too often.

I left Chancellors shortly after 2 o'clock and drove back to the office. I spent an hour or so looking through the other three folders in the notebook. One contained a list of books Alfie had read, each one with its own six line synopsis. Another detailed arrangements for holidays which he had planned but, as far as I knew, never took. Journeys worldwide, by bus, train, boat and plane, all scheduled and time-tabled. The last folder was packed with music tracks. I decided I had to share some of this with a person who excelled at conspiracy theories and could remember the shorthand he had learned as a cub reporter. I called Adam's mobile. He was on his way home. He suggested supper and the rest of the evening together. I used up another hour writing my notes on the day and dropped them into the filing cabinet under E for Emily. Easy to remember, no need to write it down. And maybe just ordinary enough for any visiting burglar to miss.

I got into the Accord and headed for Clevedon at twenty minutes past five.

CHAPTER NINETEEN

Adam and Sam hadn't come back from their late afternoon walk. Chrissie was at home alone.

"So where did you go on Saturday night?"

I hung my jacket on a peg by the door.

"Saturday?"

"Now don't start," she persisted. "You disappeared from the radar. Where did you go?"

I raised my arms in surrender and told her I had spent the night in jail. If it was possible for a chin to hit the floor, this was the moment Chrissie's did. So I regaled her with the story of my trip to the river, the encounter with Julian and my night of incarceration. I don't recall how much time it took, but by the end Chrissie was amazed, rung out and speechless.

"Only a formality the night in the cell," I said. "The service was five star and I had time to think."

She executed an exceedingly grumpy one hundred and eighty degrees and strode into the kitchen, where she made a lot of noise banging pots and cutlery about, then re-appeared in the doorway.

"Jesus Christ, Dad, what the hell am I going to do with you?"

I was spared further excoriation by the arrival home of the rest of the family. The front door opened, Sam looked around the hall, hurled himself at me, bounced off, fell back, rolled over, got his bearings, then launched himself at the stairwell and went up the stairs three at a time.

Adam said, 'Oh bollocks,' and set off in pursuit.

Chrissie stepped back into the hall. I asked where Sam was off to. She said it was something he'd done on the first day he arrived and because he'd enjoyed it so much, once in a while it occurred to him to do it again.

There was another round of joyous barking upstairs, followed by Adam shouting, "Get off the bed you hairy bugger." There was a beat before six feet pounded along the landing and into the bathroom. "Come out of the linen basket," Adam yelled. "Sam, no!"

A moment later, Sam peered round the corner at the head of the stairs with a sock in his mouth. On the landing Adam made a grab for him. Sam shimmied to his right, then hurtled down the stairs, turned sharp left, shot into the living room, did a couple of circuits, came back into the hall, looked up the stairs, saw Adam bearing down on him, dived between Chrissie and me and disappeared into the dining room.

There was silence. The three of us met, formed a posse and crept stealthily after the dog. We found him sitting under the dining table, panting furiously, tongue hanging out, the sock wrapped round his paws. Adam came up with a plan.

"You take the front end, you take the back. I'll grab the sock."

That didn't work, so we resorted to bribery with biscuits. Sam is no fool and he has been tempted by the biscuit routine on many occasions. Finally the temptation was just too powerful to resist and he dropped the sock. Adam grabbed it, headed upstairs, dropped it back into the linen basket and closed the bathroom door. Sam, satisfied that his moment of chaos had garnered reward, sat down by the kitchen door to await the arrival of his tea. Adam duly dispensed that. Sam devoured it in seconds, drank from his water bowl and offered his soaked and dripping beard for Adam to dry. Then he strolled along the hall to the bottom of the stairs, lay down, yawned and went off to sleep.

Chrissie threw Adam and me out of the kitchen. We retired to the study and I gave him the notebook and the envelope. He suggested I pour a couple of drinks while he read the material. He was on the second page of a file when I handed him two fingers of Islay malt. I went into the kitchen to add a little water to mine.

Chrissie had calmed down a bit and managed to say, "If you want to do something useful, you can peel the potatoes."

I set to it.

Ten minutes later, back in the study, Adam invited me to pull up a chair and confessed he had struggled a bit with Alfie's shorthand.

"Mine is, at best, a bit rusty, and Alfie's version is unique. But I dug out enough information to be confident I understand what's in the files. If you're sitting comfortably, then I'll begin... Alfie spent Monday, Wednesday and Thursday afternoons at an office in Queen Square, less than a hundred yards' walk from where he got off the 224 bus. And if this is indeed a true and correct record of what Alfie dug up on Gaghan Nash, and if you can reveal it without being hunted by the representatives of a coterie of people with less than satisfactory pedigrees, you may be in line for a civic reception and the highest award the new incoming Mayor can bestow. I say incoming, because the current Mayor has no chance of re-election if this is published."

"You don't get rich by being kind to widows and orphans."

"I'm serious, Jack. Even working with Howie and Mo, Gaghan would probably struggle to pass the 11 plus. But should he decide you have become a nuisance, you could spend the rest of your life in traction."

My mind flashed to a picture of Danny Malone in IC. I looked at Adam, unsure whether to suppress a grin. He wasn't smiling. He gave me time to appreciate his point of view, then continued.

"And by the way… I don't think Alfie wrote in shorthand to make his readers work hard. I think he did it to amuse himself and give the finger to anyone who was looking for explanations. If he'd wanted to make things difficult he'd have done the whole thing in code. And it would have been good enough to keep the mavericks at Bletchley busy for the duration."

"So what's in there?"

"A record of Gerald Gaghan's debts and enforcement businesses. Until July 31st anyway. Gaghan Nash was making a small fortune. And Danny Malone had been making a tidy sum here and there, until he transgressed."

"Why would Gaghan allow Alfie access to all this?"

"Most likely he didn't," Adam suggested. "Alfie found it, probably. Getting absorbed in what he was being hired to do could lead a bloke like Alfie on all sorts of missions."

Adam pointed at the pc screen.

"And there's a name here. Nick Jenner."

"Who's he?"

"He, is the Mayor's brother-in-law. An old fashioned chancer."

"Clearly fallen on hard times," I said. "At least by late July."

According to Alfie's record, Gaghan had taken over Jenner's debt on Valentine's Day from a loan shark called Marty James who had died of heart failure twenty-four hours earlier. At that moment the sum owing was £16,000. Interest on the amount was 33.3 percent per month for three months, thereafter 10 percent a week. By July 31st, the mayor's brother in law owed Gerald Gaghan £31,840

"We have no idea how concrete Jenner's guts are," Adam said. "But the idea that a debt could increase over 150 percent in the space of five months, must be enough to terrify anyone with the smallest concern over his bowel control."

I must have looked as if I was thinking, because he waited for a response. Actually, I was gobsmacked by the maths. Adam cleared his throat and came up with another question.

"Why does the paperwork stop at the end of July? I mean, did Alfie have a road to Damascus moment? Did he think 'what the hell I can't be bothered with this any longer'? Did Gaghan sack him?"

"Alfie's record ends five and a bit weeks before he died," I said.

"Then perhaps his death has nothing to do with what's in it," Adam said.

"Perhaps," I said. "Nick Jenner... Where is he now and what is he doing? Has he settled his debt? What will it be now if he hasn't?"

Adam pondered. "Another five weeks at 10 percent. Erm..." He did some calculations in his head. "Another £20,000 plus... Bloody hell..."

"What do you know about him? Apart from the fact he's the Mayor's brother-in-law."

Adam turned to his pc and Googled the Bristol Chamber of Commerce. To be offered a list of half a dozen companies, all but one with registered offices in the Isle of Man. His locally based business *FW Trusts* had an office in Queen Square. Two doors along the terrace from where Alfie had worked.

"Is there an *FW Trusts* website?"

Adam googled the address. He was rewarded with pages of organisations with FW in their titles, the words trust and trustees, and associated stuff like 'trusting in the Lord', and a movie from 1990 called *Trust*, in which a pregnant teenager encounters a moody, grenade carrying, electronics geek and takes him home to meet her folks.

No *FW Trusts* website. And no Twitter address or Facebook page.

"That's odd," Adam said. "On the other hand... maybe he's doing something so secretive and nefarious he doesn't want to tell the world about it. Or — and you might want to put your money on this — maybe he didn't pay his debts, and he's paid the price."

I asked him if I could use the phone. He waved at it. I dialled the company number listed under the Queen Square address. No ringing tone, no divert to messages. The line had been discontinued.

There might have been some irony to enjoy in all this. On a good day perhaps, but this wasn't it. None of it actually helped the Barnes' family. I sat back in my chair and stared at the pc screen. I was mildly attracted by the list of people in Gaghan's pocket, but there was nothing I could use here. Nothing it seemed that would lead me to Alfie's killer.

Adam stuck his press crusader ticket in his hatband.

"Can I go to town on the Nick Jenner story? Will that compromise what you're up to?"

I considered that.

"Probably not, if you do it without any reference to the source of the information. Actually that might be helpful. Anything capable of stirring up Gerald Gaghan might be good for the cause. Personally, I don't give a toss about Jenner or any of his mates. There's no disputing that most of them should be in jail. But this stuff is light years away from where I'm supposed to be. Is there anything else in there beyond collecting debts and menacing citizens into handing over their Jaguars and Bentleys?"

My mobile began ringing out in the hall. I found it in my jacket.

"We need to talk," George Hood said.

"Talk away," I said.

"No. Not right now. Tomorrow morning. Let's meet before the bad guys get out of bed. Circular Road. Do you know it?"

"Yes. On top of the Gorge. It runs from the zoo, towards Syme Park."

"I'll meet you at the point where the road swings towards the Gorge and begins to run parallel with it. At 6.30."

"In the morning?"

"It's that important, Jack."

It had to be. Nobody arranges meetings at dawn on a hunch. It occurred to me he might be winging this. All the way to nowhere possibly, if it fell apart. I told him I'd be there.

"Thanks," he said and disconnected the call.

I held the phone at arm's length, as if it were a carrier of the plague, and thumbed the red button. I walked back into the study. Adam looked at me.

"All right?"

"George Hood wants me to meet me," I said.

"So what?" he said. "Trinity Road holds no terrors for you. Should be a breeze. Especially after your recent overnight."

I was shaking my head. Adam looked straight into my eyes.

"No?... Not all right?"

231

"6.30 in the morning. Up on the Downs."

"Bloody hell." Adam paused for a moment, then came back to me. "Okay... Let me surprise you with what I stumbled on while you were out in the hall."

"Have you heard of the *British Political Action Group*?"

I sat down next to him. "Yes"

"They're based here in Bristol, according to Alfie's accounts."

"Organised by whom?"

"Doesn't say." He pointed at the pc screen and clicked the mouse. "This is concerned with organisation and finances. And they're bloody huge sums. The profit at the close of the business year back in March was 1.74 million pounds. Which must make them the third best funded political organisation in the country."

He sat back in his chair, released the mouse, picked up his whisky tumbler and swallowed practically all the whisky in his glass.

"Now then... What does BPAG intend to do with its dosh? People don't gather this much money in secret without having serious business on their agenda. And where did Alfie dig this stuff up? He wasn't working with them surely."

I thought about that. Linda and Val had explained Alfie's way of looking at the world. His pride in his distinctive abilities to make everything work his way. Severely impaired in some aspects he might have been, but he was mightily superior in others. Most of the time he showed little or no interest in the regimen of days the rest of us tackle. But he didn't need to. His days were highly organised and very 'normal' to him. He may have seemed lonely, but that was a problem of other people's perception, not Alfie's. Because he appeared totally uninterested in responding to the questions of others and rarely joined in a conversation, everyone outside his loop, except for his family myself, Chrissie and Val, imagined he was lonely. The relationships Alfie did have were strong and deep and destined to last. What appeared to be compulsive behaviour was intended and followed the rules he had set for himself. What seemed to be ritualistic, was simply an unvarying daily pattern of activities.

"These people are Islamophobes," I heard Adam say. "Preaching their own brand of violence. Along with a touch of ethnic cleansing as the support act. And it would seem that other people with huge chunks of dosh are paying them to do it."

"You can't arrest people because they have big bank accounts," I said. "Even if they call themselves the 'We Intend to Hang Every Muslim Party'. Unless they organise a monster rally and beat up everyone who attends."

"That's not unlikely," Adam said.

Chrissie appeared in the doorway.

"Three minutes," she said. "So save what you're working on and present yourselves at the dining table."

Adam logged out and switched off the pc.

"I haven't looked at the printed sheets yet. We'll make copies of everything before you go." He pointed at the notebook. "What do we do with this?"

"Copy the files on to a stick, then lock the notebook away somewhere. Hang on to it for a day or two until I can organise a safety net. And then, at some point, we'll hand it over to George Hood."

Adam looked as if he was about to object.

"Yes I know, it's one hell of a story..."

"You think?"

"But let's get it onto its feet before we do anything with it. Then we can deal with Hood. For the story, and for the price of plastic surgery and new identities."

* * *

Dinner passed as all dinners should. Soberly and enjoyably. I was forbidden to help clear the table, so when Adam and Chrissie disappeared into the kitchen I walked out of the French windows and on to the lawn. It was the sort of pre-autumn equinox night that painters paint and poets write about. A dazzling full moon on a navy blue background pocked with stars.

Chrissie spoke from behind me.

"Dad..."

I turned to face her. She took a couple of steps forward.

"I'm sorry about earlier. I over-reacted. Not necessarily the best response to learning that your father has just spent a night in jail."

It took me a while, but I found something to say.

"I don't know what I'm going to do. Adam has a story, the police will be able to throw a couple of dozen people in jail, but I don't have anything. I'm up against a man who thinks he's fire proof. And maybe he is."

"And maybe he isn't. You didn't get this far by accident."

"I've stumbled around a lot."

"I mean, aren't you just a bit interested in all this? The city's awash with racists and their ill-gotten gains."

"Not entirely…"

"And the money is going into the pockets of Gaghan's associates and the plan for his new Thousand Year Reich."

She stopped and spread her arms wide, the palms of her hands outwards. It behoved me to say something now.

"I've never heard this sort of stuff from you," I said.

"Yes well…I'm developing a taste for indignation. Besides, I'm only following your example. And don't look at me with such mock surprise… How many weeks of your life do you spend on lost causes? Rooting around in the detritus of other people's misery, digging up scraps of information for which, in a good year, a bunch of clients pay you what? Twenty grand?"

I considered the notion. Chrissie summed up.

"Certainly not much more."

"I'm not sure if all that rates as a compliment or an insult."

"Neither am I." She grinned at me, then changed the subject. "I want to show you something."

She led the way into the living room. There was an old cardboard box, two feet square, sitting on the carpet by the armchair to the right of the fireplace. The flaps of the lid were torn and there was a faded label on one side.

"Remember this?" Chrissie asked. "I found it a couple of days ago when I was cleaning out the cupboard under the stairs."

The Family Box.

Chrissie filled it with stuff she found in the house, a couple of weeks after Emily died. She took charge of it because she was much more organised at the time than I was. We sat on the rug in front of the fire, the box between us.

Sam joined Adam in the study, while Chrissie and I did the things we hadn't done in five years. We looked at pictures and holiday souvenirs and old letters and school prize certificates and a selection of battered toys, including a teddy bear worn smooth by years of play and cuddling. And we laughed a great deal, recalling the best of Chrissie's memories of growing up.

By 10 o'clock we were tired and all talked out. Adam came into the living room. He asked me if I was staying over. I told him I'd never make the 6.30 rendezvous if I did.

"What 6.30 rendezvous?" Chrissie asked.

"I'm taking Sam out for his late night walk," Adam said and left the room swiftly.

Chrissie repeated the question. We heard Adam call Sam into the hall. Listened to the panting and the squeaking and the rattle of his dog tags as Adam roped him with the choke chain. Then the front door opened and closed.

Chrissie gave me the look that was pure Emily. "Well?"

"A meeting with George Hood."

"About what?"

"No idea. But he obviously has news to impart which he thinks should be done out of the sight and sound of others."

The phone rang in the hall. Chrissie looked at her watch.

"Somebody's calling late."

She got to her feet and left the room. The phone stopped ringing. I heard her say, 'Oh hi,' and then 'No of course not,' followed by 'Yes he is.' Seconds later she was back in the living room. She handed me the phone receiver.

"Your next grilling."

She grinned, and went way to find something else to do.

"I'm glad you're still in one piece," Linda said with some edge in her voice. "I assume you were going to call me."

"Yes I was."

She took a beat.

"Jack, what are you doing?" she asked

"Getting closer to finding Alfie's killer," I said. "Things are progressing."

Which wasn't strictly true, but it seemed the best thing to say under the circumstances. Linda cracked the code.

"And true to form," she said, "you're probably going to do something really dangerous."

"Not intentionally," I said.

237

There was a longer silence this time.

"Linda…"

She closed the conversation. "Good night, Jack."

I put the receiver on the rug next to me and stared across the room. At the mementoes scattered around. I began to pick them up. I was looking into Teddy's one-eyed face when the phone rang again.

"I'm sorry," Linda said. "I shouldn't have had a go. Promise me you'll take care."

"I promise."

"I love you. Good night."

The line clicked and she was gone again. I pressed the red button. Chrissie called from the dining room.

"Was that Linda again?"

I said it was, and set about putting everything back into the box.

CHAPTER TWENTY

Take a look at any romantic, period piece of cinema and you'll see dawns galore, beautifully photographed.

Many years ago, in a posh country garden after some early hours' revelry which neither he nor I could remember very much about, a friend of mine surveyed the tangled decorations and the empty champagne bottles and declared that he hated sunrise, because the world looked like it had been up all night.

This one wasn't exactly Homer's *rosy fingered dawn* either. Mind you, he may not have said that exactly, good though it is. You can't trust the veracity of poetic images in translation. This dawn was a cold, damp, grey misted affair, the sort to be expected in this neck of the woods in late September.

I beat Hood to our rendezvous by a couple of minutes. When his car arrived I was standing by the low wall which separates visitors from the edge of the Avon Gorge and a plunge down 315 feet to the Portway below – the road to Wales and all points west. He got out of the Volvo, shivered and turned up the collar of his coat.

"Sorry to get you up here at such a God forsaken hour, but I don't want this conversation to be seen or heard."

"Why pick this place?" I asked him.

He gave me a look, half grin, half scorn.

"Would you choose it for any kind of sensible encounter at this time in the morning?"

"No," I said.

"There you are then," Hood said. "QED."

I waited for him to go on. He got straight to the point.

"The Assistant Chief Constable, the man to whom I report on a weekly basis, has marked your card," he said.

I stared at him.

"And mine, too. He summoned me to his office yesterday. Said he was concerned that I was pursuing an investigation into the life and crimes of Gerald Gaghan and by association, Peter Nash, a man he confessed he held the greatest respect for. He went on to say he could not see any benefit in continuing, and was thereby 'strongly recommending' that I cease and desist."

Hood paused, waiting for a reaction from me. I didn't have one, so he warmed to his theme.

"He also instructed me that to allow anyone else to do so, would meet the same implacable consequence. A certain private investigator, for instance. Do I have your undivided attention?"

He did. He saw the expression on my face change and went on, dropping the reportage and getting up close and personal.

"You're in the clarts, Jack," he said. "I wanted you to know, unofficially. Neither of us will find a bonus in our pay packets at the end of the month, if we continue to pursue our enquiries. Now say something."

I dug the usb stick with the Jenner stuff on it out of a jacket pocket.

"Just when I was going to give you this."

It was Hood's turns to stare. "What's on it?"

"Best I don't tell you. Then you can't act upon it, as all the best cop instincts in you would crave to do."

He didn't blink. "Look, Jack," he said. "Let's not fuck about at a time like this. We both know we have common cause here, and even if we don't act on the information received, we ought at least to acknowledge we have received it."

I asked a question. The one and only in the circumstances.

"Why is the Assistant Chief Commissioner ordering you not to do your job?"

"He's not ordering and nothing is written down. Not even an email asking me to report to him. In the car park lunchtime yesterday, I got out of my car as he was returning to his. He said it was a lovely day, asked me how I was and how I was getting on with my current case load. And before I could respond he suggested we have a chat later. Mid-afternoon he said, just pop in, no formalities. His secretary would be out visiting her husband in hospital – kidney stones, he knew what that was like. Oh and erm... we should keep this between ourselves."

Hood seemed not to realise that the longer that tale went on, the closer he came to an impersonation of the man he reported to every week. But on second thoughts, maybe he did.

He repeated, "What's on the stick?"

I had a supplementary question.

"How does Langley know I have been in conversation with Gerald Gaghan? Are they in the same lodge? Do they swap stories?"

241

"Have you?" he asked. "Conversed with Gerald Gaghan?"

"Yes."

"Why?"

I took a beat. Stared at him as the implication took hold.

"You didn't know," I said.

Hood locked his eyes onto mine. I rationalised.

"Gaghan and I are the only ones privy to a meeting on his patio. Apart from his drinks steward, Julian whom you know, and two wide-shouldered flat-nosed types who escorted me there."

"Jack..."

I held up my right hand.

"No no. I'm making a point here, George."

"Don't be ridiculous," he said.

Hood looked along the river bank westwards to the sea. The night was over, morning had crept upon us as we had been talking.

"It doesn't make any sense," he said. "Why would Langley risk a relationship with Gaghan Nash?"

"Because it's to his advantage to do so."

Hood shook his head.

"No no. I don't like Langley, but people of his rank don't take those kind of risks."

"Would you know if he was doing so?"

He thought about that. "Probably not. Until..."

"Until somebody you trusted turned up and waved the evidence of wrong doing at you." I gave him the usb stick. "Okay, take this. Check it out at home. And I have an envelope in the car. Hard copy of emails between Gaghan Nash and extreme right organisations in Europe. I'll get it."

Hood followed me to the Accord. I gave him the envelope. He looked at it.

"Who does this come from?"

"Me."

Again he didn't blink. "To you from whom?"

"That's confidential. Read the emails first."

He turned away and walked towards the Volvo, pointing the key fob at the driver's door. He opened the door, leaned inside, dropped the envelope on the front passenger seat and straightened up again. I moved towards him.

"I intend to carry on with my investigation, George," I said. "Whichever way it turns out. Thanks for the 'unofficial' warning. I'll keep you posted as I go. There may be enough in those emails to make Gaghan and Nash suspects in something or other. Which is what the ACC is trying to prevent."

The silence between us was a mile wide. I couldn't help Hood with the trouble he was in. He had a lot to process, but I needed to ask him something else.

"What does Peter Nash do?"

Hood précised the stuff which arrived by way of an answer.

"He is the man who puts together all the Gaghan Nash deals. He finds money. He's the brains of the outfit. Gaghan's brief is the less sophisticated. Nash and his family live a few hundred yards that way." He gestured over his shoulder. "But he has another house in Bruges. Spends a large chunk of his time in Belgium. When he's working there he commutes between Bruges and Geneva."

"Because that's where his money is."

"Probably. Nobody talks about that."

He breathed in and out. Took his time over the next bit. He put his hands on the roof of the Volvo and stared across the acreage of the Downs.

"Right. Have you got an unlisted mobile?"

"No. But I can borrow one."

"Good." He straightened up and turned back to face me. "Send the number to my home email address." He recited it. "Can you remember that?"

I repeated the address back to him and told him I'd have the mobile by the close of play. He nodded in agreement.

"Okay."

That was it. We were in cahoots now, and this was much more dangerous for Hood than it was for me. He sat at a desk two floors below one of the most senior men in local policing, the man we seemed about to conspire against. I looked into Hood's eyes. Nothing but resolution in them. We had decided to do this foolhardy and dangerous thing, so there was not much more to be said.

"Okay," I said. "I presume you don't want to be seen with me in the cold light of day, so I'm going home for some breakfast."

I offered my right hand. Hood held it firmly, and shook it. And that was enough for both of us.

In the Accord I dug out the pad and pen I keep in the glove box and wrote down Hood's email address. I drove home and parked in the street in front of my house. The dashboard clock said 7.12.

I made straight for the kitchen to make coffee. My mobile rang as I was raising a mug to my lips.

Adam asked me how the 6.30 had gone. I told him.

"George Hood has been leant on by Assistant Chief Commissioner Ralph Langley and told to stop his investigation into Gaghan Nash.

"Christ," Adam said. "That's not good."

"No it isn't. So I told him about my meeting with Gaghan."

"Which he didn't know anything know about," Adam said.

"Right."

"But Langley did," Adam went on. "Because Gaghan told him and asked him to deal with it. Langley thought about it, put two and two together and hauled Hood in to see him."

"Works as a theory, doesn't it?"

"Yes it does. Ah well, the game's afoot."

We both considered the prospect for a moment or two.

"George Hood is a copper of some honesty and grit," I said. "I gave him copies of my copies of the emails. And the usb stick."

There was a very slow intake of breath down the line.

"Okay," Adam said.

"We've set out a system for communicating via unlisted mobiles."

"This is a familiar tale, Jack," he said. "You declared an outlaw and then menaced by dangerous and unscrupulous people."

"It's an accepted modus operandi."

"Not by Linda and Chrissie."

"I'll just have to put on the slap and busk the crowd."

"Just be careful that's all."

"I'll be in touch."

I closed the call, picked up the mug in front of me and drank the coffee. I looked at the clock above the fireplace. 7.30. Maybe a bit too early to get people out of bed.

I made some scrambled eggs and more coffee.

* * *

I called Chris Gould an hour later. He said he was delighted to hear from me.

"Maybe not so delighted after hearing the proposal," I suggested.

But I had underestimated him. Like Joe Locke, Chris is a man with a heart as big as a football stadium. He has bright blue eyes and light curly hair. Five feet eight or nine and built like a champion fell runner – straight up and down both sides. He is ten years younger than me. We haven't known each other long, but we are kindred spirits. In the past a fully paid up member of the awkward squad, Chris now owns a pc repair company. In his downtime, he collects, fixes and ships old computers to schools in Africa. A one man *IT Aid*.

"Do you know anything about a bloke called Gerald Gaghan?" I asked.

"Nothing that I like."

"Good. I want you to help me take him down."

"When do we start?"

"To begin with, I need to borrow a loaner phone. Old and untraceable."

"No problem. What else?"

"Then we keep tabs on him."

"Do you want me to bug his phones?"

Now there was a prospect. Chris went on.

"I'm your man, Jack. A qualified and registered member of the Association of Technical Surveillance and Counter Measures Manufacturers and Traders."

"The what?"

"To put it simply, I make bugs. I'll send you a link to my new website, *imabugger.com*."

"How long did it take you to come up with that domain name?"

"All of a minute and a half. Getting lots of hits these days. Mostly because people think it's a joke. But once in a while..."

I told him I would keep this other career in mind.

"You'd be surprised how much a tradesman is allowed to do legally."

Perhaps not.

"As for illegally... I read recently that a German company has invented a gizmo which enabled anyone with *Windows 10* to track and download live, the output of CCTV cameras on any street in Europe."

I drove to Chris's workshop on the Albion Trading Estate. He took a five year old flip open 3G *Nokia* from a drawer and handed it over.

"Keep it as long as you like, Jack."

I went on to the office. Eschewed the lift and climbed the stairs, if not with confidence in the day ahead, but with at least a little more optimism and a lighter step. Linda's office door was open. She was behind her desk, typing with her eyes fixed on the pc screen.

"I'd like to be able to do that," I said.

Linda jumped in her chair. "Jack for God's sake."

I apologised for frightening her. She stood up, moved around her desk and into my arms. We held each other for a long time before we separated.

"Sit down," she said.

I did so, in one of her client chairs. The morning's copy of the *Western Daily Press* sat on her desk in front of me. It had been opened and then folded back so that page three was uppermost. Linda swung the paper so I could read it the right way up.

"That's your friend isn't it?"

I read the headline. Mickey Balfour had been found dead in his flat. From a crack cocaine induced heart attack. The police were saying the death was suspicious. The coroner had returned an open verdict.

"Mickey wasn't a user," I said. "Never. He had a drinking problem once, way back. But drugs, no."

It was reasonable to assume the hand of Gerald Gaghan in this. But what had Mickey done to give himself away? Or, worse, what had I done to help out? Either I

248

was followed to the flat, or Howard and Maurice caught the connection between Mickey and me in the midst of *The Quay* nonsense.

Mickey wasn't a villain, or a hero. He was just a reformed ex-con trying to get by. Living in a flat with thin partition walls, in a house full of people like himself; loners, couples, one parent families, existing on what was left of benefits cut to the bone; every day waking up to the same fractured existence they hoped they would leave behind each night as they fell asleep. Mickey was no threat to anyone. However, he had been talking to me. He didn't know anything, but that wasn't the point. This exercise in murder was for my benefit.

And there was no one around to mourn Mickey Balfour's death.

I left Linda's office and went into mine.

CHAPTER TWENTY-ONE

At that point Amy Turner came out of the woodwork. Or at least appeared to do so. She tweeted *Hi all Sorry for the disappearing act Am OK Back to see U soon*.

Chrissie phoned to tell me. So did Amy's mother and so did her recently sacked agent. I asked Celia if she thought the tweet was genuine. She told me yes, well it certainly came from the Twitter address logged on her iPhone. She had checked with a dozen people she and Amy had in common, who confirmed they had received the tweet. I asked her if the style of message was hers. She said it was hard to tell as it was so brief.

I phoned Neil's mobile. His voice mail asked me to leave a message. I did.

I emailed George Hood the loaner phone number. Twenty minutes later I received a number in return and a mini biography of Nick Jenner.

Not a man with a soul, Jenner, but not exactly a player either. He had made money here and there over the years, but never managed to hold on to it. Always looking for the next great deal, he threw away both well and ill-gotten gains in rapid succession. He was jailed after a series of short cons backfired miserably. Twelve months later he got out of prison, apparently having learnt nothing, or at least very little.

So the next step?

Go and pay Jenner a visit seemed to be it.

According to George Hood's latest intelligence he lived on the western side of the A370 in Flax Bourton.

There was no Mrs Jenner and no children. There had been apparently, but Mrs J had seen the light some years ago and disappeared with the twins. The house was a small double fronted, detached, stone cottage, which had seen better days. Most of the mortar needed re-pointing. Paint on the weatherboards and the window frames was peeling. The small garden in front of the house was just about under control. Jenner might have been making ends meet, but little more than that. He did have a Jaguar, but it had a Y registration. Looked the part, but these days you can buy a sixteen year old Jag for a thousand pounds. He was throwing suitcases into the boot when I pulled up on his drive. He slammed the boot lid as I got out of the Accord.

He was a couple of inches shorter than me. Broad enough to compensate perhaps, but carrying too much weight to be a useful bruiser. He had a purple-veined face, hooded eyes and what seemed like something of a nervous tic. I looked beyond and around him. He watched me.

"I'm renting," he said, as though explanations were needed.

"It's got prospects," I said.

"Are you a journalist?" he asked.

"No,"

"A cop?"

"No."

"Then piss off."

I asked him where he was going.

"None of your business," he said.

251

He stepped past me and moved to the Jaguar driver's door. I caught up with him. As the door opened I slammed it shut again. He spun to face me, rage building up. I stepped back half a pace and gave myself some room. He swung a left hook the meanest amateur would have seen coming. I swayed out of the way. He swung his right arm. I blocked it with my left, transferred weight to my right shoulder and punched him hard under his ribs. He choked, gasped for breath and sank to his knees on the gravel, his arms wrapped round his midriff.

I looked inside the car. There was a shoulder bag sitting on the front passenger seat. I opened the driver's door leaned across the car interior and picked up the bag. Inside it I found Jenner's passport, flight tickets to Thailand and a wallet full of US dollars.

"I'll keep this," I said.

He tried to get to his feet. I slapped him down again.

"Christ," he moaned.

He sat upright and banged the back of his head on the rear Jaguar door.

"Stay there," I said.

He looked up at me.

"Who are you?" he asked

"Jack Shepherd."

He pondered then shook his head.

"No. Doesn't ring any bells."

"Are you still broke?" I asked.

He stared down at the gravel on the drive. I kicked him in the ribs and he yelled in pain.

"Tell me."

"Bloody hell…" he squeezed out through gritted teeth.

"Do you want me to do that again?"

He held up his left arm in surrender.

"So talk," I said.

I prompted him and he did.

"I paid Gaghan back," he said. "Every single penny I owed. And shit, did the bastard make me work for it."

"What at?"

He stared at me in amazement. "Do you think I'm going to tell you? Christ no. More than my life's worth."

"Not much of a life is it? Looking over your shoulder all the time."

"It's not like that. I'm free and clear now."

I pulled his passport and wallet out of the flight bag. I could see the alarm creep into his eyes.

"Hey…" he managed. "What are you doing?"

"Well, I thought I'd start with the money. Tear it up." I found a cigarette lighter in the bag, "or maybe set fire to it."

"Now hang on…"

I dipped into the bag again, pulled out a fistful of notes in ten and twenty dollar bills. "How much is there in here? Two hundred dollars? Three? More?"

He started to bluster. "Look, err… I mean erm… what are you doing? What's this about?"

"I'm looking for somebody to blame."

"For what?"

"The murder of a friend of mine. Alfie Barnes."

He did his pondering and headshaking again.

"Never heard of him," he said.

253

I sighed. "Well that's the wrong answer you see. Because I can link you to Gerald Gaghan and Peter Nash, and I can link them directly to all sorts of evil doing."

He didn't say anything.

"Okay..."

I shouldered the bag, held the lighter to the money in my hand and set it on fire. Jenner, paralysed in amazement watched for seconds. The money burned quickly. He yelled at me. I dropped the dollars on the drive, now way beyond useful currency. Jenner tried to get to his feet. I kicked him again. He yelled again. Then he recovered a bit and offered me a deal.

"Look err… Jack?... Let's put a stop to this game. There's more money locked in a drawer in my desk. About three hundred euros, some more dollars and two hundred quid give or take. You can have it all. Then I'll get on a plane and you'll never see or hear of me again."

"Not without a passport," I suggested. "Unless you know someone who can sort that out for you."

He was puzzled for a moment.

"I mean, if I rip this up, pull the pages out, you're not going to leave the country. At least not today."

He started to panic. "No for God's sake… No no… No don't do that." Then he began to plead. "Please, please don't do it."

"Well here's the thing," I said. "Seems we're spoilt for choice… One, I could take up your offer, clean out your desk, wave you goodbye and say no more."

Jenner began nodding. Clearly this was his number one preference.

254

"Of course I could do all of that, not keep my end of the bargain, and talk to your former employers anyway."

He had stopped nodding his head.

"And then you'd be a bargain basement Jason Bourne. On the run in the far east, looking over your shoulder all the time. Or..." I paused for effect. "I could do as just outlined and tell the police. In which case you could end up with a posse of international crime stoppers after you as well."

The colour had completely drained from his face.

"But, finally, and the mode I suggest you take on board, we could discard all those alternatives and go straight to the police."

He began shaking his head again. I continued.

"In return for the scalps of Gaghan and Nash you could buy yourself police protection until the CPS gets them into court – which I admit might take a while, and that's possibly the slight flaw here – and once they're convicted you could parley that into a new identity and a house on an island somewhere."

He had stopped shaking his head and appeared to be trying to think.

"I mean, here we are. Your current existence can't be so wonderful that you'd miss it if offered a new one. So let's go over this again..."

"No let's not for God's sake."

He seemed to be sulking now. I wound up the discussion.

"The Special Crimes Unit is desperate to convict Gaghan and Nash. Your evidence would help a lot. And

255

you could be free and clear to spend your dollars in whatever lurid, distasteful and immoral fashion you chose."

His face was screwed up in concentration.

"Okay," I said. "I'll just burn the rest of your money, shred your passport, pass the word to Gaghan and Nash and leave you to your own devices."

Now deflated and miserable, Jenner stared at his shoes for a while. I gave him time.

"Okay," he muttered.

"What was that?" I asked.

He looked up at my face again and yelled at me.

"Okay. O fucking kay!!"

He put his elbows on his knees, held his hands up to his face and began to cry. Not edifying at all. I nudged his left ankle with the toe of my right shoe. He burbled into silence.

"Now...," I said. "Just so I have the whole picture, tell me how you worked off your debt to Gaghan Nash."

He told me. In prison he had conceived and nurtured what he came to believe was his real shot at a small fortune – a new mini version of the old Ponzi scheme. And once released, he persuaded an initial group of investors that a huge new solar project being built on the Mendips, would eventually run most of North Somerset's energy and make enormous profits for all those who were smart enough to get into the lift on the ground floor. The maths was based on paying off early investors with cash coming from the increasing number of new investors. All he had to do was make sure he got out and disappeared before the cash outflow – all of it going to him – exceeded the inflow. He miss-timed it badly and found himself being pursued by a gang of angry people. Which was when he found a saviour of sorts in Gerald Gaghan, who paid off his investors, kept him out of jail, took on his debt, tied him into impossible repayments and in return for not handing him over to his main man Julian to break his kneecaps, passed him on to Peter Nash, who gave him all kinds of accounting deals to 'sort'. Jenner was clearly no great shakes as a con artist but he knew all there was to know about creative double entry book keeping. This worked to the satisfaction of all three men; until Jenner realised that the closer he got to freeing himself from the fiscal shackles Nash had imprisoned him in, the deeper he was getting in to the mire. Sunk in desperation and considering going on the lam, he had a massive, but timely, heart attack.

He came out of hospital in no condition to continue working for Gaghan Nash and his two former persecutors pensioned him off. He had been a freelance ever since, and just about making a living. And if I didn't believe any of that story, he said, I knew what I could do.

"Nick," I said when he had finished the narrative. "You are a living, breathing, miserable, failure of a human being."

"Come on, Shepherd... for God's sake."

I took a long look at him. A shining example of a man trying to punch way above his weight. Lower than pond life, with all the irredeemable qualities of shit on a shoe. The problem was, I guessed, he hadn't the guts or the passion to work hard without a jail sentence in the offing or a gun to his head. In the end, fear of retribution from Gerald Gaghan caused his capitulation.

I fished inside the shoulder bag, found his mobile and gave it to him.

"Unlock it."

I called George Hood's non contract mobile, choosing my words carefully.

"I've got something. Or rather someone."

"Important?"

"Probably."

There was a pause. The mobile connection dipped and hissed. Then Hood spoke again.

"You mean the person you learned of earlier?"

Hood had locked into this non giveaway style conversation.

"Yes."

"And this pertains to what?"

"Fraud, extortion, scrubbing money and other serious crimes."

Jenner, who was hearing this end of the conversation, looked deeply offended. Down the phone line Hood spoke again.

"Where are you?"

"At the address I learned along with the name."

"Stay there," Hood said and ended the call.

He arrived fifteen minutes later, along with DS Henson, in an unmarked car. Cautioned Jenner and asked him for the keys to the house and his desk. Jenner handed them over. Henson handcuffed Jenner and installed him in the back seat of the car. Hood led the way towards the house. Stopped by the front door and looked at me.

"We'll leave the house alone until I get a prints officer out here to go over it. Someone I can trust to keep this off the books pro tem." He looked at me. "If anyone is going to get us further into the manure, it had better be you."

He didn't blink. Neither did I. Instead, he handed me his pair of surgical gloves. I stuffed them into a jacket pocket.

"Maggie, the prints person I have in mind, will take an hour so to get here," he said. He dropped Jenner's keys behind the plant pot to the left of the front door. "I'll tell her where to find them."

Side by side, we moved towards his car. He gestured to Henson who dutifully joined Jenner inside it. I asked Hood if his DS was in the loop.

"Yes, he is."

"Can you trust him?"

"Yes. At least, not to divulge anything of this to his fellows. He's solid. Of course he'll have to come clean if the ACC calls him in for a chat."

"Then let's hope he doesn't," I said.

Hood took a deep breath and blew the air out of his mouth.

"Okay, Jack," he said. "So far so good. You go your way, I'll go mine. And thanks for this."

I told him it was a pleasure.

He got into the front passenger seat of the car. Henson u-turned in the lane and headed back towards the main road. As conspiracies go, this one was a belter. If it went wrong, I could simply chalk it up as experience. George Hood would get ten years. I looked around the garden. An hour before Maggie arrived. That was time enough.

I put on the gloves, retrieved the keys from behind the plant pot, unlocked the front door and let myself into the house.

CHAPTER TWENTY-TWO

It was a Victorian cottage with small, square rooms and eight feet high ceilings. Like the outside, it needed something of a re-furbish. The wallpaper was past its best, paint on the skirting boards and the door frames chipped, sofa covers frayed and old carpets threadbare.

It was a solid building, but currently it looked like the cowman's cottage tied to the farm next door. There were six inch nails hammered into the plaster in the hall instead of coat hooks. Most of the picture rails in the house had been prised off the walls, probably for firewood. There was no central heating. There were old storage heaters in the rooms downstairs and cast iron fireplaces in the bedrooms up above.

I had no idea what Jenner aspired to, but it must have been more than this. Bought as a fixer upper the cottage would be cheap, but subsequently cheered up, would be worth, at a guess, around half a million. Not too ostentatious for an upper middle class aspirant, and very comfortable. Maybe Nick Jenner just didn't aspire to anything anymore. Or couldn't afford to.

I had a bit of a wander. The kitchen and scullery were as I expected them to be, stacked with the appropriate appliances, baskets and pots and pans. The downstairs loo had rising damp. The dining room held no secrets as far as I could see. The living room sofas were old fashioned, comfortable and tatty. The carpets, different sizes and colours in all the rooms, looked as if they had come from end of warehouse rolls. Upstairs, I checked the bathroom and the main bedroom first. There was nothing out of the ordinary in either place. There was nothing under the bed and the wardrobe wasn't hiding anything.

Which left only the small bedroom – a bit smaller than my office – which was dominated by a desk and padded swivel chair. Actually more like a trophy room it turned out. Darts trophies on shelves above and alongside the desk. Darts? Something else he hadn't made money at, clearly. Not my thing darts, but the game is popular enough for the International Olympics Committee to consider including it in the games every decade or so. Hardly fits the *higher faster longer stronger* brief, is my take on the subject.

I sat in the chair and tried all the keys in the all the desk drawers one at a time. It took me three or four minutes to find what Jenner had promised – inside the bottom drawer in the right hand pedestal. Money in pounds, dollars and euros, along with half a dozen sealed A4 size brown envelopes.

I swung round in the chair to face the wall I hadn't inspected.

I've always considered myself not easy to shock, but if I ever wanted a complacency check here it was. I was confronted with a poster size rendering of the BPAG badge, a slogan stencilled underneath *The Right Decision*. Along with the strap line *Do You Want Your Country Back?* at the top of the picture, and *We Do!* along the bottom. Words poured across the badge in the centre of the poster, raging at the 'colonisation' of Britain by every race which didn't happen to be white or christian. A chunk of sustained hate, majoring on what BPAG perceived as the nonsense in tolerating more than one race in one nation.

Standing next to the poster was a three-drawer filing cabinet. At the second attempt I found the right key/drawer combination. I unlocked the cabinet. It was full of copies of neo-Nazi magazines filed by volume and issue number from the top drawer to the bottom. *Nation One, European Rebel, Race Matters...*

From a brief look only, it appeared that one article covered all. There were half a dozen ideologies of hate in the documents I looked at. All brands of xenophobia, based on race, religion, colour and nationality, and pride in the determined rise of the 'New Order'. Articles with little more than names, faces and places changed, repeating the same mantra of neo-Nazi culture and aspiration. One article could have thrown a blanket over the whole oeuvre.

I looked at my watch. Fifteen minutes until Maggie was due to arrive. I'd had enough anyway and was only too glad to be out of the place. I grabbed random copies of the magazines and quit the field. I sat in the Accord for a while, a thick, clogged, dry taste in my mouth.

I have always known that the far right had a greater hold over hearts and minds than anyone on the left and in the middle of the road realised. Sitting in the car I remembered a play I studied at university, *The Fire Raisers* by the brilliant Swiss dramatist, Max Frisch. In this dark comedy, Gottlieb Biedermann's town is suffering from increasing attacks of arson. A man knocks on his door and talks his way into spending the night in his house. As the action unfolds, more people arrive and move into his attic. Biedermann watches while they pile drums of petrol above his head, refusing to accept what is happening. He even helps them measure the lengths of fuse, and finally still in denial, he hands them the matches.

Brexit has outed all the stuff once repressed and has given a voice to fear and prejudice. Now we can say what we really feel, and children can follow suit with graffiti on the walls of their schools. Donald Trump speaks directly to the hard right, and is cheered to the rafters because he legitimises their xenophobia and their racism. He gives his audiences power to pursue confrontation and to feed their hate. All the work and all the mended relationships in multi-racial communities undone. Now we can say what we really feel because we have permission to do so.

I was born in the month that Martin Luther King was assassinated and Enoch Powell delivered his *Rivers of Blood* speech. I learned about these events several years later, when my Uncle Sid was talking about his time in the Merchant Navy. He told me about the day his ship arrived at the East End Docks and a thousand dockers went on strike, marched to the Houses of Parliament carrying banners which yelled out *DON'T KNOCK ENOCH* and *BACK BRITAIN NOT BLACK BRITAIN*.

I called George Hood's unlisted number. It went straight to message *Sorry I'm not in. Leave a message or call back*. Simple and, hopefully, un-attributable, save for voice analysis. I responded in the same vein. *Stuff to tell you*.

I drove up the lane and turned left onto the main road. I was sitting at a red light in Long Ashton when George called. The traffic light changed to green. I told George to hang on while I pulled over, I drove across the junction and sild the Accord into the kerb.

"The house is a gold mine," I said.

"Our representative is in the place. She just called."

"We're both assuming the sealed brown envelopes in the desk drawer will hold something you can use. Yes?"

He agreed.

"Which will be enough to get you a search warrant, when the occupier offers 'no comment'?"

"Yes."

"Good. Because when you get into the house, go straight to the filing cabinet. It's where the occupier stores all his neo-Nazi stuff."

"His what? Did I hear right?"

"And a lot more I'm sure. Certainly enough to give you reason to take the place apart."

Hood took that in. The mobile connection crackled.

"What happens when the occupier asks for his lawyer and all this comes under scrutiny?" I asked.

"I was told, specifically, who to leave alone. As far as SCU is concerned, this investigation is another case altogether."

"Yes, well good luck with that," I said.

"You keep a sharp lookout too," he said, and ended the call.

I realised I hadn't eaten since breakfast, way back in the day. I picked up a couple of sandwiches at a Spar grocery and drove to the office.

It was uncomfortable eating sandwiches and reading the magazines I'd just collected. Actually it was more than uncomfortable, and would have been so had I been wearing lederhosen and drinking Bavarian beer.

I rang Adam to tell him the SCU had picked up Jenner, but to keep it off the record for now. I also told him about the magazines I'd picked up. He asked to see them. I invited him for tea. He said he would bring some cake.

So we switched from sandwiches to Swiss Roll. Not that the change of diet helped.

I began with *Race Matters*, Adam took the copy of *Nation One*. We read in silence for a while, sitting on opposite sides of my desk. Until the diatribe became too preposterous to take without some invective of our own. 'Jesus Christ', Adam said at one point, followed a couple of minutes later by 'Hell no' and seconds later by 'That's such bollocks'. Meanwhile I was discovering that all active groups in Europe − or so it seemed − however large or small, share the same twisted nationalist vision. A lot of the raison d'être is based on semi-legitimate historical theories, some of it propped up by distortions of academic scholarship. Especially for groups in Germany and Belgium, and in the Balkans where the recent past dies hard.

Both of us signalled our ultimate irritation at all the nonsense, when Adam said, "I can't read any more of this shite!"

He looked at me. "Jim Daniels," he said. "Heard of him?"

"No."

"Well he's from around here you'll be delighted to know. He's just set up his own anti-Islamic Christian group, *Believers in Truth*. Listen to this... *Liberalism in all forms is rapidly leading to the destruction of all values held to be eternal throughout the world*."

"Does he realise he kind of agrees with IS there?"

"He goes on to say... *Including Christianity*. Followed a few lines later by... where is it? Oh yes... *It is not anti-Semitic to oppose, with force if necessary, the spread of Zionism*. And listen to this headline, and I apologise for quoting it verbatim... *Niggers lie and lie and lie*." He looked up at me. "This is free speech."

"You don't seem to be defending to the death his right to say it."

"This isn't funny, Jack."

"No it isn't." I looked again at the magazine I was reading. "There's a piece here about our very own BPAG." I offered a précis. "Delegates, along with others from the English Defence League, the BNP, Greece's Golden Dawn and Germany's National Democrats are taking part in a European far right pro-Kremlin forum in St Petersburg next month. About the intention to strengthen links with other groups throughout Europe and define a common agenda."

"Shall we attend?" Adam asked. "Easy enough to get in I expect. Give ourselves an offensive name and we'll be welcome."

"And there's a bit more... *BPAG members are currently in eastern Ukraine, monitoring the work of -* "

"Monitoring?"

"Wait for the rest of it... *Monitoring the work of pro-Russian separatists in the struggle to legitimise their rule against the excessive and unacceptable condemnation from Kyiv and the governments of Western Europe.*"

We both sat in alarmed silence for a while. Adam spoke first.

"The thing is... Thugs and agitators these people may be, but, and this is the frightening bit, they are more than followers, they are true believers. And all it takes for their pernicious influence to grow, is for the rest of us to dismiss them as nutters, rioters and trouble makers, and advocate time in prison. Meanwhile, hate crime is enjoying glory days. And it's not just 'Poles go home' stuff. It's way more sinister. And it's written on school toilet walls, for Christ's sake. Who's guiding the kids who assume they can do that?" He waved his copy of *Nation One* at me. "I'll leave you with more from the aforementioned local hero Jim Daniels. *"I believe in this crusade as the only way of driving back the dark and destructive forces of liberalism."* So let's cheer the bastard on, shall we? It seems a hell of a lot of other people are doing that."

The forty minutes of down time with tea and Swiss Roll and Nazis had done nothing for our day. We stowed the magazines in the bottom of the filing cabinet. I made some more tea, knocked on Linda's door and invited her to join us. Adam asked Linda how she was. She was gracious. She smiled at him and said she was well. The tea and Swiss Roll tasted better after that.

* * *

The three of us of us talked – finding enjoyment in being together for the first time since Alfie's funeral. Adam left for Clevedon an hour later. I didn't give Linda details of my day. There was no point in breaking the spell of the afternoon.

We left the office, walked across the old iron bridge and into the park. To meet Bertie again. His small owner recognised me and sent the frisbee in my direction. I caught it, moments before Bertie was on me. He put on the brakes like Scooby Doo. I sent the frisbee back in the direction from whence it came. The girl half caught it, dropped it and saw it whisked away from her in a split second.

Linda and I sat on the bench and watched the girl and her dog play. Her mother walked into the park, saw me and waved. I waved back.

The loaner phone rang. George Hood was brief and to the point.

"The evidence looks useful. We've been allowed to entertain our friend for an extra twenty-four hours while we figure out what to charge him with. All this might work. Thanks."

I thanked him and pressed the red button. Linda caught the vibe.

"Good news?"

"It just might be," I said.

"What are you doing tonight?" she asked.

"Nothing. Why?"

"Would you care to spend it with me?"

It was the best offer I'd had in many a day. We locked the office doors, climbed into our cars and drove, line eastern, to Portishead.

We cooked together, something else we hadn't done in a while. Conversation was light and we were easy again. I remembered something I hadn't told Linda.

"Adam and Chrissie are getting married."

She stirred the contents of her pan. "That's good."

We served up the casserole and took it outside into the garden. We ate it and watched the sun go down.

CHAPTER TWENTY-THREE

Linda appeared to sleep well. I lay awake a long time, with as much patience as I could muster. The digital alarm on the cabinet at my side of the bed ticked on. At 2 o'clock, I slid out from under the duvet and crept downstairs into the kitchen. Warm milk with a touch of whiskey is held by some to remedy situations like this. Probably not in this case, but it tasted all right. As I got back into bed, Linda breathed deeply and turned over to face me, but didn't wake. The last time I recall looking at the clock it said 2.43.

At Wednesday morning breakfast Linda looked better than she had done for a while. She told me I looked awful. I said 'thank you'. We avoided talking about progress and prognosis with regard to the Alfie investigation.

"I have a potential client to see in Oxford today," she said. "I'll be back late afternoon."

I drove into the office. Adam had emailed me a link to a website called *New Crusader*. I closed the office door – I normally leave it open – and took a look.

The website was cloning the hate which had burned for centuries, moments in time as kindling, sometimes as embers, but regretfully for long seasons pure and implacable. The Home page began with a note attempting to open eyes to the threat posed to all Christian futures by Islam. And then got swiftly to the point.

Muslims. This is for you. If you are going to buy houses in my part of town, knock on my door, call me a knobhead, or tell me you are going to fuck my mother or

sister, or threaten to behead members of my family...
Don't bother, I've heard it all before. Though, on second
thoughts, maybe I'll have to do something about it.

I logged out. The knee-jerk instinct of any decent
human being. I left the office went along to the kitchen to
make some coffee. I sat down again with the mug at my
right elbow, called up Adam's email once more, clicked
the link and read on. In the second paragraph the
'crusader' turned his ire to communists, anti-fascists,
Marxists and 'Muslim appeasers.'

If hearing the truth about Islam offends you – TOUGH.
If you think emailing me your bullshit bothers me in any
way, then think again. Basically I don't give a fuck. And if
what you are reading here concerns you more than the
bombings and beheadings being committed by Islam, then
you have serious problems you cunts.

The Contacts page offered Twitter and Facebook links.
The latter glorying in another chunk of bile, exhorting all
those who doubted the crusader's message to *open their*
eyes.

There was a page headed 'Muslim Stuff' which I
clicked on, then off again after the opening paragraph. A
Blog which contained the same kind of diatribe as the
Home page. A list of links to like-minded individuals and
presumably supporters of this raging nonsense.

I sat back in my chair, took several deep breaths and
drank the rest of my coffee.

In spite of their headlines about sleaze and the
behaviour of politicians and celebrities behind locked
doors, this was the kind of free speech the red tops would

abhor. And rightly so. Freedom of the press and the right of all news organisations to run their own affairs is a given, or should be, but let's not assume that is the be all and end all of the free speech issue. Yes, it's a long road from exposés and dominatrix headlines to the deeply felt shite pedalled by the crusader, but in the end the creeping perversion of evil is only a question of degree. How do people get to be so full of hate? Nurture perhaps. No one is born hating – well maybe 0.01 percent of the population. People have to be taught to hate. But why? Is it actually fear?

The sound of the telephone ringing dragged me out of the nightmare.

Neil Shore said he had my message. I assured him that Amy's tweet was progress. He said he also had something which might help.

"I think I know where Amy might be," he began.

"Where?"

"In Bristol."

"Where in Bristol?"

"Ah…" he said.

That was a less helpful revelation than it might have been, but nil desperandum. I tried another question.

"Why do you think she's in the city?"

"Right…" Neil said, and began to pull his thoughts together. "You remember the drugs in the kitchen cabinet?"

"Yes," I said.

"Well they're still there of course," he said. "What I mean is, Amy didn't arrive at the beach house and she

273

didn't use them. Which could mean she's clean and not in trouble."

"Or it could mean she isn't and she's gone to her supplier to get some more."

"I thought of that, too. He's likely to be in Bristol. Because where else would she get them? Working the punishing shooting schedule she does, she'd need her supplier close. No time to go tear-arsing round the West Country."

My turn to agree. "Okay…"

"I don't know many people in *The Causeway* crew," Neil went on. "But I do know an assistant director called Brian. I worked with him a couple of years ago when I was told my star was on the rise. I called him and we talked late last night. He chose his words carefully. Began by saying he didn't know anything about Amy's private time. But he did agree that it was in everybody's interest to find her. Then he gave up a story. He said that on one occasion, late into an evening shoot, he took a visitor to her trailer. A man, tall, youngish, who 'looked like a pimp', Brian said." He paused. I waited for him to wind up. "Don't you see," he said. "He must have been her dealer."

I gave that a second or two.

"It doesn't follow that he - "

He interrupted me. "I know, I know. But Brian said he looked full of himself. 'Too flash by half' he called him. An impression that was given credence by the car the bloke drove up in – a white BMW Series 5 Li. They cost the best part of £75,000, Brian said. He knows about cars, apparently."

"He didn't by any chance note the registration number."

"I asked him that. He said no. But he did say it was unusual. A personal reg number. You know, the ones you pay loads of money for. He remembers it being four numbers and two letters... A date and some initials maybe."

"Yes, that would figure," I said.

Suddenly Neil seemed to lose confidence.

"Doesn't help as much as I thought, does it?"

"Not yet, but it might do. As long as we ask the right bloke the right questions."

"And who would the right bloke be?"

"The BMW dealer who sold our man the car."

"Of course," he said. "Because all car dealers have reg numbers and chassis numbers and owners on their franchise database."

"Got it first time, Sherlock."

"This is good isn't it?" Neil said.

"Not if it doesn't work. We have to trawl the BMW dealers in the area and then persuade them to 'fess up."

"And how do we do that?"

"A little lying and deceiving is the usual method. But right now, I have an arrangement with the Special Crimes Unit, so let's try upright and honest first. I'll get onto this and call you back when I have something."

"Oh..."

He sounded disappointed. I assured him it was good thinking. He accepted that and said he'd wait for my call. I asked him how the new script was coming along. He said it wasn't really. He was still working on the third act and it was a mess. Who was doing what, with, and to whom, was still a mystery. I told him I knew how he felt.

I checked out the websites of the registered BMW dealers closest to home. Two in Bristol, one in Bath, one in Newport just across the water, and two others in Bridgwater and Swindon.

I called George Hood on the loaner phone. He answered on the third ring.

"Are you open for requests?" I asked.

"Maybe," he said.

"Can you to check out a car owner for me? It's linked to my investigation into the disappearance of Amy Turner."

He offered me a guarded 'okay'.

"There's no need to work under the radar for this," I said. "But it may be an SCU matter down the road."

"Okay, I'll get Henson on to it."

"How did it go with Nick Jenner?"

"His lawyer got him out this morning. But in the meantime we searched his house and we've charged him with a couple of offences. Right on cue for my weekly report. I emailed it to the top floor and included the Jenner info. I was acknowledged and thanked by return. Got to go."

Henson called five minutes later. I told him as much as I knew. He didn't sigh or gripe. No buts, no reluctant okays. Said he'd call me back. I thanked him and disconnected the call.

So I was back to waiting again. I trundled along the corridor to make some coffee. Three quarters of an hour later Henson called again.

"I'm sending you an email," he said. "All white 5 series Li BMWs sold in the region over the last two years. You may have no need to look beyond the Bath dealership. Go to that list first. And DI Hood says keep him in the picture."

"Give him my regards," I said.

Henson was right. The Bath dealership list had a sale which was a gift to the case. Owner, name, address and phone numbers. A white 5 series car had been sold nine months earlier, to one Ridley Benjamin Gaghan. Registration number 8899 RG.

What a score. Neil's information had morphed into gold. I rang him.

He chortled in glee. "Shit. We have a lead man... This is a lead, isn't it?"

"I'd bet my pension on it," I said.

"Your pension will probably be worth bugger all in twenty years," he said.

Nevertheless the lift in morale deserved lunch, and time to sit down and think. I left the office and walked two hundred yards to the dock side restaurant under the approach road to the Cumberland Basin swing bridge. Once an illegally parked, white van roadside bacon bar, then a larger mobile home size trailer, it is now a proper eaterie with stainless steel cutlery and tablecloths. The chef's special is a knockout plate of bangers and mash.

* * *

There was more research to be done on Gaghan and Nash, together and separately. Company and personal stuff. But working on the old maxim that a change is as good as a rest, I settled on an alternative way of spending the afternoon.

I decided to doorstep Ridley.

CHAPTER TWENTY-FOUR

Doorsteps are doorsteps. But Ridley Gaghan's doorstep was something else. It was the only one in the street with a porch – just this side of flamboyant. The local authority wields a big stick when it comes to transforming the cityscape of a World Heritage Centre. Or so the planners proudly boast. There are many who disagree. According to the person living next door to Ridley, the porch was an eyesore. He had a home printed sign in his window which claimed so. And underneath the strapline, some words I struggled to read from my position on the pavement, saying that money, however ill gotten, was all that was needed to have the person who mattered put a tick in your planning box. Inside his living room, a grey haired man in his 60s, I guessed, saw me reading the proclamation and raced to his front door.

"Do you agree?" he asked.

"Absolutely," I said.

"And with the bit about council corruption?"

"That bit especially."

I looked to my left and asked him if a Mr Gaghan lived next door.

"That's right," he said. "Got the council in his pocket. Someone he knows has a connection in the Planning Department. So don't tell me there's no greasing of palms going on."

I assured him I wouldn't and wished him all the best with his campaign. He thanked me and went back indoors.

At least Ridley's porch was built, like the rest of the street, out of Bath stone. Small by comparison with other Regency dwellings in the city, the end of terrace house had a stone wall surrounding the side which faced the park at the top of Sion Hill, and something of a garden at the back. Clearly young master Gaghan lived here in some comfort, away from the baleful influence of his father. I stepped up to the front door and rang the bell. I heard it ring in the hall, but the sound produced no result. I rang again, my finger holding down the button longer this time. To no avail. So I resolved to do something of which I genuinely don't approve. A spot of breaking and entering.

An arched doorway gave access to the garden. It was locked, so my incursion would have to be over the six foot high garden wall. The blocks of stone were evenly cut and laid, but there was the odd hole in the mortar here and there. I walked the few yards back to the corner. Nobody approaching. I scanned the park beyond the railings. It was sparsely populated, the nearest person was a good seventy or eighty yards away. I retreated to the edge of the pavement, angled a run at the wall like a high jumper, sprang up, grabbed the top of the wall, found a toe hole and hauled myself up and over. The landing wasn't as spectacular. I dropped into a substantial pile of grass cuttings then rolled onto the lawn.

I lay still for a minute or two, looking up at a terrific blue sky. I rolled onto my face, transferred my weight backwards, got to my knees and stood up straight. I had grass cuttings in my hair, filling my pockets and stuck to my trousers. I combed through my hair with my hands, took off my jacket and shook it, flapped at my trouser legs and attempted to extract the grass from underneath my collar. All with the minimum of success.

I was facing the back of the house. A basement, with three floors above it and steps down from the lawn into a small courtyard. Access into the house from the courtyard was via French windows and a Regency style half glazed door. In the yard, to my left, was a stone shed which seemed to be attached to the wall adjoining the property of the man with the protest in his window. Probably once a fuel store. It took me ten minutes to find a key in a plant pot under a stack of shelves. I unlocked the back door and stepped into the basement.

This was one room, about twenty feet long and fifteen feet across. At the far end, a bespoke kitchen took up half the available space. The remainder was occupied by an expensive light oak table and half a dozen matching chairs. I took the open tread staircase up to the ground floor and stepped into the hall; onto a polished oak floor, midway between the front door and the rear window looking out on to the garden. The stairs up to the first floor were behind me. Opposite the stairwell, a sash window looked across the road and into the park. To my left the living room door was open.

Like the hall, the room occupied the whole floor, from the street at the front of the house to the garden at the back. More oak floorboards, with big, expensive pile rugs in selected places, the plaster ceiling rose featuring nymphs and shepherds or some such, the cornices and the marble fireplace restored. There were floor to ceiling bookshelves each side of the fireplace and a major painting each side of the doorway I had just stepped through. All the woodwork was painted white, the walls a moss green colour.

The thought occurred - Ridley might be an over-indulged, over-aged delinquent, but if this room was his work the boy had class at least.

I went up to the first floor, which boasted two bedrooms with elegant en-suite facilities, and then up the last flight of stairs. The first room I reached on the top floor was a third bedroom. Next to it was a bathroom. And a small room full of empty cardboard boxes.

The bedroom was locked.

To the left of the door was a long, low, ancient, dark oak blanket chest. On top of it was a Wedgewood bowl, eighteen inches in diameter. There was a key sitting in the centre of the bowl. I picked it up. Unlocked the bedroom door and pushed it with my left hand. The room was dark, the curtains or shutters closed. I listened. Heard no sound. I stepped into the room and waited for my eyes to accustom to the light. I looked around me.

There were no pictures on the walls, no ornaments or dressings, no cupboards, no wardrobe. The only pieces of furniture were a chest of drawers and a duvet covered bed.

There was someone asleep in the bed. Breathing deeply but quietly.

I stood glued to the spot for a long time before I decided to get closer. The sleeper was facing my direction, a black bob of hair covering most of the features. I stooped, leaned forward and drew the hair back.

And looked into the face of Amy Turner.

I straightened up. My immediate reaction was simply 'Well I've found her. Now that's done'. Swiftly followed by a massive surge of relief that she was still alive, and – although a little difficult to assess under the duvet – apparently all in one piece. I reversed quietly out of the room and pulled the door closed. On the landing, I leant against the wall, slid down it and sat on the floor.

The best way to avoid scaring Amy to death as I woke her, was to do the waking from out here. If I knocked on the door, her first reaction would be to assume that her guardian was back. No surprise perhaps, but thinking about it not necessarily a consummation devoutly to be wished. Hamlet would have been just as confused and irresolute as me right now. What to do or what not to do? That was the question. What the hell...

I knocked on the door. There was no response.

I knocked again and waited. I heard shuffling and the creak of a badly sprung mattress.

"Amy," I called out. "My name is Jack Shepherd. I'm working for your family. I'll repeat that. My name is Jack Shepherd. I'm a private investigator, hired to find you."

I stood motionless. There was no sound from the room. Maybe that translated into no panic.

"I have the door key," I said. "I'm coming in."

Amy wasn't panicking. She was sitting up, leaning back against the bedhead, staring in the direction of the door. In the gloom, I couldn't see the expression on her face. Her cracked voice reached me across the room.

"Jack who?"

"Shepherd. Jack Shepherd."

"Where's Ridley?" she asked.

"He's not here," I said.

"How did you get in?"

"I found the back door key."

Her voice dropped again and she said something I didn't hear. I looked towards the window.

"May I let some light in?"

"Yes," she said.

I crossed the room. Drew back the curtains. Turned to look at Amy. Her skin was the colour of my grey shirt. There were beads of sweat standing on her forehead. Her eyes ringed by deep purple, had sunk to the bottom of two hollows in her face. Her lips were pale and seemed to be receding into her mouth, as though she'd had her teeth pulled out. She took time to focus on me, then struggled a little further upright in the bed.

I couldn't find anything to say. There seemed to be no ambient sound in the room. And nothing seeping in from outside. She took it upon herself to help the conversation along.

"I look like this every morning before I go into make-up," she managed to say; her voice fuller this time, but hoarse.

I managed to dredge up something in reply.

"How long have you been here?"

"I don't know. What day is it?"

284

"Saturday."

Amy counted back.

"Eight, er no, nine days," she said. "Why do you have grass in your hair?"

She was together enough to notice that. I shook my head and scraped my scalp again.

She groaned, took a huge breath, shivered, rolled across the bed and threw up into the plastic bowl at my feet. She spat into the bowl, swallowed, heaved again, and spoonfuls of bile dropped into the bowl. She dry heaved once more and this time nothing came out. She worked her lips and spat into the bowl again.

"Yeeurch," she muttered – or something translatable as such.

I helped her back onto the bed and pulled the duvet over her again. She began to shake, so violently that the mattress bounced and the headboard thumped against the wall. I reached out to her. She shook her head and tried to yell 'No'. I stepped back. Thirty seconds or so later, the shaking began to wind down. A couple of minutes and it stopped altogether. I watched all this, standing by the bed.

The first three investigations I was involved in as a young DC were to do with drugs. A street robbery, a burglary and a case of aggravated assault. Each one to buy money to feed the perpetrator's habit. Those cases, followed shortly after by twelve months working in Vice, taught me a lot about drugs in a very short time. The brain works like a spring. Drugs push the spring down and suppress the production of neuro transmitters. Which is the intention, given the high required. And it works just as the user wants it to. The high is fabulous, but it needs a regular supply to keep things running that way. And the time comes when the high is constantly needed and the addiction is complete. And then begins the descent into hell. Control over mind and life and limb becomes impossible.

The decision made to quit is both courageous and foolish. Take away the drugs and the brain re-bounds into action, producing surges of adrenalin which generate withdrawal symptoms, delirium and hallucinations, even seizures and heart attacks. The acute withdrawal stage can be as short as forty-eight hours, but the next stage is more problematic. It can take weeks to get clean and free. Energy levels drop and rise, and nights of disturbed sleep lead to restlessness and deep depressions. Then there are mood swings and poor concentration. No actor, especially a network darling, needs that sort of baggage to carry.

Amy had chosen cold turkey, because checking into a clinic, however secretly, becomes common knowledge at the first tweet. Self-medication − in this instance effectively no medication − was the only way to keep her move to the US alive. Hollywood producers allow superstars to fall from grace, particularly if their shows are selling millions of bucks worldwide, but no one takes on a newcomer with addiction problems from the get go, no matter how talented.

Amy was doing this the hardest of hard ways.

I'm not a man with a strong stomach, but I managed to pick up the bowl, take it into the bathroom, empty the contents down the toilet, flush it, drop the bowl into the bath and clean it under the taps. I picked up a hand towel hanging on the rail next to the wash basin and soaked it in cold water. When I got back to the bedroom she was sitting up again.

"Do I look any better?" she stage whispered at me.

"Not much in all honesty," I said.

She almost manged a grin. "Not a fan huh?"

Right now I was her biggest fan. She was wrestling with a mansion full of miseries and demons. She'd been doing it for nine days and nights. And rotten though she looked at this moment, she was probably winning.

"Did Ridley lock you in here?"

She nodded at me, then at the window.

"He locked that too," she said, her voice stronger now. "He's been looking after me. Trying to get food and water into me, cleaning me up, then cleaning the duvet cover and the bedding. At least, the diarrhoea's stopped. And I don't throw up as much as I did. I think I'm kicking it."

"Ridley's here most of the time then?"

She nodded. And that helped to explain why I hadn't seen him since the fracas at *The Quay*.

"Why is he doing this?" I asked.

"We're old friends," she said and tried to smile. "He's in love with me."

I looked at her. Ridley wasn't supplying Amy, he was trying to get her well. I asked her how long she had known him.

"Since we were teenagers. We were at school together."

"Are you up to answering some questions?"

"You can give it a try."

"Do you know that Neil is at the beach house?"

"You know about the house?"

"I've been there. He's looking for you too."

Amy swallowed, looked as though she might be about to throw up again. I waited. She swallowed for a second time and shook her head.

"I'm only here because of something Neil worked out," I said.

I gave Amy the story of my introduction to Neil, his evening with Julian, and our assumption that Ridley was supplying her drugs.

She managed the half smile again.

"No. Not Ridley. He's not a dealer."

"So why did he visit you on set late one night?"

"What night?"

She shot me a look as steadfast as she could manage.

"I'm here," I said, "because a friend of mine traced Ridley's car."

She choked. She was beginning to sweat again. I pressed the hand towel to her forehead. It warmed up instantly. I wiped the rest of her face with it.

"So who is, was your dealer?"

She shook her head. "I'm not going back to him."

"Does he know where you are?"

"No. Ridley made sure of that."

I asked her if she knew Gerald Gaghan. Amy said she'd never met him, and from what she'd heard about the man, it was clear Ridley was never going to make an introduction any time soon. She shook her head again, trying to clear it. She was growing tired. She asked me if I intended to wait for Ridley to come back. Then she shivered, groaned, rolled to her left and back again. This time I kept my distance. The spasms were stronger than before, but over in less time.

I considered what might happen if I waited for Ridley to arrive. His default response would be to beat the hell out of me first and ask questions if, and when, I regained consciousness. On the other hand, if I was sitting in his living room with the Wedgwood and the Lalique and the pictures, reading one of his early editions, maybe he'd be less inclined to break up the place.

"You don't have to wait here," Amy said. "I'm not going anywhere."

I made another trip to the bathroom, re-soaked the hand towel and gave it to Amy. At the bedroom door she asked me not to get into a fight, assuring me that Ridley would listen to everything I had to say. I closed the bedroom door, returned the key to the bowl on the chest went down the stairs. In the living room, I found an Everyman edition of *A Tale of Two Cities*. Arranged myself at a useful angle to the door, in a chair next to a side table with a Lalique rose bowl on it, and settled down to read.

It was the best of times, it was the worst of times, it was the age of wisdom, it was the age of foolishness, it was the season of Light, it was the season of Darkness, it was the spring of hope, it was the winter of despair, we had everything before us, we had nothing before us...

Did Dickens write this yesterday?

I turned from page five to page six as Ridley unlocked the front door and stepped into the hall. I called out to him. He arrived in the living room doorway, froze and stared at me. I matched the stare with one of my own.

"Who the hell are you?" he asked.

"Jack Shepherd," I said. Lifted the book and waved at the bookshelves. "Have you read all these?"

He nodded. "Most of them. Jack who?"

"I'm a private investigator, working for Amy's family. They hired me to find her."

Ridley morphed from angry to confused. So I helped him out.

"I don't want a confrontation," I said. "It would be a shame to damage any of the beautiful things in here. But I need to talk with you."

He took a step into the room. I dropped the book on my lap and picked up the rose bowl. He asked the same question as Amy.

"How did you get in?"

I gave him the same answer.

"I've seen you before somewhere," he said.

"Briefly," I said. "You were busy causing an affray at the time."

Enlightenment dawned. "Ah yes. In *The Quay*. Well, I was pissed and angry."

"Maybe. But there was no need to bust up the place."

"Why did Howie and Mo arrive?" he asked.

"Mickey called them."

The expression on Ridley's face changed. "Mickey..."

"He was a friend of mine," I said. "I think he was killed because he talked to me."

That seemed to make an impression.

"For God's sake, Shepherd, put the rose bowl down. There's no point in either of us trying to prove how tough we are. Unless you want to take this out onto the lawn."

None of this was playing as I had expected. Ridley was standing in front of me, offering a passable imitation of the most reasonable man in the world. Well spoken, no accent in his voice – but then he'd probably had the best private education money could buy. No sign of the wayward child, drunken hooligan, or awkward bastard of legend. He was around the same height as me, long of limb and square of shoulder. Looked as if he worked out.

I declined his offer. He asked me if I would like a drink. I ordered a small glass of malt. He crossed the room to a drinks table. Held up a bottle of Laphroaig.

"This do?"

"More than acceptable."

He poured drinks for both of us, walked back to my chair, handed me a glass, stepped back a pace or two and sat down on the sofa on the other side of the fireplace.

I told Ridley that Amy was awake. He looked momentarily concerned. I said she was okay apart from the two spasms I had witnessed. The concern increased. He downed his drink and got to his feet.

"Stay there," he said, and left the room.

So... Was this the real Ridley Gaghan? Reasoned, caring, a collector of fine objects, a reader of books. Or was he uber bipolar and merely in a good place at this moment? The presentation I'd just been given didn't jibe with the reputation he had, and the foolishness I had witnessed in *The Quay*. The biographies I'd been offered were those of a renegade son, living on some money from his father, some drug dealing and a pimping operation he had going. Received opinion said that fortitude was never his ace, that boozing with his mates, aggressive behaviour and bad tempers were at the heart of his default setting.

I put Dickens back on his shelf. Wandered round the room checking on the silverware. There was a selection of porcelain cow creamers in a shelved, glass fronted cupboard. I looked out of the window across Sion Hill Park. This really was a handsome address.

Ridley returned two or three minutes later.

"Amy's over the worst. She's getting stronger," he said.

I asked him who her supplier was.

"Didn't she tell you?"

"No."

"Doesn't matter. Somebody dealt with that situation apparently. Put a bullet into his leg. He's on remand and he's not dealing anymore."

Well, there was a question answered. Julian, freelancing on Gerald Gaghan's time. I must have pondered silently for a while because Ridley took hold of the narrative.

"Look," he said. "The best that we can do is let this play out. Amy will be back in the real world in a day or two. I'll make sure of that. She'll go back to work with a story prepared, and the lost days will be forgotten. I suggest you do nothing to interfere."

"Her family needs to know she is safe," I said.

"Then tell them so. But not where she is." He looked at me for a long time. Then decided on a direct course of action. "If you give us away, I'll come looking for you."

No idle boast that. Ridley seemed like the real deal. He was delivering more than a simple playout of the feckless hard case people had attested to and I had seen in action. I chose my words carefully.

"Is that threat designed to preserve Amy's agenda or your own?" I asked.

"Doesn't matter," he assured me.

This was beginning to feel like a version of the old Danny Malone one two. Only more nerve wracking, in the sense that I could read the signs with Malone. I had no idea how Ridley's modus operandi might work. He extended his arm in the direction of the door.

"So if you don't mind..."

"I need some assurances about Amy," I said.

"You've had those. Believe me or don't. Your choice. It's no matter to me. Just go. And don't come within a hundred yards of this house again, unless you're invited."

That was it. The only way Amy was going to get well was to be left alone to complete the job. With Ridley. Telling the police she was here wouldn't help in the slightest. I had to trust Ridley unconditionally. All of us with her welfare at heart had to do so.

There was a final subject I needed to broach. So I took a risk.

"Did you know Alfie Barnes?" I asked.

He didn't say anything. I persisted.

"Do you know anything about the circumstances surrounding the death of Alfie Barnes?"

He still didn't say anything.

"Is your father implicated in the death of Alfie Barnes?"

This time he responded.

"I wouldn't be surprised."

Then he pointed to the door again.

CHAPTER TWENTY-FIVE

I called Thelma Turner from the car. She was at home. I told her I had found Amy and answered all the questions about her well-being while deflecting those concerning her whereabouts. The conversation was hard work; the grandma asking all the pertinent questions, the private investigator prevaricating. I ended with the umpteenth repetition of 'I promise you she's fine.'

"Please tell her mother," I said. "I'm going to call her agent."

I rang Celia's mobile. It went straight to a message. I told her I had good news about Amy and asked her to call me back soonest.

A little blurring of the edges there, but at this stage...

I called Neil. Left the message with him, too.

I looked at my watch. 12.40. I went for a ramble around Sion Hill Park. After I'd rambled a bit, I sat on the grass and looked south over the city. The afternoon sun was warm and embracing.

Celia was the first to return my calls. I told her the whole story. Something of a soliloquy. She didn't speak until I had finished.

"And you're sure Amy's all right?" she asked.

"Yes," I said. "Given the circumstances."

"And will this Ridley bloke be as good as his word?"

"Yes. He knows I'll go to the police if anything untoward happens. In which case, he will get pulled and the police will get a warrant to search his house. The last thing he would desire is a horde of coppers turning his place upside down."

"Thank you, Jack," she said. "Do I owe you anything?"

"Talk with Amy again as soon as she re-surfaces."

"Of course."

"I'll keep you posted."

She thanked me again and we ended the conversation.

It occurred to me I hadn't had lunch. There were no takeaways and sandwich bars in this part of the parish. I went back to the Accord. I called at the *7 til 10 Store* on Bristol Road, bought a jumbo sausage roll, a cheese and pickle sandwich and a bottle of fizzy water. Stopped in a lay-by once I had cleared the city and sampled the fare. Neil called. I swallowed a mouthful of sausage roll and picked the mobile up off the passenger seat. I gave him the story I told Celia, almost word for word. He asked the same question when I finished.

"Ridley. Can we trust him to do as he says?"

I told him 'yes'. He took that with some suspicion and asked why. I reminded him that Ridley and Amy were old friends. He worried about that, too. I suggested he stay at the seaside. At least for a few days.

"Relax, unwind and then get back to your script," I said. "I'll call you as soon as Amy is up and about."

"As long as you keep an eye on the situation."

I pressed the call cancel button and a nano-second later the phone rang in my hand. One of those moments when you jump in surprise, like a man who's just sat bare-arsed on an electric storage heater.

"Are you sure Amy is all right?" Rachel asked.

I conducted version four of the 'everything's okay' conversation. A reprise of the one with Thelma, omitting Ridley and the drugs. Rachel asked a not unreasonable question.

"Why won't she talk to us?"

"She's busy working stuff out," I insisted. "She will be back in touch within days. There is no problem. She is perfectly all right."

Another version of 'the saving lie'. It was never going to go down well, with any recipient. Thankfully, Rachel was the last in the queue. I finished my simple repast, switched on the motor and drove back to Bristol. I talked with myself on the way. I decided I knew more than enough about Gerald Gaghan, and ought to get to grips with his associate instead.

I sat down in front of my office pc and googled Peter Nash. The Bristol connections told a simple tale of local success and a business philosophy to please all sides of any debate. Gaghan Nash was the leading member of a consortium of West Country, M4 corridor and South Wales companies, all involved in the same line of business. PR consultancies, media advisers, lobbyists and fixers – and in Gaghan Nash's case also periodical publishers – boasting contacts in all major European capitals. More Nash than Gaghan all of this. More national high profile success than local debt enforcement. This was Peter Nash's forte. And he was no shrinking violet. Out and proud, mixing with all sorts, low and high.

I was offered another site called *Business in Bruges*. Nash had an office in the city, the headquarters of a company called *Modern European* with an address in a prominent business quarter. So did Gaghan Nash, and another company listed at the same address called, simply, Now. The latter published monthly magazines in English, French, Flemish, Dutch and German. I flashed back to the magazines I had found in Nick Jenner's filing cabinet and for a moment a wave of optimism took hold. But the half a dozen periodicals listed seemed to be concerned with up market lifestyle stuff. All the businesses were part of the Modern European Group. The group head office and registered address were in Geneva.

To be informed is to be well armed, or so I've read. In this case maybe not. It was difficult to work out what to do with this information. It always helps to know the strength of the opposition, but the real plus is having a strategy to deal with it. And I didn't have a sack full of riches at my end.

However, a super sleuth never admits to running out of ideas. And I had a Belgian contact on the books. I called Val and asked if we could meet. She suggested an early evening drink in a pub in Clifton we both knew, called The Well Wisher. She was sitting in a corner of the lounge by the time I got there.

I told her everything the good guys had discovered about Gerald Gaghan and Peter Nash. She knew of the *Modern European Group*. A friend of hers had worked in Geneva, translating yearly reports for the shareholders and group partnership contracts.

"Boring work, albeit well paid. Translators avoid it if possible. Reports and contracts have to be one hundred per cent legally perfect. No paraphrases or colloquialisms. The party of the first part's obligations to the party of the second part can't have so much as a syllable out of place. And some annual reports run to hundreds of pages."

"Are there any blots on the Peter Nash escutcheon that you know of? Any whiff of the smallest irregularity?"

"Nothing that's come my way. Mind you, I haven't been digging. It's possible that er…"

Her attention was suddenly distracted.

"Oh God…"

She was looking across the room, beyond the right side of my head. She got to her feet and launched herself towards the bar, yelling at the barman to turn up the TV sound. There was a picture of a man on the screen. As the volume rose the studio Anchor handed over to the channel's European Editor.

"Yanis Mertens' passport was taken away from him after his arrest in Molenbeek…"

I joined Val at the bar and listened as the journalist continued.

"But it may be he has another passport and is currently operating under an alias. Interpol and national police forces are working together to trace his whereabouts, with the assistance of Security Organisations in Belgium, France, Germany and here in the UK. He is described by the Belgian State Security Service as a 'very dangerous man'."

Val turned away from the screen, leaned against the bar and stared at me. The barman asked her if that was all? She nodded. The TV volume was turned down again. I waited for her to speak.

"Yanis Mertens," she said eventually. "If he has disappeared from Belgian State Security radar, then he's on a mission. Somewhere."

We moved back to our table. Val elaborated a little.

"Something I didn't tell you the other day... Back in the spring, when tens of thousands of people walked in silence through the streets of central Brussels in a march against terror and hate, CCTV picked out Mertens in the crowd lining the road. He followed the route of the march all the way. And that was probably the last time he was seen. If he is in England, or anywhere in the UK, you can bet your house and all the family silver he's not here on holiday."

She swallowed the rest of her gin and tonic. I asked her if she wanted another.

* * *

We walked to the parked cars. I aimed the key fob at the Accord. It bleeped. I faced Val again.

"I've not asked you this," I said. "Are you a practising Muslim?"

"Mostly I am. A little hard to justify perhaps, considering the arrangement at Chancellors Hotel. But I read the Koran. I believe in Mohammed."

"How do you react to anti-Muslim slogans?"

"Islamophobia is a very confused entity. Sometimes it pops up as a kind of mild embarrassment. You know...

300

Shouldn't we take a look at this? Then there's the clear nudge in the ribs; like the tweet I read last week which asked the question *Do you get paranoid when there's a Muslim around?* And then another response, from the heart of extreme right prejudice; a picture of an atom bomb exploding, with the caption *Some cancers need to be treated with radiation. Islam is one of them*. There's no disguising the message in that is there?"

Val opened the driver's door in the Vauxhall. Paused, then swung to face me again.

"I've been asked if I feel responsible for Islam. Of course I don't. I don't feel obliged to apologise for IS attacks. I won't be held accountable for a fanatical re-imagining of the Koran."

"A friend of my daughter is an American," I said. "He feels compelled to apologise for the USA foisting Donald Trump on the world."

Val grinned. "Maybe there's mileage in that."

She got into her car, then looked back at me

"Like the bible, the Koran says 'love thy neighbour', too. The clothes you wear, the food you eat, the books you read, the faith you believe in... all those things are to be shared with others. Did you know that the leaders of a Mosque in the city are opening its doors to Christians? Saying that they are welcome to come in and pray. And why not? Muslims should be encouraged to pray in churches. There are beliefs and lessons to be passed on regardless of your religion."

"Is the city ready for that?"

"The first mosque opened its doors in Bristol in 1967. Fifty years ago. At the time, nobody paraded outside it warning citizens of the dangers of Islam. And during the 80s and the 90s, nobody talked of Jihadi plots to take over city schools, or the radicalisation of teenagers. It could have happened but it didn't. Why? Because there was, and still is, no reason for it. Currently it's fashionable. But it's driven by prejudice and ignorance. Take a straw poll in any part of the city and you'll discover that those who claim Islam is dangerous are just repeating stuff they've heard or read in the headlines."

"It has enough substance to stir up trouble from the right," I suggested.

"Only when a right wing event is scheduled, like the march this weekend."

"Will there be trouble?"

"Yes, I'm afraid. It might even be choreographed into the thing. A disruptive moment in the crowd will spread and lead to a reaction among the marchers. A lot of abusive chanting will be generated, a tussle will break out somewhere and hey presto..."

"Will you be there?"

"Yes. At some place on the route."

"Why?"

"Because extremists on both sides have to be made to see that violence isn't the way forward. Communities in Manchester and Borough Market and Finsbury Park did that."

"But it doesn't stop the violence. Not on the streets."

Val looked at me, disappointed.

"Do you really believe that, Jack?"

"I'd rather not, but I think I do."

"Then come with me on Saturday."

I stared at her. She closed the car door and wound down the window.

"Ring me," she said.

She turned on the ignition, wrapped herself in the safety belt, looked back at me and smiled, selected first gear and pulled away. I watched the car being swallowed up by the traffic.

Join Val at the march... That would be a hell of a date.

I drove home. A sandwich board on the pavement outside the newsagent's grabbed my attention - MARCH TO GO AHEAD IN SPITE OF PROTESTS. I parked the car and bought a copy of the Post.

Community leaders had lost a last ditch plea for the BPAG march to be cancelled. Nonetheless, there was a meeting scheduled for 10.30 the following day to be hosted by the police. To furnish details of the route, explain the marshalling and safety procedures and to assure the public, particularly those living along the route, that all would pass sensibly and peacefully.

Genuine guarantee, spin, or pie in the sky?

I phoned Adam. He was cooking, so I began the conversation with Chrissie. Asked her about work. She said she was enjoying every minute of every day. The more cynical among the staff were applauding her zeal and enthusiasm, she said, but advising her that during the thirty or forty years ahead she might come to revise her notions. Unlikely she said. That's what I thought, too.

Chrissie is Emily's daughter. Clever, tough, committed to the things she believes in, generous with her time and serious about teaching. She starts at the top of an idea and works down, if necessary, under protest. Unlike her father, whose labours begin more often than not at the bottom, with a client's despair or a cry for help. Chrissie approaches all she signs up for with passion and a total belief in the outcome. This isn't naivety, it's the desire of a twenty-three year old to take on the world. For which I admire and love her.

She handed the phone to Adam and took over kitchen duty.

"Are you going to be at the march meeting tomorrow?" I asked.

"Yes," he said. "Why don't you come with me? The intention is to reach everyone who might be involved. All interested parties. Which is why it's being held at the Victoria Rooms and not in a police station. The purpose is to create a less formal, friendlier vibe."

My gut reaction to that last sentence was suspicion. Chrissie would have found more optimism in it.

"I'll come to you," Adam said. "We'll leave the cars at your place and take a cab."

He wished me a good evening. Linda was expecting us to spend it together. I called her.

"Shall I bring some takeaway with me?" I asked.

"Yes, great. My choice would be from the *Thai House*."

The phone in the hall rang as I was opening the front door. I had one of those 'shall I or shan't I?' moments. I left the door open, stepped back and reached for the receiver.

"Jack," Amy said. "Ridley left in a foul temper, about an hour ago. I don't know what he's about to do. He's pumped up and angry. I wanted to ring you earlier, but I didn't have your number and had to go via my mother. She was at grandma's. They kept me talking."

"Is Ridley coming back later?"

"I suppose so. If he does, he's likely to be unstable at best."

"Will he hurt you?"

"He never has. I just thought that..." She paused, thinking something through. "Will you come over? Please, Jack."

"How are you?"

"I'm okay. On my feet and up and about. Not very strong, but I'll be fine..." She paused for a second or two. "If we have to leave."

I looked at my watch. 6.35. I could get to Sion Hill inside half an hour, if the traffic was helpful. I could accomplish both evening excursions. Look after Amy and still get to Linda's. The Hamlet moment again. Leave Amy in trouble or suffer the slings and arrows of outrage from Linda by charging to the rescue. I chose Amy. Told her I'd be there as fast as I could. Called Linda. She appeared sympathetic. Said that was the only course open to me. I could picture her saying so through gritted teeth. The Thai food was probably a lost cause. I told her to eat and said I'd sort something out for myself later.

Traffic was light from the city centre to Temple Meads Station, along the Bath Road and out onto the Keynsham by-pass. But I came to a full stop in Saltford, held hostage by red lights and stationary vehicles. I travelled a mile and a bit in six or seven minutes. I floored the pedal on the only bit of dual carriageway available, braked from eighty miles an hour to thirty, peeled left, crossed the river into Newbridge and on through the western suburbs of Bath. I roared up Sion Hill at close to fifty miles an hour, parked on double yellows and rang Ridley's doorbell.

Amy looked a lot better. I told her so. She smiled. I asked her if she had any idea where Ridley had gone.

"He was in the kind of rage he gets into when his father crops up in conversation. Perhaps he's... I don't know."

I suggested we should leave. Amy took a deep breath.

"Yes. Okay. Let me get a couple of things."

She went up the stairs carefully, at a measured pace, looking in remarkable shape. My watch said 7.25.

"What are you doing here, Shepherd?" Ridley said from the doorway.

I turned to face him. He repeated the question. This time with less surprise and more fury.

"Tell me before I peel the skin off your face."

I heard Amy coming down the stairs. I glanced behind me. She paused on the floor landing. Ridley yelled at her.

"And where the hell are you going?"

There was a moment's hiatus, before Ridley moved towards me. Gave me time to shift slightly to my left, to offer him room and invite him to pass. A yard short of me he swung a hefty right cross, designed to take my head off. I ducked under it. Momentum drove Ridley's body clockwise until he was at right angles to me. I balled my right fist and punched him hard in his right kidney. He yelled and staggered away from me. Amy stepped to my side. I grabbed her right hand and dragged her in the direction of the front door. Ridley made a grab for Amy. I pulled her past me, she lost balance and stumbled into the door frame. Ridley was a couple of paces away from me. I stepped backwards, off the hall carpet runner, bent down, grabbed the end of it and heaved. It pulled Ridley's legs out from under him, his arms windmilled, he lost contact with the floor and dropped backwards onto the tiles. There was a crunch as his skull made contact with the Italian ceramics, followed by a yell of pain. He rolled over onto his side, blood seeping through his hair. Amy moved towards me. There was a cut above her left eye. She wiped the blood from her forehead.

"Don't worry," she said. "Just the side of the door frame."

She knelt down beside Ridley. He groaned and passed out.

I picked up the phone receiver. Dialled 999. The call was answered on the fourth ring. I was asked which service I required. I told the operator. There was a click, a momentary buzz and the ambulance operator came on the line.

"There is a man lying on the tiles in the hallway of his house, unconscious, and bleeding from a serious wound to the back of his head."

I gave the operator Ridley's address. She said the ambulance had only a mile to travel and would be on its way in moments. She suggested I do all I could to stop the bleeding. Asked if I wanted her to stay on the line. I said no. There was a beat's rest, then she finished by saying the ambulance ETA was three minutes.

Amy came out of the kitchen with a handful of wet tea towels. She knelt beside Ridley, folded one of them, clamped it onto his head with her left hand and pressed hard. With another towel she began wiping the blood from his neck. I knelt on the floor to Ridley's left, exchanged the bloody towel for a clean one. The blood flow began to slow down.

Ridley regained consciousness. He looked at Amy, all anger spent.

"Let him look after you," he whispered.

I stepped into his eye line. He managed to look in my direction without moving his head.

"And you... Go and face my father. And his partner. Stop the bastards doing..." He took a deep breath. "...Doing what they plan to do... Be careful though, they have friends who..."

He passed out again.

A siren faded up under the ambient street noise. I stepped outside. Got into the Accord and moved it a couple of car lengths closer to the corner. The noise of the siren bounced off the Bath stone as the ambulance turned into the terrace. I stood behind the Accord and waved my arms like a man with paddles at the airport.

The ambulance sped towards me and pulled into the kerb.

The paramedics worked on Ridley for a couple of minutes, staunching the blood completely, protecting the wound and then putting him into a head and neck brace. Which gave Amy and me time to consider.

"What do you think Ridley meant? That bit about his father?" she asked.

"No idea," I said. "But Ridley's no saint, so if it offends his code of honour, it won't be something to cherish."

"Then we have to stop it. Whatever it is."

I looked at her. Her face was flushed with excitement – the first time I'd seen colour in her cheeks.

"Not we," I said. "Me. You go to hospital with Ridley. I'll call your mother and tell her to pick you up."

She looked down at the man regarded as a villain by many in the shire.

"Okay," she said, then looked back at me. "You take care. Ring me when you can. I'll stay at my mother's."

"And do something else for me. Phone Neil. And Celia. She's worried, she cares and she wants to talk with you."

Amy grimaced. "I doubt it. I behaved very badly. Acted like some juvenile prima donna. She didn't deserve to be on the receiving end of my stamping and yelling."

"She paid me to find you," I said.

Amy stared at me. I grinned at her.

"And I don't come cheap."

"I bet that's never the motive for anything you do, Jack Shepherd."

"You'd be surprised what I'll do for money."

"I don't believe it," she said.

"I won't kill for it and I won't marry for it. But I'm open to most other offers."

Now she grinned at me.

"That's better," I said. "That's a great smile. A little frayed around the edges, maybe. So get in some practice."

The paramedics lifted Ridley onto the stretcher. He woke up again as they carried him into the street. Amy was by his side. She reached out and pressed his right arm. I watched them all get into the ambulance. The siren roared into life again, the ambulance pulled away from the kerb, passed the Accord and sped off in the direction of the Royal United Hospital, four or five minutes away.

I phoned Rachel Turner. She said would leave the house immediately.

I pulled up outside Linda's garage at twenty minutes to nine. The apology and the explanation took some time, but Linda's ire cooled swiftly. She pointed me in the direction of the kitchen, a slice of pork pie, some cold ham and cheese.

We went to bed forty-five minutes later.

CHAPTER TWENTY-SIX

"The marchers will gather in Rose Park in Montpelier".

Superintendent Robbins, the officer in charge of policing the event, pointed a stick at the map on the interactive whiteboard.

"They will walk down Cheltenham Road, along Jamaica Street, on to Upper Maudlin Street, past the BRI, along Park Row, then left into King's Road, left again on to Park Street and on down to College Green. Where they will congregate for a maximum of thirty minutes to hear from speakers."

He turned back to those of us on the floor of the small banqueting room. Approximately fifty souls. Local and national journalists, local and network TV crews. Muslim and Christian leaders of the mosques and churches along the route. Shopkeepers, concerned citizens, some onlookers at the back and me.

I counted four TV cameras live in the hall.

"I'll take questions now," Robbins said and sat down at the table in front of him.

His second in command, Chief Inspector Helen Smart, sat to his left and beyond her a Police Community Liaison Officer. At Robbins' right elbow was the civilian PR person Eve Wilmore, and to her right, towards the end of the table, ACC Langley made up the row of protagonists.

A man sitting in the middle of the gathering raised his right hand.

Eve Wilmore pointed at him. "Yes, John…"

"How many uniformed officers will be shepherding the marchers?" he asked.

Eve Wilmore looked at CI Smart. She took up the cudgel.

"One hundred," she said.

"Is that enough? Given the recent disturbances we have witnessed – the bombing and the knife attacks."

"We believe so, yes."

A woman in the second row of seats stuck up her hand. She caught Wilmore's attention.

"Elaine..."

"How many members of the *British Political Action Group* do you expect to attend this march?"

"Thirty or forty," Smart said.

There was a rustle and a snort from the back of the hall.

"Seventy to eighty," a male voice called out.

Heads turned, cameras panned and lenses zoomed in. A man with a close cropped haircut, heavy eyebrows, and an unruly moustache, stood up in the back row of chairs. He was around six feet tall, wide-shouldered and barrel-chested. The man next to him stood up too. He was longer and thinner.

"Maybe more," he said.

The sound level in the room rose. Eve Wilmore stood up and asked for their names.

"David Bairstowe," the moustache said. "But you can call me Dave."

A reporter on the front row asked, "Are you a member of the *British Political Action Group*?"

"Yes," he said. "Proud of it."

"How can you be confident of that size of turnout?" someone else asked.

"This event is important to all local members of the party."

His mate nodded in support. "They'll be present."

Other people attempted to get into the conversation, each one drowning the other out. ACC Langley watched, stiff and impassive. Making no show of interest. C I Smart banged the table with a block of wood, the noise rising above all else. She stood up.

"One at a time, please. We would like everyone in here to operate according to the system we agreed."

The noise in the hall diminished. Smart continued.

"Thank you for your input, Mr Turner."

Turner shrugged. He and his mate sat down again. Smart continued.

"A patrol car and three motor bikes will lead the march. Two more patrol cars will bring up the rear. The rest of the uniformed offices will walk with the marchers. There will be another fifty officers stationed on College Green, along with vehicles from the Police Urban Security Force."

She sat down again. Wilmore pointed in the direction of a network reporter. He stood up and introduced himself.

"Mark Danvers, *ITV News*," he said. He addressed Robbins. "Do you actually believe that the BPAG merits this amount of attention?"

"The beliefs of the BPAG are of no interest to me," Robbins said. "Nor to most of the people in this hall today. Please consider - "

There was shout from the back row. "Bollocks."

Robbins ignored it and carried on. "Please consider why you asked that question. I would suggest that this march has been over-hyped because you and your colleagues are here. You are giving this event all the publicity that Mr Bairstowe at the back, could wish for."

Bairstowe and his mate applauded.

There was brief reaction from Wilmore. She glanced at ACC Langley, who betrayed no emotion at all. Then she singled out a reporter to her left. The lady stood up.

"Eve Shelton," she said. *BBC Points West*... Is it not true, that in allowing this march to proceed, you are actually giving support to the likes of the man I spoke with yesterday? Who said *"I'm English till I die. I don't want any more of Islam in my country"*."

"I repeat... We are not supporting what anyone has to say," Robbins said. "We are simply allowing them to say it. Which is their legal and constitutional right."

There was a bellow of "Hear hear" from the back of the room.

Another reporter jumped in with, "How can you possibly agree that the people who say "We don't want mosques in the city, they preach hate", have a right to a hearing?"

Smart got her feet again. "No one at this table is agreeing with that."

Then the whole melodrama gathered momentum.

314

Another journalist stood up. "Is it correct to say that the cost of policing this event will be in the region of £250,000?"

Robbins, Smart and Wilmore looked at ACC Langley. He shook his head, barely but significantly, like a man keeping a secret. On a roll, the journalist ploughed on.

"Shouldn't this request from the BPAG have been turned down, the march forbidden and the money spent sensibly elsewhere?"

Wilmore replied on behalf of the rest of the table.

"We are not able to reveal the costs of policing the event at this time."

And so the briefing developed. I told Adam I had something to do. Got up out of my seat and moved to the back of the hall, from where I could keep an eye on Dave Bairstowe and his mate. They didn't make another contribution to the debate, satisfied they had made their point and more than happy to witness the discomfort of the representatives of the Avon and Somerset Constabulary.

Five minutes later, the two men left the hall. I followed.

Outside the building, they turned right, walked one hundred yards up Queens Road, then turned right again into Westbourne Road – a terrace of three-storey Victorian houses, with cars parked on both sides. I watched the two men get into a grey Nissan. The driver started the engine, pulled the car out into the centre of the road and drove away from me. I made a note of the registration number.

I walked back to the Victoria Rooms. Sat on the wall surrounding the hideous Victorian retro-Corinthian, cherub laden fountain at the front of the building. I called George Hood on the loaner mobile.

"How are things?" he asked.

"I've just been watching your colleagues getting a mauling from the fourth estate and a couple of BPAG heavies."

He asked where I was. I told him. He grunted down the line.

"I watched the broken noses leave the Victoria Rooms and get into a grey Nissan," I said.

I gave him the registration number. He told me to stay on the line. I waited. He came back to me.

"The car owner is known to us. We have pictures here along with other associates. Can you come in and take a look at them?"

"Sure. Give me forty minutes or so."

I called a cab, then left a message on Adam's mobile. The cab picked me up five minutes later and conveyed me home. I drove to Trinity Road.

Dave Bairstowe was thirty-nine years old and had an interesting list of misdemeanours on his sheet. Twocking, joyriding and dangerous driving. A bit of robbery. And a number of racist incidents at football matches. His compadre, Carl Defoe, the car owner, had a similar if slightly more colourful CV, which included two convictions for aggravated assault.

"A pair of real charmers," Henson said.

Hood dropped a couple of A4 sheets onto the desk in front of me.

"Copies of their records for you take away and enjoy," he said.

"Can you pick these two up?"

Hood shook his head.

"Nothing to pick them up for. We'll probably do that on Saturday, after they've kicked the shite out of a group of bystanders; an outcome as certain as day follows night. But by then they will have had their afternoon of excitement."

I stood up to leave. Hood shot me a warning look.

"Be very careful in what you're about to do," he said.

"And what would that be?"

"Let's not give voice to it. Otherwise I will have to intervene."

Hood was giving me a lot of rope here. More than enough to hang both of us. Henson escorted me to the lift.

Defoe's address was an apartment in what was once a pub in Ashley Down. It sat at the bottom of Lilstock Avenue, which sloped down from the cricket ground to where a railway station had once existed, built for the sole purpose of enabling W G Grace to get to work. It was said that his walk up and down the hill was the only exercise he ever took. The Nissan wasn't parked in front of the building or in the yard behind it.

Bairstowe's semi was in a short residential cul de sac in Bishopston. A small two bedroomed place, as cute as all the other houses in the street, with a carefully manicured front garden and a bright red, newly painted, front door. It looked resolutely middle class and infinitely respectable. The Nissan was outside the garden gate. I drove to the end of the cul de sac, u-turned, parked on the opposite side of the road and began considering what to do next.

Yanis Mertens took the decision for me.

He stepped out of the house. Moved along the path and aimed a key fob at the Nissan. The car flashed and beeped. Mertens closed the garden gate behind him, crossed the pavement and slid into the car. He then copied my U turn and moments later drove past me. I started the Accord and followed.

All the way to within a hundred yards of Gerald Gaghan's house.

I parked the Accord as Mertens turned into the drive. Grabbed the loaner phone and called George Hood. No response. This couldn't wait, so security went out of the window. I dialled Hood's landline. DS Henson answered the call.

"Can I talk to? - " was a far as I got.

"Let me call you back," Henson whispered down the line.

I sat in the car staring though the windscreen. Henson was back to me inside forty-five seconds.

"Sorry, Shepherd," he said. "The skipper's calls are being re-directed to me right now. He's got Langley in his office."

"Can you tell if the conversation looks measured," I asked. "Or is George getting a bollocking?"

"Don't know at this moment. I'm out in the yard."

"Do you think you can interrupt proceedings?"

"More than my life's worth?"

"More than the whereabouts of Yanis Mertens?"

There was a beat. The line gently hissed.

"Christ. You know where he is?"

"He's just called on Gerald Gaghan."

"You mean he's in the house? Right, okay."

He ended the call. I looked at my watch. 12.40. I straightened up. Pressed the CD player button. The stacker clicked and offered Bruce Springsteen and *Darkness on the Edge of Town*. The track is four minutes and twenty seconds long. If we got to the end without Yanis Mertens appearing again...

During the second verse, about secrets dragging you down, I looked at my watch again. 12.43. The mobile rang. I grabbed it.

"We're on the way," George Hood said. "Sirens and blues. We'll switch them off before we get close enough for Gaghan to hear."

The Promised Land followed. Four minutes forty-one seconds later, I looked at my watch again. 12.48.

Into the second chorus of *The River* I looked at my watch for the umpteenth time. 12.51.

I opened the car glove box. Found the CD case. The next track *Hungry Heart* was a bit shorter. As Springsteen went into the last chorus I looked at my watch and did some maths. Nine minutes since the conversation with Hood. And Mertens hadn't left the house.

Two verses into *Human Touch* I heard the sound of police sirens. I wound Springsteen's volume down. The sirens cut out. I looked into the rear-view mirror. Suddenly it was filled with police cars. I scrambled out of the Accord and stood in the road. The leading patrol car stopped five or six paces in front of me. George Hood's Volvo slid to a halt alongside. Henson was driving. There were three more unmarked cars behind the Volvo and another patrol car.

Hood's window slid down. I ducked my head and asked him if he'd ever called upon Gaghan. He said no. I pointed across the road.

"The drive is the only way in and out."

Henson pressed the window button to his right. He looked into the patrol car alongside and made a circle in the air with his right forefinger. The front passenger window slid down.

The PC said, "Sir..."

"Once the rest of us have moved onto the drive," Henson said, "park across the gateway and block it. Then get out of the car and wait. Tell the guys behind."

The PC opened the patrol car door. Hood talked to me again.

"Stay with the patrol car. If this was a run of the mill collar I'd invite you along. But this is too important for input from the private sector."

I stepped back. Hood looked at Henson.

"Let's go."

Henson let in the clutch, gunned the motor, swung the Volvo across the road and into Gaghan's drive. Tailgated by the other four cars. The patrol car slid across the front of the drive. I walked across the road. Two patrols of detectives and uniforms moved left and right and around the house.

Hood and Henson and two of the heaviest coppers I'd ever seen, walked up to the front door. Hood rang the bell. The man in the white jacket who had served Gaghan and me drinks on the terrace, a lifetime ago it seemed, opened the door. Hood waved his ID and the man invited the group into the house. The door closed.

Then nothing happened. A monster anti-climax enveloped those of us at the gate. No bellowing and shouting, no sound of commotion, nothing breaking, no gun shots. Five minutes later, Yanis Mertens handcuffed by left and right wrists between the two huge detectives, was ushered out of the house, followed by a second car load of coppers. The uniform next to me got into the patrol car and reversed it clear of the gate. As Mertens and his escort passed me, Henson appeared in the doorway and waved. I walked towards the house.

Everybody was out on the terrace – Gaghan, Howie and Mo, the man in the steward's jacket, Hood, Henson and six other coppers. Hood looked at me and pointed at Gaghan.

"Do you know this man?"

I said I did.

He motioned in the direction of Howard and Maurice.

"Are these the men who collected you from your trip on the ferry and brought you up here?"

I said they were.

"By polite invitation," Gaghan growled.

Hood surveyed the miscreants.

"I am now asking that you accompany these officers to Trinity Road Police Station for questioning regarding your relationship with Yanis Mertens, a fugitive wanted by Interpol and the police and security services of Belgium and Holland."

Five minutes later, the miscreants were inside a custody wagon, under guard and heading for the city. Hood, Henson and I were left standing on the terrace. Hood looked at the refreshments trolley parked in the shade.

"I think we deserve a drink," he said.

Suitably comfortable, sitting in the sun loungers grabbing some rays with gin and tonics all round, Hood led the summing up.

"We've got half a dozen EU and Interpol warrants for Mertens. So we can consider him nicked. The lawyers will have Gaghan and his mates out after breakfast. But ultimately, they can't deny they were here on the terrace, drinking with the most wanted man in the Low Countries."

Henson raised his glass.

"Cheers."

Hood continued with a question to both of us.

"And are we still convinced that Gaghan had people in his employ, or under contract, beat the shit out of Danny Malone?"

Henson swallowed a mouthful of gin and nodded his head. I did the same. Hood looked at me.

322

"Not that this is an SCU remit... But do you still think Gaghan ordered the killing of Alfie Barnes?"

"I'm sure of it," I said. "Mickey Balfour's murder too."

"And can you take a stab at who might have accomplished the deeds?"

"Take your pick," I said. "There's Julian..."

"Currently on remand for attempting to shoot you," Henson said.

"And until recently earning pocket money as a part time recreational drugs supplier," I said.

Hood stared at me for a moment, then opened his mouth to question the voracity of that info. I went on quickly.

"Howard and Maurice," I said "Gaghan himself..."

Henson, face tilted up into the sun, opened his eyes, turned his head and squinted at me.

"Ridley?"

"I originally had him down as public enemy number one," I said. "But not now. He may be a cast in bronze menace, but there's only one person he wants to kill, and that's his father."

Henson's mobile rang. He answered it. Then sat bolt upright in the lounger.

"Yes... What... Where?... Yeah, thanks." He looked at Hood and me. "That's two less Nazis for the march on Saturday. Bairstowe and Defoe have been found."

He paused, to ensure he had our complete and undivided attention.

"In the cupboard under the stairs in Bairstowe's house. Sitting upright, back to back, roped to kitchen chairs with gaffer tape. Both considerably worse for wear. The current theory is, that after coming out at this morning's meeting, Mertens decided they were a liability. There's evidence that he's has been staying in the house. Perhaps for several weeks."

"That's helpful," I suggested.

The other two nodded. I looked at Hood.

"Mind you, none of this is guaranteed to get you two out from under ACC Langley. And you have his mate in overnight this time."

"So what's he going to do?" Henson asked. "Upbraid us for flouting instructions with one of Europe's most wanted in his lap?"

Hood nodded at the drinks trolley

"Shall we have another?"

CHAPTER TWENTY-SEVEN

I was breakfasting with Linda around the time Gaghan's high end lawyer was ushering his clients into his Lexus. It was another Friday morning and I had Alfie on my mind.

It was three weeks since his murder. Four days since Mickey Balfour had suffered the same fate. Assuming that Gaghan had a hand in both killings, maybe I was closer to uncovering the how and the why than I seemed to be. But I would have to sit on the man to find out.

Meanwhile, everybody was in the clarts. Bad guys and good guys. Hood and Henson had disobeyed orders, although the seizure of an internationally wanted criminal was bound to help their position. Langley was no doubt taking the day to re-position himself. Gaghan, happily, was now a prime suspect in a lot of stuff. His main man, Julian, was in a remand cell in Horfield prison. Ridley was out of hospital and back home with a bandage round his head. Slightly better off than Danny Malone who was still in a coma. Howard and Maurice were on gardening leave. And if it could stretch across the city as far as my front door, I'd be on the carpet too.

"Penny for them," Linda said.

We were in the dining room, a pot of coffee and the remains of breakfast between us.

I looked at Linda and told her that I loved her. It took her by surprise. Me too, just a bit. She got to her feet, moved around the table, stood behind me, wrapped her arms round my shoulders leaned down and kissed my neck.

"And I love you," she murmured.

"Well that is all right at least." I took a beat, then turned in my chair to look up at her. "I'm going to the neo-Nazi thing tomorrow with Val."

Linda looked straight into my eyes. "Are you going to do something knightly but dangerous?"

"Not if I can help it."

She shook her head. "I must learn not to ask such foolish questions."

I made a stab at spinning the exercise.

"All we are going to do is follow the march some of the way," I said. "Then stand on College Green for half an hour and listen to some half arsed rant about lebensraum."

She stared at me. "Do you really think those two sentences you have just uttered have any base in reality?"

"Adam will be there, too."

"He's possibly just a little less foolish than you."

"The whole thing is being policed."

"Oh right. A hundred uniformed constables on double time and just along for the inevitable punch up."

"It's hardly likely to be a re-run of the Battle of Orgreave."

She started to clear the dining table. As a gesture of defiance I re-filled my coffee cup.

* * *

I don't know why I went to my office. I could just as easily have done nothing at home. Maybe because Linda was going to the same place. I suggested we car share. She said she needed the Golf because she had a client to visit in Taunton late morning.

Amy called. Her voice sounded strong and confident. She invited Linda and me to Sunday lunch with her mother and grandmother. I said we would be delighted to attend. Neil Shore called. He said that Amy had phoned him and he was coming to lunch, also. After which, they would both go to the beach house for a couple of days.

"Oh and by the way," he said, "I've started working on the screenplay again."

I told him I was pleased. I sipped a lot of coffee and stared out of my window at the traffic beyond the river on Coronation Road. Hugged Linda before she left for Taunton. Did some more window staring. Then there was a polite knock on the open door. I turned round. Val was standing in the doorway.

"Come in," I said. "Most of the crowd has left for the day."

Val stepped into the office. Asked me how I was. I said I was okay.

"Not true," she said, reading the mood. "You are pissed off and frustrated."

"How can I be?" I asked. "I'm Interpol's current darling."

She waited for an explanation. It occurred to me I hadn't told her about the arrest of Yanis Mertens. So I asked her to sit down, and I did.

"Why isn't this front page news?" she asked when I had finished. *"Bristol PI accomplishes what hundreds of European policemen failed to do."*

"To be honest, he made it dead easy. Or rather, two of his mates did. I happened to be outside the house he was bivouacking in when he stepped out of the door."

"Where he is now?"

"The last time I saw him was at Gerald Gaghan's front door shackled to the England second row. He's probably back in Belgium already. Avon and Somerset Constabulary, whilst basking in the glory of the collar, couldn't wait to offload him. Interpol have thrown a blanket over the whole thing. No announcements, no bragging, nothing attributed to anyone, until Mertens is formally charged. And nothing will be revealed locally until the weekend is over and tomorrow's event will proceed as planned. The powers don't want the local Nazis inflamed any more than they already are."

Val took a deep breath and said, "I have a theory."

"Not just the province of private investigators," I said.

"Those A4 pages of Alfie's... Maybe they're movement orders. Details of the next piece of action scheduled. Telling the composers what when and where. Did you notice, each of them is dated?"

I fished my copies out of the centre desk drawer. Looked again at the sheet on top of the pile next to me. It was dated March 19th.

"That's ten days before the riots in Molenbeek. Suppose that page is Mertens' moving orders for *Action Politique*. Suppose he is... Who's mentioned?"

I checked the page. "Richard, Franz and Fred."

Val went on, her enthusiasm for this theory gaining heat.

"So… One of these pages goes out before each scheduled piece of action. There's a brief acknowledgement. No need to do more, because the groups are organised and can get up to speed inside ten days… Tell me I'm not just fantasising here, Jack."

"You may be, but it doesn't mean we're wide of the mark. I have one outstanding question, though. Why is all this coded communication done in German?"

This was Val's territory. "Next to English, German is the most readily spoken language in Europe. It's precise, more ordered than French, or even English… the Latinate structure, verbs at the end of sentences. If you try, you can get to the point quicker in German."

"Okay, but maybe the explanation's simpler than that," I said. "Maybe Alfie's pages went to a German source, where they were translated and then sent on to the foot soldiers."

"That's an unnecessary complication surely."

"Maybe not, if security is a big thing."

"Alfie spoke it fluently," Val said. "Maybe it was just another of his wrinkles and Gaghan thought it clever."

I scooped the receiver out of the base of my desk phone. Called Adam's mobile. It diverted to his office at the *Post*.

"Val and I have a theory," I said. "It needs lifting onto its feet and propping up a bit. And maybe you're the man…"

I explained. Adam listened. He spoke when I had finished.

"Google *eventsintime.com*.   A real gift to journalism, this site," he said.

I thanked him and looked back at Val.

"That was Adam, my putative son-in-law. He's a little sore. He's sitting on the story of the decade and he can't publish yet. He'll be with us tomorrow."

The website came up on my pc screen. I passed the sheets of paper to Val.

"Give me a date."

She picked up one of the pages and offered me January the 2nd 2016. I typed January 12th into the search box. The standout entry was Barack Obama's final attempt to get his by then considerably diluted welfare legislation through the US Senate. There was another piece about a statement from the IMF. Further down the list I came across a report in *Le Républicain*. My French was good enough to understand the headline. I clicked the 'translation' icon and the theory was made flesh. An incident in Lyon in which a mosque was vandalised, which escalated, according to the following day's edition of the paper, into violent reactions in three of the city's suburbs.

"Try this," Val said. "February 21st."

I fast forwarded to March 3rd. To the headline item. A piece about revellers being bombed out of a club in an African quarter of Rotterdam.

Late May's incident was an anti-immigration march in Palermo, which caused chaos, confusion, running street battles, and attempts to lay blame on every known and imagined disaffected organisation, including the Mafia.

Val offered me Alfie's June 23rd page. This time, two deaths in a knife attack on a quartet of Iranians in Graz.

The penultimate incident was well documented. A neo-Nazi rally in Munich – where else? – during which, attendees beat the living daylights out of anti-Nazi protestors, three of whom were run down by a speeding car while trying to avoid getting stomped on. A woman died in the gutter where she fell, a man died later in hospital, the third had a leg amputated.

The unique thing about all these events was that no organisation had claimed responsibility; usually the first act by the perpetrators, eager to get their names in the frame.

The last page of instructions was issued on August 22nd. And on the evening of September 1st, a street of houses being re-developed in Leipzig was burnt to the ground, along with the newsagent's shop on the corner.

"September 9th," Val said. "Three days before Alfie's murder."

We sat quietly for a long time, two minds absorbing all of the nonsense and trying to quantify it. Until another question popped up.

"How were Alfie's pages delivered to the composers?" Val asked. "Not by email surely. Not secure enough."

We both concentrated on the question. I came up with the answer.

"By post," I said.

Val stared at me.

"Nobody sends letters by post these days," she said.

"That's right," I said. "They don't. It's the internet which gets all the attention, from ISPs, senders, security people and hackers. The post is so old fashioned no one monitors it any more. The age of steaming open letters is long gone."

"No no," Val said. "You don't run a revolution by post."

"Why not. Hitler did. And Lenin and Castro."

"That was light years ago."

"That's what I said. So?..."

We sat in silence for a moment or two. Val spoke first.

"No. It's barmy... It's..."

She tailed off. I grinned at her.

"You can't finish that sentence can you?"

She didn't reply.

"I think we should let this idea fester," I suggested. "Then come back to it after tomorrow's march."

We both walked along to the kitchen, where we made some coffee. On the wander back to the office Val suggested we follow the march from the point where it would emerge onto Cheltenham Road.

"I don't want to spend any time with them while they gather in Rose Park. They'll be more palatable on the move. As to College Green... weirdly, I'm kind of looking forward to the grisly climax."

I didn't acknowledge that. Didn't really take any of it in.

"You're pre-occupied again," she said. "Is it Alfie? Are you anywhere near a solution to your investigation?"

"No." I shook my head. "I know it has something to do with Gerald Gaghan. I think there is a lot more to come from that direction. But right now, nobody's giving anything away. Do you want to go for a drive?"

"Where to?"

"I don't know. Anywhere. The seaside. Weston, for fish and chips."

She smiled at me. And for the first time I realised that smile would work in the most jam-packed of crowded rooms. Make the recipient feel like the only person in the place. Some women can do that. I remember an old journalist – now long retired but still alive in the West Country somewhere – telling me about the moment he met Christine Keeler in a corridor in Fleet Street. Electricity was coming out of her and sparking he said. She was the sexiest lady on the planet and she was pumping out enough power to charge the national grid. All for him, personally.

"Why not?" Val said. "To Weston then."

* * *

We both enjoyed the interlude. The fish and chips and the walk along the beach afterwards. The donkeys still at work. Not quite the end of their year. The Weston donkeys have been on the beach since 1886, the business run from the beginning by the Mager family. How's that for tenure?

Val and I talked like old friends, not new acquaintances. Nothing we said was guarded, or spoken like it was being tested. She was cool, relaxed and funny. I asked her about the gentleman who shared the top floor at Chancellors Hotel with her.

"Edward is a multi-millionaire," she said. "He owns property all over the world. Even a whole seaside resort on the Australian east coast. But he doesn't flaunt it. Gives millions away each year to a group of children's charities. His money has saved the lives of more at risk kids than you can possibly imagine. Right now, he is funding three teams of aid workers in the Aegean."

"Doesn't he ever get compassion fatigue?"

Val shook her head.

"No. He gets angry. And he hurts like no one else I know. But he never despairs. Because inside the whole bloody maelstrom there are always highs and joys. Edward is, quite simply, a truly decent man."

"Sounds like you're a bit in love with him."

"I am a bit."

"When did his wife die?"

"Back in the 90s. He is Tutsi, they both were. They lived in London. They went on a visit to Aurora's family in Rwanda. At totally the wrong time. They left the kids at home, fortunately. Edward's wife was killed. Along with 800,000 others during the Hutu massacres... A forgotten scandal now. By no means the UN's finest hour." She paused. "You'd think, wouldn't you, that someone who had suffered so, would stay away from the source of his grief and try to blot it all out. But not Edward. He goes back to Rwanda regularly and works there for a month or two at a time."

"How long have you know him?"

"Five or six years."

"Where did you meet?"

"In Brussels. He was lobbying his MEP at the time. Nothing happened. The useless tosser was a member of UKIP."

We lapsed into silence. And for the first time, silence felt uncomfortable. Val reached out her left hand, took hold of my right arm and stopped walking.

"I don't want to say this Alfie thing will work out. I've never been one to use 'It'll be fine' as routine. We haven't know each other long, but I do sense you're not a quitter. And right know, Gaghan must be on the back foot. And vulnerable."

She smiled her one hundred gigawatt smile.

"Go get him, Jack."

CHAPTER TWENTY-EIGHT

Saturday morning.

Adam and I shared the Accord again. We parked in Cotham on a fellow reporter's drive, walked down to the Arches, where Cheltenham Road and Gloucester Road meet. There wasn't a trace of excitement in the air. No hint of 'Here come the Nazis'. The place looked and felt like any other Saturday - a line of traffic moving north out of the city and everybody not in cars shopping. Nothing was moving into town. This section of inbound traffic had been diverted. We decided to follow the march into the city centre from the outbound side of the road.

Val tugged at my elbow.

"Good morning."

I said 'hello' and introduced her to Adam. She smiled and shook his right hand. Adam looked at his watch.

"10.45," he said. "Any time now."

A police motorbike rolled out from under the Arches and onto Cheltenham Road. The rider pulled into the kerb, stopped, put his toes on the ground, leaned into the pavement and propped the bike up with his left leg. He looked ahead, to his right and to his left and over both shoulders. Apparently satisfied that nothing untoward was brewing, he relaxed back onto the bike seat and waited.

A minute or two later, the noise of drums banging and voices chanting faded up and added to the ambient noise. A police patrol car swung onto Cheltenham Road, passed the motorbike rider who waved in acknowledgement, and coasted to a stop about fifty yards ahead of him. Two other bike riders materialised, followed by the protestors flanked by uniformed police officers. The chanting was competing well with the drums in the volume stakes, but roared so loud the words was undecipherable

The three motorbikes moved on towards the patrol car. We started moving to keep pace with the marchers. I began to read what the banners were proclaiming. *IS DEALS IN DEATH, THE KORAN PREACHES HATE, MUSLIMS SUPPORT JIHADIS, CUT OUT THE CANCER OF ISLAM*. Along with the second division hate material about sending immigrants back to the hovels from whence they came, keeping white Anglo-Saxon blood pure, body searching everyone with a beard who comes ashore, and the long established mantra about England for the English.

"I've counted seventy-six of them," Adam yelled into my ear. "As Bairstowe and Defoe promised."

Barely a tenth of the number of junior doctors and supporters who had marched down Park Street five months earlier. And even allowing for the local constabulary's miscalculation, the ratio of cops to marchers was still high. Ahead of us, the motor bikes overtook the patrol car and sped on towards the traffic lights at the junction with Ashley Road, five hundred yards away.

There is a mosque on the west side of Cheltenham Road fifty yards from the lights. The march inched closer to it. The doors were open. An A board sat on the pavement, hand painted with the words *All Are Welcome*. There was no one standing in front of the mosque. No one for the marchers to yell at. Nonetheless the parade refused to pass by without venting spleen. One of the marchers, broke through the police line at his side, raced across the road, picked up the A board and hurled it through the mosque doorway. He turned back to face his compatriots, held up his right arm in a Nazi salute and the marchers roared approval. Two uniforms bore down on him, grabbed him and dragged him back across the road.

"At least that was fairly harmless," Adam shouted.

Val shouted back. "Just the beginning. There's always a sortie or minor skirmish early on in the proceedings. Those two policemen know that, so they were careful."

The traffic lights were held at green, as the march moved into Stokes Croft. There was a group of black men and women who had walked up to the junction from the heart of Saint Paul's to jeer at the Nazis. A comical moment essentially, as they waved placards with cartoons painted on them. One of them a confused, jackbooted, Great War German survivor, with a strap-line under him, echoing back to the original socialist beginnings of Hitler's organisation *DOES HE KNOW HIS LEFT FROM HIS REICH?*

The police pressed the marchers onwards. Ahead of them, the patrol car swung broadside on at the junction with Jamaica Road. Another car, coasting up towards the junction from the city, temporarily blocked the carriageway. The driver got out. The march turned right. The patrol car at the rear stopped for a moment or two. The passenger side window rolled down. The cop in the passenger seat shouted something at the driver, who nodded, yelled something back and raised his right thumb.

In Jamaica Road another patrol car pulled out from the kerb and stationed itself in front of the marchers. The motorbike cops sped on to the junction with Upper Maudlin Street. At the last minute, both lanes from the BRI to the right and the Bus Station to the left were held up by red lights. The march turned right again and headed past the BRI and onto Park Row. And from Park Row, left and left again onto Park Street.

And suddenly we had a crowd. Both left and right hand side pavements were choked with people, mostly students. More ran down towards Park Street from the university buildings two hundred yards away. The marchers were jeered at the rest of the way down Park Street and onto College Green. More police patrol cars and a big arrest wagon were parked on the western perimeter of the green, in front of the Library and the Cathedral. There was a ten foot square podium sitting on the grass in front of the Council House, a hefty speaker each side of the podium and a PA console behind it.

The marchers trooped onto the green and gathered in front of the podium. The students followed and congregated behind them. Val, Adam and I moved to the Cathedral side of the green and stood at the back of the crowd, twenty yards or so in front of the police wall which now ringed the area.

We waited. A long, thin man with neatly ordered hair, holding two radio mics, stepped onto the podium from behind it.

"That's Jim Daniels," Adam said. "Our home grown neo-Nazi."

Another man, detached himself from the crowd and joined Daniels on the platform. Daniels handed him one of the mics. A kind of hush fell, underscored by the sound of traffic running up and down Park Street once more.

Daniels beamed round at the crowd.

"Welcome," he called into the mic. "Brilliant to have so many supporters and like-minded souls here this morning."

There was a roar from the crowd, immediately drowned out by student chants of "Nazis Out."

Then it happened.

At the edge of the crowd to our left, fifteen or so paces from the podium, Ridley Gaghan moved forwards. He was wearing a Petr Chec head protector. He took everybody, the marchers, the speakers and the police, by surprise. He leapt onto the podium, grabbed at the microphone held by Daniels, who wouldn't let go. He swung his left arm across his chest, then slammed his elbow into Daniels' throat. Daniels let go of the mic, staggered backwards and fell off the podium. Ridley bellowed into the mic.

"Ladies and gentlemen. Don't listen to these bastards. They - " was as far as he got.

The co-speaker lunged at him. Ridley balled his left fist, swung it up in arc to connect with the underside of the co-speaker's chin. The force almost lifted the man off his feet. He bit his tongue, screamed in pain, and fell into

340

the arms of the crowd surging forward. Moments later Ridley was swamped.

By now the police were on the move. A line of them surged past us. The students backed away, as if choreographed. The police waded into the marchers and a bit of a commotion began. Four of the marchers broke through the cordon and fled towards us.

The blade of the knife in the leading marcher's hand flicked open. And something kicked in. An image from twenty-five years earlier at a football match, when an irate fan turned on me with a knife he pulled out of a holster fastened around his ankle. The marcher closed on me without slackening momentum. The man at the right of the quartet peeled away and disappeared from my line of sight. I stepped to my left, hoping to create space between myself and Val and Adam. It worked, in the sense that the man's focus on me didn't waver. But the space I created left Val and Adam to deal with the other two.

The man was all charge and no finesse. Thankfully no knife expert either. He might have appeared to be so among his mates in some back yard, but he was just a stooge who felt good and big and important with a stiletto in his fist. He was left handed. Better for me, because the knife came at me from my right and I was probably his first attempt at glory. Most of the knife attacks the police come across are slasher affairs – multiple stabbings by rushed and angry attackers. I saw a kind of lust in his eyes as his charge at me slowed. And suddenly he didn't know what to do. He looked like he was going to aim a poke at my midriff.

I lunged to my left. He swept the knife in an arc from his right. I raised my left arm and swung my body though forty-five degrees and hard in to his.

This isn't one of my signature moves. Rather something I had never mastered in attack and defence sessions in the Trinity Road gymnasium and it certainly was no balletic move now. But I did succeed in making enough contact to get beyond the arm wielding the knife and propel him backwards. He hit the ground before I did. Rolled away and stood up. I did too. We both looked around for his knife. Neither of us could see it. I charged at him. Startled and defeated he turned and ran away.

Val screamed behind me. I turned round. She dropped to her knees, clutching her stomach. There was blood seeping through her fingers. In front of her was another knife owner. She was an easy target and he sort of knew what he was doing. He aimed the knife at Val again and it sank into her rib cage.

I hit him as he pulled the blade out, with my shoulders, arms and as much body weight as I could muster. He went down underneath me. The back of his head hit the grass, but the ground underneath was hard and the fall hurt him, I grabbed his hair – no razor cut here – lifted his head and banged it back onto the grass. He lay still. I picked up his knife and looked to my left. Adam had taken off his fleece rolled it into as compact a shape as he could make and was holding it against Val's stomach. Blood was seeping from between her ribs.

I heard a voice yell, "Okay, sir, we're here."

A paramedic was sprinting towards us across College Green. Behind him, an ambulance was reversing fast and closing at speed. The paramedic dropped onto his knees beside Val. Adam stood up and stepped back, but didn't look away. He was shaking so much his teeth were chattering.

"Jesus Christ..."

The paramedics worked on Val for five or six minutes, finally stopping the blood flow. By which time she was unconscious. Two uniformed coppers helped to get Val onto a stretcher and into the ambulance, slowly and very carefully.

Adam had stopped shaking.

"You go with Val," he said. "I'll get the car and meet you at the hospital."

I climbed into the ambulance. One of the policemen closed the door. The medic next to Val called forward to his mate in the driving seat.

"Okay. Let's go."

The engine fired up, the siren came on and the ambulance picked up speed across College Green. It occurred to me I had been responsible for two ambulance rides during the last seventy-two hours.

* * *

Adam joined me in the A & E theatre waiting room.

"How is she?"

"One of the doctor's said they were dealing with an internal bleed, but offered no more than that."

Adam sat down next to me.

343

"I called Chrissie and Linda," he said. "They know where we are. I've never been in a knife fight before. Well any serious fight at all. You did everything you could, Jack."

"If Val dies, I didn't do anything."

"I'll go and find us something to drink," he said.

We supped drinks machine coffee from plastic cups. Walked up and down a lot. Looked at the clock on the wall endlessly. Checked the door which led to the operating theatre every time it opened.

An hour and a half after Val had been admitted, a surgeon stepped into the waiting room. We stood up. He moved towards us.

"Miss Haroun is stable," he said. "We made repairs to her stomach wall, lower bowel and her punctured lung. The internal bleeding has stopped. At least for now. She is on her way to Intensive Care. I need to ask, is either of you related to her?"

"No," I said. "She has a sister in Clifton. And a close friend."

"Can you call them? Let them know what has happened. But stress that no one can see her for at least thirty-six hours. The attendance nurse at the desk over there, will give you a direct line number for IC. Call at any time. And please be assured she is getting the best of care."

Adam led me to where he had parked the Accord. He handed me the key fob, I unlocked the car and we got into it.

"Now what do we do?" Adam asked.

"I know what I have to do," I said. "I'll take you back to your car and you will go home to Chrissie."

"Which will leave you doing what?"

"Going after the bastard responsible for all this."

I turned the engine over, found first gear, wound up the revs, let the clutch go and pulled out onto St Michael's Hill. Adam picked up his car outside my house and left for Clevedon.

I called Terri James. Work, home and mobile. Only to listen to three versions of 'Please leave a message or call later'. But 'Hi, your sister's in hospital and it's touch and go' is no message to leave. I would have to call later.

I sat in the living room for a while to work out how to do the next bit.

CHAPTER TWENTY-NINE

Gerald Gaghan or Peter Nash?

The former was at the heart of everything that had happened to me and those around me over the last fortnight. But all the sleuthing I had done, all the information I had gathered about Alfie, had led me in the direction of Gaghan's door without the slightest sign of a smoking gun. It would take me all night to regale someone with the stuff I had learned since the moment Danny Malone materialised in my office. Yet despite all the menacing, threatening, thumping, and brawling, Gaghan was unlikely to go down for the murder of Alfie Barnes unless I did something extra special to facilitate it. Gaghan could afford to play a long game, I couldn't. A return visit to his house on the hillside was the major proposition. That was pro-active, in a dangerous sort of way, but ought to lead somewhere at least.

Conversely, I knew precious little about Peter Nash, so perhaps that was the direction in which my zeal should lead me. And perhaps a meeting of minds would be less foolhardy than a confrontation between an irresistible force and an immovable object.

As that great baseball philosopher Yogi Berra said... *When you come to the fork in the road, take it.*

To Nash Towers then. He was, at least, more likely to be alone. By all accounts there was no family living in his house. He probably had at least two secretaries and a butler, maybe multiple butlers, but that was a risk I'd have to take. I could simply go blundering in of course – a modus operandi not unfamiliar – and let events unfold as they may. But an ace detective who charges two hundred and fifty pounds a day ought to be more professional than that. I had no idea what I was going to stir up.

"Improvise, Shepherd," I said out loud. Sounded better than 'blunder in'. And swiftly, because the sooner I accomplished this foolish thing the better.

I drove up to Cilfton Down, past the mansions that really did have multiple staff members and turned into Peace Vale Road. I counted the alarmed cast iron gates, parked a couple of chunks of real estate before Nash's pile, and took stock.

Somehow it was fitting that he lived in this neck of the woods. An enclave built by immensely wealthy men without a moral bone in their bodies who made their fortunes from one of the most evil trades of all time, and built more churches in Bristol than any other city could boast, to salve their collective conscience. There was a time when slavery was perceived as an honest business, because foreigners, especially those from the 'Dark Continent', rated very low on the human scale. And now, Gerald Gaghan and Peter Nash, men with all the principles of Bashar-al-Assad, were living high on the hog and had taken up the cudgel.

A beech hedge to the right of the gate masked my approach to the place, but I'd never get across the lawn without being seen. To the right and around the side would appear to be the preferred route. Which meant climbing the stone boundary wall and creeping though the topiary.

I had done climbing walls three days ago in Bath. So I did a re-run, with almost exactly the same outcome. On top of the wall I lost grip and fell into a forsythia bush, scraping my forehead, scratching both cheeks and drawing blood.

It took me five or six minutes to get around the house. I took a deep breath, ducked under the kitchen windows and moved to the back door. I put my ear to the frosted glass pane and listened. I couldn't hear a sound, so I wiped my sweating palms on the seat of my trousers, took hold of the door handle and pushed down. The door opened as I leaned against it.

Inside the kitchen, I stood rooted to the floor for a minute or so. The door leading into the hall was open and beyond it I could hear voices.

Two men.

There was nowhere to go but onwards. I moved across the kitchen and stepped into the hall, where I came face to face with myself in a huge gilt edged mirror. The blood from the scratches had dried and smudged. Like war paint. Crazy Horse must have looked much like this at the Little Big Horn. It was a terrifying sight. At least, if push came to shove, I could probably frighten Nash into submission.

The ten paces from the mirror to the living room door, took as much time as the journey across the street. The door was open a couple of inches. I leaned against the wall and listened.

The voice I couldn't recognise was probably Nash's. The one I did know was Gerald Gaghan's.

He was responding to something Nash had said.

"We're still in control."

"No we're not. We have… had, a plan. A pan-European scheme with financial and political clout. I didn't spent endless weeks in Belgium and Switzerland to rejoice as it slips away from us."

"It won't," Gaghan said

"It is doing precisely that."

"No. It's fixable."

"Face it, Gerald."

"Okay… If you hadn't gone off half cocked," Gerald replied, "we wouldn't, I wouldn't, be staring at a court appearance."

"How many of those have you avoided in your life?" Nash said. "You have lawyers who know every trick in the book. Objections, matters of procedure, injunctions, appeals. They can keep this case out of court for years. And, if and when you do come up before a judge, everyone involved will be too old to care. Besides you're well practiced in the art of dealing with witnesses and suborning juries."

The pitch of Gaghan's voice rose and the volume soared.

"You senseless fucking arsehole," he yelled. "It's a no-brainer. Just go and take a holiday, then stay out of my way for the rest of the fucking year."

Nash's voice was calmer.

"If only it were that simple… We have too much at risk, Gerald. So start getting things right."

349

One of them must have leapt into some sort of action at that point. There was a rumbling noise, something dropped to the floor, then something else, then there was a sequence of rattles and breaks like ornaments falling off a shelf. Then a crunching sound and a mighty cry of pain.

I stepped into the room. Nash had his arms round his associate's neck. He pointed Gaghan at the left edge of the stone fireplace and bounced the top of his head off it, re-producing the sound I'd heard five or six seconds ago. He released Gaghan, who slumped to his knees, fell forwards into the fireplace, keeled over to his left, and slid head first into the wood basket.

The shelf above the fireplace was empty. All the objets d'art were lying broken in the hearth. Nash picked up a poker, two feet long, with a barb on the end for grabbing at logs on a lit fire. He raised the poker and measured the stroke from the barb to Gaghan's head, like a golfer practicing his swing.

I decided it was time to speak up.

"He won't feel it," I said.

Nash froze. Then his head whipped round through ninety degrees. He stayed in that position for a second or two, then straightened up and turned the whole of his body to face me.

"Who are you?" he asked.

"Jack Shepherd," I said.

"Ah…" he said. "The private investigator."

"And you must be Peter Nash," I said.

He dipped his head in acknowledgement.

"I told Gerald not to under-estimate you. But then not being too clever himself, he more often than not fails to see the attribute in others."

Nash was a couple of inches shorter than me. Slim, but straight backed, with thick black hair, dark eyes and Denis Healy eyebrows. His grey wool suit had been tailored by an artist. And any closer to him I'd have been able to see my reflection in his highly polished black shoes.

"Is there anyone else in the house?"

"No. Banwell has the evening off."

I had only one other question I wanted to ask, so I cut to the climax.

"Who killed Alfie Barnes?"

"Yanis Mertens," he said without hesitating.

"Under orders from whom?"

"Me. Under my orders," he said and stiffened even straighter.

"Why?"

He offered what could only be his New Reich stare.

"The boy was impure," he said. "An idiot."

"He spoke German," I said. "Was a mathematical genius. He wrote computer code for games."

"He was an intellectual gimp. Born the wrong way round or something."

"Put the poker down," I said. "Or I'll take it from you and make you eat it inch by inch."

He shook his head. "I think I'll hang onto it a bit longer."

"Tell me about Alfie," I said. "You hired him."

"Not exactly. Gerald did. He was impressed. The odd little bastard could speak Russian."

"He could only count in Russian."

Nash sneered. "There you are then. People like that pollute the gene pool."

I stared at him. "The what?"

"There is no point in trying to cure disease by simply doctoring the symptoms. You agree?"

"Yes."

He grinned. I'd neatly cued up his guiding principle.

"In truth," he said, "the best way to eradicate disease is to identify those who carry it and eliminate them and the disease at source. Do that, devote yourself to preserving the best elements of racial stock and be the standout model for all others to follow. And it's time for England to lead the way."

He didn't believe this bollocks surely...

"Our movement will always remain conscious of the nature of its struggle, embrace the true values of national personality and racial purity, and order its words and deeds to that end."

He segued into full flow.

"We are patriots who will continue to fight for our ideals, despite receiving no recognition from our contemporaries. We have tapped into the soul of the nation. People are no longer frightened of the truth. They are coming out of hiding, strong and proud. And the more they do so, the clearer and simpler the issues become."

He paused and looked at me dead centre.

"The Barnes boy should have been eliminated at birth."

That was enough. I picked up a sofa cushion and stormed at Nash. He didn't know what to do with the poker, tried to step away and lost his balance. The poker slid from his grasp. I dropped the cushion, grabbed Nash by his expensive lapels, spun him around and propelled him backwards across the Axminster into an eighteenth century walnut dresser. The glass in the doors shattered, showering us both with expensive porcelain.

"Shepherd," he shouted. "For Christ's sake."

I pulled him towards me, then slammed him back into the dresser again. I let go of him and stepped back, crunching cups and saucers into the carpet. He began pulling shards of glass out of his hair. His neck and face were bleeding. He dropped to his knees and surveyed the mess around us.

"Look at this..."

"Is this your leadership in action, Nash? You've ordered one hit that I know of and Christ knows how many more, you're close to attempted murder – or to the real thing if your partner over there dies – and you're worried about the Crown Derby."

"It was a present from Gerald."

"Maybe if he comes round, you can apologise."

"At least he handed it to me. Somebody else bought it, obviously."

He must have caught the amazed look on my face.

"I can't talk to you," he went on. "People like you don't ever accomplish anything. You have neither the vision to see the future, nor the strength to put it into action."

I looked around me. With my right hand I picked up the biggest ashtray I could see; a sculptured design in marble and as heavy as I had imagined it would be. I adjusted my grip on it and bounced my wrist up and down.

"Okay," I said. "I can see you're on your knees, begging for mercy. So let's see how much strength we can put into this."

Nash broke in an instant. He started yelling at me. I stepped close to him. He stayed on his knees, a glass and porcelain covered supplicant. There was a phone on the table at my side of the sofa. I picked up the receiver.

"One more question, Nash." I dialled 999. "Why was Alfie killed?"

The operator asked which service I required. I left Nash to come up with a response while I ordered an ambulance. Another one. That done, I yelled at him.

"Well?"

Nash stared at the floor, shaking his head. I raised the ashtray. He looked at me and held up his arms in surrender.

"Lie down," I said. "Face down. And don't move."

He tried to brush shards of glass out of the carpet where his face would be. All he did was cut his fingers.

"Lie down," I said.

He bowed to the inevitable and did so.

"Comfortable?"

He muttered something, his voice muffled by the pile.

I picked up the phone receiver again and called Harvey Butler's office number, expecting it to divert to whatever mobile he was using.

"Murder Investigation Team," DS Mailer said.

"Liz," I said.

"Jack," she said. "How are you?"

"Just fine," I said. "I have the man who ordered the killing of Alfie Barnes. And his business associate."

There was a long pause.

"Where?" she asked.

"The house of Peter Nash. Gerald Gaghan is lying with his head in the wood basket by the fire. He may be dead. I've been too busy to check. Nash is lying on the carpet in front of me."

"Is he dead?"

"No. Just sulking. Like all deflated bullies and dictators."

"What has? - "

I interrupted her.

"Everything when you get here. I've already called an ambulance."

I ended the call. I searched around for the poker, located it, exchanged it for the ashtray and hovered over Nash again. I repeated the question.

"Why was Alfie killed?"

"He instructed members of my own task force to burn down some property I was re-developing in Leipzig. The best part of a whole bloody street. A multi-million investment up in smoke."

That was that explained.

"I don't know how he imagined he would get away with it, but that's disabled people for you. I was proved right. I didn't want an obsessed, automated, intellectual cripple working in my organisation. And the gimp hacked into our database as well. No problem to him, I have to give him that. In the end he couldn't put two sentences together, but he was clever enough to take the piss and make all of us vulnerable. Mertens was in Bristol, on hand. He beat the Barnes kid to death. Him and his two neanderthals Bairstowe and Defoe. It wasn't difficult to set up. Everybody knew where the retarded little sod walked every morning."

"And they dealt with Danny Malone, too?"

"Yes. But that was Gerald's idea. He said it was 'neat'."

"Face down again," I ordered.

Nash closed his eyes and pressed his forehead into the carpet.

I heard the sound of an ambulance siren in the distance.

* * *

Gaghan was taken away by the paramedics, only just alive. DS Mailer dragged me to Trinity Road, where I made a statement and signed it. From there I drove to Chancellors Hotel. There was a dark skinned, bearded man behind the reception desk

"Is the gentleman who owns the hotel in the building?" I asked.

"No, sir. He's in France. But we do expect him back here mid-morning on Monday. Would you like to leave a message for him?"

"No," I said. "I'll call back."

EPILOGUE

Sunday lunch was enjoyable. Everyone around the table smiled throughout the meal and on into the afternoon. Nobody made any reference to the events of the previous fortnight.

Amy and her re-engaged representation spent a long time on the phone on Sunday evening. *The Causeway* wanted her back and to extend her contract. Celia told the producers that was unlikely. They said if it was a question of money... Celia said no it wasn't.

Neil announced he wanted to go to the US with Amy. Celia made him swear he would look after her. In return she gave him a list of names & address − contacts in LA for him to seek out − and she promised to email all of them by way of introduction.

Auntie Joyce, Uncle Sid and I talked via skype. The results of the Alzheimer's tests were inconclusive. Which represented something of a stay of execution while the neurologists pondered.

Monday morning's *Western Daily Press* ran a garbled and uneven story of Saturday's events. Adam kept his own counsel; he had a much better story for later.

The Avon and Somerset Constabulary PR department praised the forces of law and order for the way in which they had policed the march. And emphasised that the commotion on College Green had been a minor affair, although half a dozen arrests had been made.

I made good my promise to Joe Locke and bought him lunch.

George Hood called me. He said he had just come out of a meeting. ACC Langley had gathered the whole SCU team into a room on the top floor, sung their praises and thanked them for the work they had done in helping to make the streets of Bristol safer.

Mid-afternoon, I called at Chancellors Hotel again. Edward came down into the lobby to talk. He was all that Val had said, and more. Gracious, quietly spoken, and yet clearly a man who could command any room anywhere. I drove him to the BRI and conducted him to Intensive Care. Val was asleep, hooked up to drips and gizmos and monitors. Edward picked up a chair, moved it to the bedside, reached for Val's left hand and spoke to her, softly. The nurse conducted me away from the bedside. I asked her what the prognosis was. In the doorway, she said 'not good, to be honest'.

I tip-toed out of the room.

In IC reception I ran into Doctor Alison again.

"Ah, Mr Shepherd," she said. "I heard you were here. Mr Malone woke up an hour ago. Would you like to see him?"

THE END

Closing The Distance – The first Jack Shepherd Thriller

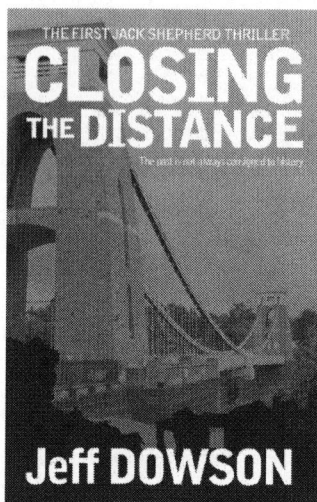

"I want you to find someone," Deborah said.
"And who would that be?" I asked.
"Me," she said. *"I want you to find me."*

Jack Shepherd takes on this odd commission and his client promptly disappears. A body surfaces in the mud of the Severn Estuary and is identified as Deborah's therapist and a former client of Shepherd.

He comes up against a local second string villain, attempting to punch above his weight as a dog fight promoter and the UK end of a trafficking business run by a pair of ex pat Serbs.

Shepherd battles to stay on the right side of the law as he struggles to locate his client. In the process, he unearths a story which goes back 12 years to a bloody massacre in a Kosovan village.

Closing the Distance is a clever modern thriller where nothing is as it first seems.

- Cathi Unsworth

Changing The Odds – A Jack Shepherd Thriller

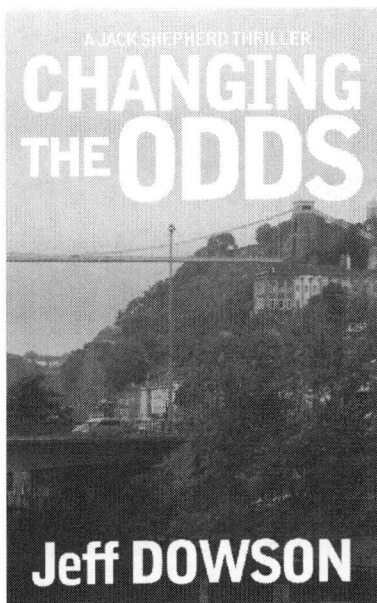

"Prominent Syme Park Millionaire Disappears ... The story of the Bristol PI and the blood stained parquet floor grows curiouser and curiouser."

As the headlines grow more cynical by the day, Jack Shepherd knows that his search for a missing retired bookie can only end in misery.

But in accepting May Marsh's commission to find her husband, Shepherd doesn't anticipate just how high the odds stacked against him are, as he is pitched into a world of ruthless exploitation, unbending violence, and a heart-stopping confrontation with old enemies – the city's criminal royalty, the Settle family.

Fast paced with an explosive ending, this is compelling reading

- Mystery People Magazine

76491231R00223

Made in the USA
Columbia, SC
07 September 2017